They continued their ride silently for a while when Richard suggested they might dismount and sit on a convenient stone wall as the day was quite bright and sunny. Fabia agreed, and he handed her down and secured their horses before joining her.

"So difficult to talk when you are riding," he complained.

"But the object is exercise, not chatting," Fabia teased, quite content to follow his lead, but not entirely willing to let him have it all his way.

"Well, I haven't much time. My ship should be ready in a few weeks," Richard informed her with a wealth of meaning in his tone and glance.

"Time for what?" Fabia asked, deliberately misunderstanding, but not displeased at his hint.

"I want to get to know you, to impress upon you what a marvelous fellow I am before I sail away," Richard replied lightly, but his eyes belied the frivolity of his words.

"Are you a marvelous fellow?"

"I doubt it, but I would like you to think so." Then, surprising her, he leaned over and kissed her gently on the lips . . .

ZEBRA REGENCIES
ARE
THE TALK OF THE TON!

A REFORMED RAKE   (4499, $3.99)
by Jeanne Savery

After governess Harriet Cole helped her young charge flee to France—and the designs of a despicable suitor, more trouble soon arrived in the person of a London rake. Sir Frederick Carrington insisted on providing safe escort back to England. Harriet deemed Carrington more dangerous than any band of brigands, but secretly relished matching wits with him. But after being taken in his arms for a tender kiss, she found herself wondering— *could* a lady find love with an irresistible rogue?

A SCANDALOUS PROPOSAL   (4504, $4.99)
by Teresa DesJardien

After only two weeks into the London season, Lady Pamela Premington has already received her first offer of marriage. If only it hadn't come from the *ton's* most notorious rake, Lord Marchmont. Pamela had already set her sights on the distinguished Lieutenant Penford, who had the heroism and honor that made him the ideal match. Now she had to keep from falling under the spell of the seductive Lord so she could pursue the man more worthy of her love. Or was he?

A LADY'S CHAMPION   (4535, $3.99)
by Janice Bennett

Miss Daphne, art mistress of the Selwood Academy for Young Ladies, greeted the notion of ghosts haunting the academy with skepticism. However, to avoid rumors frightening off students, she found herself turning to Mr. Adrian Carstairs, sent by her uncle to be her "protector" against the "ghosts." Although, Daphne would accept no interference in her life, she *would* accept aid in exposing any spectral spirits. What she never expected was for Adrian to expose the secret wishes of her hidden heart . . .

CHARITY'S GAMBIT   (4537, $3.99)
by Marcy Stewart

Charity Abercrombie reluctantly embarks on a London season in hopes of making a suitable match. However she cannot forget the mysterious Dominic Castille—and the kiss they shared—when he fell from a tree as she strolled through the woods. Charity does not know that the dark and dashing captain harbors a dangerous secret that will ensnare them both in its web—leaving Charity to risk certain ruin and losing the man she so passionately loves . . .

Available wherever paperbacks are sold, or order direct from the Publisher. Send cover price plus 50¢ per copy for mailing and handling to Penguin USA, P.O. Box 999, c/o Dept. 17109, Bergenfield, NJ 07621. Residents of New York and Tennessee must include sales tax. DO NOT SEND CASH.

Fabia's Choice
Violet Hamilton

ZEBRA BOOKS
KENSINGTON PUBLISHING CORP.

ZEBRA BOOKS are published by

Kensington Publishing Corp.
850 Third Avenue
New York, NY 10022

First Printing: August, 1994

Printed in the United States of America

Prologue

Native waiters padded softly about the paneled room, removing the heavy white linen cloth from the mahogany table, replacing the silver candelabra and setting out the decanters of port. Roger Thurston, host for this celebratory dinner, looked about with a benign smile. He knew that few of the guests or even his fellow plantation owners could offer such lavish hospitality.

Thurston, a plump, red-faced, balding gentleman whose green eyes sparkled with enjoyment, had every reason for complacency. Tomorrow his elder daughter, Stella, would wed Paul Beaumont, a handsome and respectable young Englishman, who had consented to remain at Eden Hall here in Nevis, where he would eventually inherit the sugar plantation from his father-in-law. Thurston, who had mourned the lack of sons, felt much more cheerful at the prospect of Stella and Paul's children, his grandchildren, growing up on the island, recipients of the profits from his own dedicated work. This wedding was the culmination of his life's dream. And in appreciation of that, half a mile from Eden Hall stood a new smaller gray stone replica of the mansion, fully furnished in the latest style from

England, awaiting the young couple's residence. It was his gift to his daughter.

Tonight, twenty-four guests had sat down to a luxurious meal of island crayfish, prime beef, various savories, and a spun sugar confection which had brought appreciative gasps from the diners. Vintage wines, imported from France, had been poured generously throughout the meal, and now many of the celebrants were feeling the effect of overindulgence.

Stella, her cheeks flushed with anticipation, sat next to her bridegroom, looking a very picture, her father thought. No wonder Paul, the target of matchmaking mothers and daughters since his arrival on Nevis six months ago, had spurned them all in favor of his lovely Stella. What a handsome couple they made. Every man here must envy Paul, especially their most august guest, Captain Horatio Nelson, whose own recent bride, a Nevis widow, could hardly rival Stella. Gossips insisted that the ambitious Nelson had married her because he understood she would inherit Montpelier from her uncle. Of course, although Montpelier was a fine estate, it was not to be compared with Eden Hall.

A slight breeze stirred the pale blue silk draperies pulled back from the wide windows, but hardly cooled the revelers, who now were quite boisterous. Hearing some of the remarks, Thurston, who was inclined to allow a certain license on this special evening, frowned as he noticed his wide-eyed younger daughter sitting halfway down the table. As he watched, a red-faced young planter's son leaned over and bussed her furtively on the cheek to roars of approval from his neighbors.

Fabia was too young for this type of entertainment. Roger raised his eyebrows and made a dismissing motion to his wife, who rose and approached Fabia. "Come, Fabia, time for you to retire. You will want to be fresh for your duties tomorrow," Maria Thurston advised.

Twelve-year-old Fabia made a small movement of protest, but rose to obey her mother. This had been her first grown-up party, and if the adult behavior had become a bit ribald, she had still enjoyed it. Even silly Bobbie Sefton kissing her had been exciting, although she had not thought his wine-ladened breath or wet lips very appealing.

Making her polite good-nights to the company, Fabia looked admiringly at Stella. She had often mourned the fate that denied her the same buxom blond beauty and instead inflicted her with straight chestnut hair and a scrawny figure, not improved by the frilly white muslin dress of her mother's choice. Stella had inherited her looks from their mother, although little of Maria Thurston's early appeal was evident now in the faded matron whose once creamy cheeks had coarsened under the tropic climate and the cares of plantation life.

Fabia's only claim to future attention lay in her large green eyes, now wide with innocent pleasure as she wistfully passed a backward glance over the scene. Her withdrawal caused no comment, for as the decanters passed to and fro, ebullient spirits exceeded the bounds of even the most indulgent propriety, and tempers and voices became heated.

Indeed, Paul Beaumont and Randal Goring, a young man of intemperate habits and a jealous na-

ture, were engaging in a furious argument. Thurston wondered if he should intervene, especially as
the subject must be embarrassing to Captain Nelson.
The dispute appeared to concern the futility of the
British Navy's attempts to enforce the Navigation
Acts. The Acts had been passed as a war measure
against the former American colonies, to prevent
the West Indies planters from selling their sugar
crops to the enemy. Paul insisted that the government was not only foolish, but unsuccessful, a view
endorsed by most planters. Goring fulminated
against the lack of patriotism, if not outright treason of such a stance.

However, despite Thurston's fears, Captain Nelson made no effort to push his case or His Majesty's, remembering no doubt the islanders' earlier
anger when he had compelled their compliance. It
seemed that in the West Indies, and in Nevis especially, the American colonies were not regarded as
treasonable rebels, but eager markets. Patriotism
must cede to profits, most of the planters felt. Nelson had been diligent in enforcing the law but had
earned many of the planters' scorn and sullen defiance, their captains eluding his patrolling ships
whenever possible. It was apparent that he believed
a prudent silence might serve him better on this
occasion.

If Nelson was unusually forebearing, so was Roger
Thurston, who was inclined to give young bucks
their head. He was beginning to realize, though,
that both Paul and Randal were verging on violence,
neither in any condition to control their tempers.

"Damn it, Beaumont, you condone breaking the

law because you are now in a position to enjoy the
fruits of illegal trade," Randal accused, his face red-
dening with the force of his fury. More than politics
were behind his quarrel with Paul. He had tried
for Stella's hand, and his lack of success had embittered him, although until now he had tried to
conceal it.

"It's an idiotic law which deserves to be broken,"
Paul retorted, unmindful of Stella's conciliatory
hand on his arm and a protest from Captain Nelson. If his temper had not been aroused, Paul might
have heeded both demurs, as well as the guest who
murmured, "Remember, Beaumont, there are ladies
present."

However, Paul's natural good manners and his respect for Thurston's guests were not proof against
Goring's taunts. Nor was Randal in any condition
to observe the niceties of polite behavior.

"Are you saying I am idiotic for honoring it?"
Randal raged, his hand groping for his glass.

"If you wish to take it that way," Paul answered,
refusing to back down.

"How dare you insult me!" Randal shouted. All
sense of decorum abandoned, he threw the contents
of his wineglass in Paul's face.

Paul rose to his feet, grasped Randal's collar, and
dragged him to his feet. "I won't stand for this."

"You are a yellow coward, all bluster, no action,"
Randal cried, while trying to wrest himself from
Paul's grasp.

"Coward, am I? Well, you will answer for that
slur on the field of honor. I challenge you to a
duel," Paul answered, ignoring Stella's protest and

the guests' gasps. Suddenly the festive dinner had disintegrated into a sobering crisis.

"No, Paul, you can't. What are you thinking of? Tomorrow is our wedding day." Stella's shocked words fell into the sudden silence.

Thurston walked around the table to confront the two antagonists, now facing each other with hard eyes, neither willing to retreat from the disastrous situation brought about by their drunken dispute.

"Come now, Paul, Goring, it is just the wine urging you to these excesses. Shake hands and forget this pointless argument," Thurston pleaded.

Most of the guests averted their eyes, reluctant to intervene, although the seriousness of the situation was apparent to them all. Perhaps Paul might have surrendered to his host's suggestion or Stella's pleas, but one look at Goring's sneering face stiffened his resolve. He would not be branded a coward by this poltroon.

"No, Roger, he accused me of cowardice. I cannot ignore that," Paul insisted stubbornly. "We will meet at dawn, get this settled. The ceremony is not until noon, and by that time I will have had my revenge. Unless you want to apologize, Goring," he suggested. Both young men had been pushed into a corner from which their only escape was to fight or offer an apology that pride would not allow.

"Not at all. Your servant, sir. I will choose my seconds," Goring answered stiffly, turning away to search for two supporters.

Roger Thurston, appalled at the deterioration of his cheerful dinner party, tried to set matters right, but the two young men were deaf to his efforts.

Nor did Stella's moans have any effect. The party broke up hurriedly, the guests eager to distance themselves from this unhappy circumstance. Stella, still pleading, threw herself into Paul's arms, heedless of the onlookers, while Goring stood by, insolence hiding a sudden apprehension as he watched the pair. Stubborn and willful, both young men, sobered now by the contemplation of tomorrow, might have wished to retract, but honor prevented this sensible resolution to the affair.

The duel was scheduled for the first light, a few hours away, and Goring departed with some neighbors to pass the few troubled hours before dawn. Whatever Paul felt, he put on a brave face before Stella and Roger, assuring them he would dispatch his victim and then eagerly await his bride at the church.

Across the rows of gleaming green cane, the strong June sunlight was just beginning to make its force felt when Fabia was jolted from her deep sleep by dreadful screams. At first she thought she was dreaming, but as the horrible cries and moaning continued, she realized that some frightful tragedy had occurred. Stumbling from her bed, she ran into the hall looking frantically for the cause of such agony. Across the corridor, in her sister's room, came her mother's soothing voice, and Fabia opened the door to a pitiful sight. Her sister, tearing at her nightdress, was crying over and over, "No, no, it's not true," in their mother's arms while her father stood by helplessly.

"What's wrong? What has happened?" Fabia asked.

Her father, pale, turned dazedly. "Paul is dead, shot in the duel," he explained dully, confusion and shock in his voice.

"Paul dead, shot in a duel! He is marrying Stella in a few hours. How can this be?" Fabia's voice trembled.

"He and young Goring had an argument, and the fools decided to fight. Paul is dead and Goring severely wounded. There will be no wedding," he said baldly, unable to soften the blow.

"Get Fabia out of here, Roger. She should not be seeing this," Maria Thurston ordered. "And help me with Stella. We must get some laudanum in her. She cannot suffer this way."

"Go to your room, Fabia. I will come to you later. We must all help Stella now," Thurston pleaded.

Fabia hesitated, wanting to comfort her unhappy sister but still confused, unwilling to accept what her father had told her. Just a few hours ago happiness and gaiety had reigned, all promising fair for the young couple. Now Stella, a victim of this unaccountable tragedy, would not be wed today or any day. Why had her father not prevented it? Accustomed to looking upon her father as all powerful, never at a loss in any emergency, she could not accept this sudden reversal. There must be some mistake.

But there was no mistake. Later in the morning, Fabia crept into the library where Paul's body lay in a coffin. Her parents had forbidden her to enter the room, but she had to be sure that this was not some terrible nightmare. He lay there in his wedding finery, the bullet hole in his chest covered by a shawl. He seemed calm, as if asleep. Only his pale features and cool folded hands gave lie to her first impression. Paul was dead and Stella would never be his bride.

Fabia bowed her head, a prayer for Paul, for Stella, for all of them on her lips. A feeling of deep hatred for Randal Goring filled her heart. He was responsible for this, and she would never forget that he was the instrument of her family's tragedy.

One

Fabia stood in the narthex of the minster, looking east down the nave, soothed by the timeless beauty of the church. She badly needed this respite after her tiresome hour arranging the flowers for the Sunday service under the direction of Sybil Milford-Smythe, one of the parish's most redoubtable dowagers and head of the Altar Society. Normally Fabia dodged this duty, but her Aunt Honoria, wife of Wimborne Minster's rector, Aubrey Wetherell, had begged her indulgence. Aunt Honoria had taken to her bed with one of her megrims, and Petra Wetherell, Fabia's cousin, had refused to substitute for her mother. Such a nasty April day, too. As Fabia fastened her pelisse and walked out of the north porch, she gave a rueful look at the daffodils bowing their delicate heads before a cruel wind. A fine mist was falling, and she struggled down the path, remembering she still had another chore to complete for her aunt.

On days like this she yearned for the bright sun and clear skies of her island birthplace, although it was seven years since she had left Nevis. The tragedy which had impelled her parents to take ship for England remained but a hazy memory, as did her parents themselves. A bout of scarlet fever had wiped those tragic days from her mind. And even more tragedy had followed, for her sister Stella and her parents had taken ship for the island and their sugar plantation before Fabia had fully recovered, only to be lost at sea in a storm off Bermuda. Since leaving her school in Cheltenham, Fabia had lived with her uncle and aunt, the Wetherells, and her cousins, Petra and Trevor, in this Dorset minster town.

Although she knew she should be grateful for the efforts of her relatives to make her welcome, she often felt a distance from them and their life, so removed from the halcyon years of her childhood. The duel that had robbed Stella of her bridegroom and the subsequent horrible days remained blurred and frightening, and she wondered why this gray April day should recall them to her mind. Then she had been a child, a scrawny, wide-eyed scrap of a girl with none of her sister's beauty. Of course, the plantation, Eden Hall, still stood in Nevis, managed by a factor her uncle had engaged. But somehow she had never wanted to return and face the ghosts of that long-ago felicity. Shaking off her sense of uneasiness, she strode resolutely into the wind, bound for the shop on the errand her aunt had commissioned.

Her head down against the whirling mist and gusts, she stumbled on the uneven cobblestones outside the drapers on Market Street, colliding with a gentleman who grasped her by the arm.

"Have you hurt yourself?" he asked anxiously.

"I don't think so. Providentially you saved me from a painful spill. I am in your debt, sir," Fabia replied, looking into the strong weather-beaten face and kind, deep blue eyes of her rescuer.

"Very inclement weather. You should take shelter. Perhaps I might escort you home," he suggested persuasively.

She should be shocked at such a blatant attempt to make her acquaintance, but another glance at the tall gentleman reassured her. He appeared to be quite respectable, not at all undesirable. He had taken off his tall beaver hat and, heedless of the mist dampening his dark brown hair, was gazing at her hopefully. "I am Captain Richard Goring, thoroughly respectable," he assured her, as if answering her unspoken doubts.

Fabia hesitated, and then recklessly offered her own name. "Fabia Thurston. And I must stop first at this shop to match some silks, but thank you for your offer," she said, smiling at his beseeching face. She might have guessed he was a naval officer. He had that farsighted gaze redolent of staring for hours at the distant seas.

"Let me come in with you. I am a master at matching silks. My mother is dedicated to her tapestry," he said with a smile.

Without more ado he held open the door of the shop, and Fabia, shrugging her shoulders, preceded him into the Misses Beasleys' establishment.

Hurrying from the back of the shop, a white-haired gnome of a woman bustled forward to wait on her customers.

"Ah, Miss Thurston, here you are on such a miserable day. What can I do for you?" Miss Anne Beasley asked, eyeing the tall gentleman escorting

Fabia with curiosity. Within hours Fabia knew it would be all over the town that the rector's niece had been accompanied by a strange but handsome gentleman into the Beasley shop. Oh well, as long as she had taken this irregular course, she must carry it off with aplomb.

Ignoring Miss Beasley's avid inspection of her escort, she quickly dispatched her business with some droll suggestions from the captain, whose knowledge of embroidery silks produced hilarious suggestions of a nauseous puce and a violent yellow. Choosing more decorous colors, Fabia completed her purchases and made her farewells, not forgetting to inquire politely about the health of the other Miss Beasley.

Once outside the shop, where the wind and mist appeared to be slackening, she turned to the captain and scolded him. "Miss Beasley will think the worst, I am sure."

"Do you mind?" he asked guilelessly, and to her surprise, Fabia discovered she did not. "And now may I escort you home and make my duty to your parents?"

"My aunt and uncle, and I must warn you he is the rector at the minster and very careful of my reputation," she corrected.

"As he should be. Such a lovely young woman should not be wandering around town, liable to eager attempts by suspicious naval officers to make her acquaintance. But let me assure you that I have impeccable references even if my conduct is shocking," he joked, taking her arm firmly as they walked down the street.

Delighted that he should think her lovely, for Fabia had no great conceit about her looks, she gave him a speaking glance of reproof. "Well, the least we can do is offer you refreshment after you have come so gallantly to my rescue," she conceded. "I suppose you are on leave and a bit bored," she offered with an impish grin.

"I was bored, but I am not now. And I am on leave, visiting my parents some miles from here. I came in to meet a fellow officer at the Wimborne Arms, but he left a message to say he could not make it," he explained, as they took a left turn onto a nearby street lined with Georgian houses.

"It's not too far now," Fabia promised, wondering what her aunt would think about this sudden incursion of a strange naval officer into their midst. Petra would be delighted, she knew, since her cousin's main purpose in life seemed to be the pursuit and capture of desirable young men.

"Here we are," she said, as they approached a tall brick house guarded by delicate iron gatework and showing a smooth bland facade to passersby. Mounting the marble steps, Fabia knocked and then entered with Captain Goring hard on her heels.

Hollins, the Wetherell butler and factotum, appeared through the green baize door at the end of the long narrow hall and gazed at Fabia with mild reproof. He disliked not being on hand to admit visitors.

Ignoring Hollins's intimidating mien, Fabia gave him her cloak and bonnet and indicated that Captain Goring should hand over his greatcoat and hat to the butler.

"We would like some tea, Hollins. Is my aunt in the drawing room?" Fabia asked. Then, realizing that Hollins would take umbrage if not allowed to announce her guest, she said, "This is Captain Goring."

"Good afternoon, sir," Hollins acknowledged. "Mrs. Wetherell is still confined to her room, but the master and Miss Petra are in the drawing room."

Following Hollins to a set of double doors on the right of the rather dark hall, Fabia made a rueful moue at the butler's unbending back. An insouciant shrug of her shoulders suggested that she found the man's pomposity amusing.

Captain Goring admired her casual attitude and the trim lines of her figure now that she had doffed her outdoor clothes. She was dressed simply in a bottled green cashmere redingote faced in cream, a warm and practical gown which testified to her preference for comfort over fashion. Captain Goring approved, eyeing her neat ankles with an appreciative glance.

Hollins opened one door of the drawing room and announced in a sepulchral tone, suited he believed to an ecclesiastical household, "Miss Fabia and Captain Goring," then stood aside to let them enter.

The Reverend Aubrey Wetherell rose to greet his niece. He was the epitome of an Anglican rector, tall, with a lined face and a shock of graying hair.

"Good afternoon, my dear," he greeted mellifluously, the same soothing voice serving him well in the pulpit. Putting out his hand to the captain, he said, "Your servant, sir." Then, turning to the girl seated before the fire, he said, "My daughter Petra."

"Delighted to meet you both. And I only hope I am not intruding. Your niece almost suffered a fall outside a shop on Market Street, and I was able to rescue her, which she kindly believed entitled me to escort her home."

"How good of you, sir. Fabia is apt to be impetuous," Petra cooed, looking up at him with a melting glance from her blue eyes and smoothing her blond curls complacently. A far different type than her cousin, full of artifice and an eye to the main chance, the captain concluded shrewdly.

"Yes, indeed. I hope you suffered no ill effects, my dear," the rector said anxiously. Genuinely fond of his niece, he often found her company more soothing than that of his flirtatious daughter. Petra's conversation seemed limited to fashions, gossip, and men who admired her. He wished she took more of an interest in the minster and parish duties. And he often wondered how he and his somewhat staid wife had produced such a flibbertigibbet.

"No, Uncle, but it is quite a nasty day, and I was not taking proper care. Do you suppose we might have some tea? I think Captain Goring deserves some refreshment after his knight-errantry," Fabia said, seating herself on a bergère chair across from Petra, who patted the space beside her on the settee indicating that the captain might sit beside her. Fabia repressed a smile. She had expected Petra to take advantage of this unexpected diversion.

"Yes, of course, my dear. I appreciate you assuming Honoria's duties with the flowers. Unfortunately my wife is feeling not quite the thing, and Fabia kindly deputized for her on this blustery day," the rector explained to his guest as he gave a tug to the tapestry bellpull by the fireside.

"Not at all, Uncle. I was happy to oblige," Fabia said, watching with some amusement her cousin's interest in the caller.

Petra presided over the teacups with grace, waiting on the captain with assiduous charm, fluttering her hands, and generally displaying her assets for their visitor's delectation, virtually ignoring Fabia and her father.

Accustomed to her cousin's ploys, Fabia turned her attention to her uncle, inquiring after her aunt, and then giving him a droll account of her passage at arms with Mrs. Milford-Smythe.

"Can you believe it, Uncle Aubrey, she wanted huge banks of arum lilies hiding the pulpit steps. I knew you would be annoyed at having to push your way through such an obstacle, and I protested vigorously," Fabia reported, munching heartily on a scone. She had a very healthy appetite and none of the mincing manners of her cousin.

"And did you win the battle, my dear?" the rector enquired. He felt he should defend Mrs. Milford-Smythe, but he could sympathize with his niece. He often found the lady trying himself, although he knew it was his duty to accept her devotion to the church and, alas, to him with Christian charity.

"Yes, after a struggle. She was won over when I pointed out how dreadful she would feel if you tripped on your way to the pulpit," Fabia confessed gaily. She was determined not to vie with Petra for

the captain's attention. In the year she had lived
with her relatives after leaving school, she had endeavored to become friends with her cousin, but
she found her airs tiresome and her conversation
frivolous.

"Captain Goring tells me he is on leave and will
be in the neighborhood for some weeks," Petra interrupted, casting a promising look at the captain.
His attitude toward her was a careful blend of courtesy and appreciation, but Fabia noticed he did not
seem particularly taken with her attempts at flirtation. For some reason this pleased her, and she reproved herself for caring. Petra could no more help
trying to attach any eligible man than she could
stop breathing, and it would be foolish to hope that
the captain would be more impervious than any
other to her attractions. Fabia never tried to challenge her cousin in these situations.

But the Reverend Mr. Wetherell, delighted to
have a naval man in his drawing room, immediately
claimed Goring's attention, plying him with questions about his service and experience.

"My ship, the *Andromeda*, is at Portland, sir, being
refitted after a small encounter with the French
outside Brest. I hope to rejoin my chief, Admiral
Nelson, in the Mediterranean before too long. The
French, as you know, have been causing a great deal
of trouble there," Captain Goring explained.
"Meanwhile I am staying with my parents, perhaps
you know them, at Beechwood some miles from
Wimborne."

"Goring, Goring, yes, I think I have met your
father, Sir Thomas. Not a member of the parish,

of course, but a good churchman. A warden at St.
Mary's, I believe," the Reverend Mr. Wetherell remembered.

Petra, piqued at being ignored, rushed into the
conversation. "Oh, do tell us about the admiral and
Lady Hamilton. We hear such scandalous gossip
about them. Is it true?" Petra questioned, avid to
hear the details of the liaison that had London agog.

"Sir William and Lady Hamilton have been most
hospitable to all the officers of His Majesty's Navy
when they dock in Naples. You should not heed
rumors, Miss Wetherell. Admiral Nelson is a brave
and clever officer. I am fortunate to be attached to
his command. Until now I have been with Admiral
Rodney in the Caribbean," he informed her gravely.
Miss Wetherell's blatant attempts to flirt with him
had not won his approval, and he glanced from her
to her quieter cousin and thought how much more
appealing she was.

"Oh, pooh, you men are all alike, defending one
another whatever the scandal. Lady Hamilton is a
common opportunist and years younger than Sir
William. Not at all respectable," Petra insisted.

"That will do, Petra. It is unseemly for you to be
discussing matters of which you know nothing. Far
more important is Nelson's defense of the realm.
Without him and men like him, England would be
in grave peril," Mr. Wetherell intoned in his best
lecturing voice.

Petra, belatedly realizing that her interest in the
Hamilton affair was not winning Captain Goring's
approval, hurried to change her tactics.

"Since you will be in the neighborhood for some

time, Captain Goring, I hope you will visit us again. Wimborne is a rather boring little town, but we do have a nice assembly which meets every Friday evening now that the season is upon us," Petra simpered, angling for a request for dances and future meetings.

"What an attractive prospect," Captain Goring agreed, but he looked at Fabia, not Petra, promising that this would not be their final encounter.

Fabia, who wanted to ask him about his Caribbean adventures and whether he had ever visited Nevis, hesitated, and then her chance was lost as the captain rose and made his adieus.

"Thank you, sir, for welcoming me so kindly. I would enjoy telling you of some of our naval engagements at a later date. Perhaps I may prevail on your hospitality again," he asked politely.

"Of course, Captain Goring. It has been a treat for us, in this backwater, to entertain such a gallant defender of our country. Do drop in whenever you are in the neighborhood," the Reverend Mr. Wetherell pressed. His words, however, masked a disquietude which had just come to him. Goring. Suddenly the name stirred distant and unpleasant memories. On the other hand he was apt to be absent-minded. Perhaps he was mistaken. Throwing off his unease, he warmly invited the captain to call again, echoed by Petra, who had every expectation of adding the caller to her roster of beaux.

Fabia smiled and thanked him again for coming to her rescue, but said nothing of a future meeting. If the captain was put out by this omission, he showed no evidence of it and, bowing to the ladies, took his leave.

Two

Conversation that evening at the Wetherell dinner table naturally concerned the new acquaintance, Captain Richard Goring. If the Reverend Aubrey Wetherell appeared a bit distant, his family saw nothing amiss in his manner, supposing he was thinking about his Sunday sermon.

Petra, inappropriately gowned in a green silk dress elaborately trimmed in lace, wanted to discuss the captain, ignoring both Fabia and her father's reluctance to pursue the topic. Petra quite naturally supposed the captain would be returning to pursue her and resolutely ignored any claims Fabia might have to the attentions of Captain Goring. She regaled her mother, who had made the effort to appear at the table although she ate little and seemed still affected by her megrim, with the captain's interest in her. They had been unexpectedly joined by Petra's brother, a sober young man who was reading law in a local solicitor's office.

"Trevor, you must meet Captain Goring. He is so different from the rather dreary men one meets around here. If only I could have a London season, I might attach a man of his type," Petra moaned, not for the first time.

"And what makes this stranger so fascinating?" Trevor asked dryly, giving his cousin Fabia a speaking look.

"For one he's a naval hero, and for another his father is a baronet. I expect he is his heir to some tidy acres," Fabia informed him with a smile. She was fond of Trevor and shared his view of Petra's opportunistic ploys to find a husband.

"And how did this paragon happen to call upon you?" Trevor asked as he carefully peeled a hothouse peach.

"Fabia ran into him on Market Street," Petra admitted. Then feeling that perhaps more was called for, she added, "Then she brought him home to tea."

"So, Fabia, *you* were the attraction," Trevor suggested, knowing this would irritate his sister.

"Not at all. He hardly spoke to her," Petra said sulkily. The notion that any man could prefer her cousin to herself was ridiculous.

"I stupidly stumbled outside the Misses Beasley's shop and he saved me from a nasty fall. Naturally I invited him home to meet the family. He's quite unexceptional," Fabia explained, not eager to challenge Petra. Far easier to let her believe she had made a conquest. It made for peace.

"I believe you have met Lady Goring, my dear," Aubrey Wetherell interrupted, turning to his wife.

"Have I? I don't recall," Honoria offered vaguely.

"Well, I look forward to the next installment of this exciting drama," Trevor said with some amusement. He found his sister's avid attempts to catch a husband boring and only hoped she would soon succeed so that the family would be relieved of her presence. Like his father, he much preferred the company of his cousin to his vapid sister, although he viewed her with a certain amount of tolerance.

"I believe I will retire. I am still feeling quite poorly," Mrs. Wetherell said. She rose, and Fabia and Petra accompanied her to the door.

Trevor, having risen to open the door for the ladies, returned to his seat and poured himself a half-glass of port. He was fond of his father and had noticed his abstraction over dinner. Obviously some problem was occupying the rector's mind. Trevor sensed his father wanted to discuss it but was reluctant to begin. They had a good understanding of one another, and the Reverend Mr. Wetherell often talked over parish matters with his son, valuing his common sense and dry worldly approach to affairs that the rector often found troubling.

"Well, Father, out with it. You have been brooding all through dinner. Has some straying member of your flock come to you for assistance?" Trevor asked.

The rector frowned, not sure he should air his fears. Not that he doubted his confidences would be betrayed, but he felt the affair was too delicate even for Trevor's practical views.

"I may be wrong, but this Captain Goring. I wonder if he could be related to the young man who brought such tragedy to Fabia's sister," he confided, casting aside his doubts and hoping for reassurance.

"I never knew the whole story, and Fabia seems happily to have forgotten most of it, due to that bout of scarlet fever. Was the miscreant's name Goring?" Trevor asked, somewhat disturbed by the idea.

"Yes, I think it was. And I wouldn't like to shatter the dear girl's peace of mind and recall those dreadful days without good cause. I think she has found a measure of contentment among us; and goodness knows, after the death of her family and all that preceded it, I would be remiss in my responsibilities if I needlessly reminded her of the unhappy past."

The rector's indecision often annoyed Trevor, who did not share this defect, but he was genuinely fond of his father and wanted to help him. "Then your problem is whether to tell Fabia of your suspicions and so thwart what might become a friendship between the noble captain and my cousin," Trevor said with admirable clarity.

"Quite. I would not want to be uncharitable. Probably this is not the same man, although his age makes it possible. And he did say he served in the Caribbean. But I gather that the Goring in question was rather a ne'er-do-well, not at all a description I would give to the captain," the rector added, worry darkening his face as he contemplated his various courses of action.

"Poor Fabia. She meets a desirable young man, and Petra wants to annex him and you think he killed her sister's betrothed. A dilemma indeed," Trevor offered, putting the matter in the starkest terms. He thought his father had stirred up a tempest over nothing. If it were true, it would be the strangest of coincidences, and Trevor did not believe in a malign fate. Still, his father was distressed and he must help him.

"I would say nothing, Father. Best to leave it

alone. This Goring may just be a distant relative or
no connection at all. Justice demands you ignore
it," Trevor decided.

"Yes, you are probably right. I will keep my own
counsel for the moment. No good will come from
stirring those troubling memories. Needless to say,
I can rely on your own silence," the rector insisted.

"Of course. And I truly believe your doubts are
groundless," Trevor agreed, hoping to put his father's mind at rest.

Fabia, having settled her aunt for the night—a taxing chore, Mrs. Wetherell complaining about her hot
water bottle, her vinaigrette, and her still-present
headache—went to her own room with a sigh of relief.
Aunt Honoria could be a trial, one which her daughter refused to accept, which left Fabia to offer consolation and sympathy. She was not unmindful of her
duty, but wished she felt the affection for her aunt
and cousin Petra that she had no difficulty in extend-
ing to her uncle and Trevor.

Alone at last, Fabia undressed and settled herself
before the fire, a necessity on this cool April night,
intent on reading the latest novel by Mrs. Radcliffe.
But somehow she was not engrossed by the horrific
adventures of the heroine, her mind wandering to
her meeting with Captain Goring.

She hoped she was not becoming infected with
Petra's obsession with finding a husband. And what
was she thinking of, dreaming of the officer after
one meeting? For all she knew she would never see
him again, or if she did, it would just be as a spec-

tator to Petra's efforts to attach him. Fabia knew
that young men often lost their sense when confronted with an attractive young woman intent on
throwing out lures. And Petra was a beauty, despite
her less endearing traits. Any man might find her
delectable. Fabia had no great conceit of her own
charms and admitted it was entirely possible that
Captain Goring had been attracted to her cousin,
for which he could not be blamed. It was a pity,
for Petra would be no wife for a serving officer. At
that, Fabia chided herself for behaving like a jealous
harpy and returned resolutely to Mrs. Radcliffe's
heroine.

Contrary to her belief that she would not see the
captain again, Richard Goring appeared at the
Wetherell door just two days after the initial meeting with Fabia. And he did not ask for Petra, instead requesting Fabia, to her surprise and
gratification. April, that capricious month, had
turned warm, and Captain Goring suggested that a
ride in his curricle toward Kingston Lacy might afford her some pleasure. Fabia agreed, donning her
bonnet and a warm pelisse.

Beech trees, lining the tops of the chalkland val-
leys which led from the town, were in bud, promising generous shade in the coming months. A
gentle breeze waved their generous branches.

"I have a message to deliver to Aunt Frances from
my mother, and I thought you might enjoy visiting
Kingston Lacy, the Banks home. It's a splendid pile,
over a century old, but still a family house. A bit

too grand, perhaps. But you may have visited it already?" he enquired, as they rode out of town, leaving behind the imposing grandeur of the minster, whose two squat towers dominated the landscape.

"I have ridden by, of course, and I agree it's a dramatic house with those serried rows of great windows overlooking the parkland. I would very much like a closer view," Fabia agreed.

"Aunt Frances is not really a relative. She's my godmother. Uncle Henry represents Corfe Castle in Parliament and is something of a scholar and art collector," Goring explained.

"Yes, I knew that. Uncle Aubrey greatly respects Mr. Banks's High Tory views," she replied with a slight grimace.

"Well, I don't. He's much too hidebound and unwilling to give any aid to the distressed agricultural workers, a stand he will yet rue, I believe," Goring returned. He smiled then as if to seek her indulgence. "But politics is a dreary subject for such a day and not at all suitable entertainment for a young lady, I am sure."

"Nonsense. I come from farming people myself and quite agree that farm workers here deserve some relief," Fabia protested. She did not want Richard Goring to think she was some silly female with no interests beside fashion and gossip.

"Well, fortunately Uncle Henry is in London, so we need not fear any arguments today. Very unseemly of me as an officer of His Majesty's Navy to be holding radical political views," Richard quipped, not at all displeased by Fabia's comment.

He wanted to learn more of her family, but hesitated to ask.

Fabia, sensing that he was looking for a way to ask about her situation, offered a brief history. "I was born on Nevis, one of the sugar islands. Perhaps you know it?"

"Yes, my ship docked there some years ago, an idyllic place. You must miss it?" he answered smoothly, not eager to pursue the matter if Fabia disliked speaking of her childhood, a feeling he had received from her reticence. He was unusually perceptive and did not want this charming girl to think he was prying.

"Sometimes, especially on a blustery winter day. But my family is all gone, and there is nothing to call me back. I am fortunate in having such affectionate and generous relatives," Fabia said carefully.

"Your Uncle Aubrey seems a good and honest man. I like him."

"So do I. And my cousin Trevor is a darling. Both Aunt Honoria and Petra have been very kind to me," she added, after a significant pause. Was this the captain's roundabout way of asking about Petra? If so, he decided not to pursue the matter. Perhaps because they were now driving up the long avenue toward the red brick Caroline house with its impressive portico.

A groom, upon hearing their approach, hurried from the stables to take Captain Goring's horses, and Fabia was escorted from the curricle up the wide stone steps to the door where they were received with cordiality by the butler.

"Good morning, Langley. Is Mrs. Banks at

home?" Captain Goring asked, as they entered the rather dark hall, accented by Doric columns and a molded ceiling.

"She left yesterday to join the master in London, Captain Goring. But I know she would insist on offering you and the young lady some refreshment," Langley invited, intent on hospitality.

"This is Miss Thurston, Langley, and I am sure she would like a peek at the drawing room and a short tour of the other rooms," Goring replied.

"Isn't this an intrusion?" Fabia whispered, having surrendered her cloak and bonnet to the butler and following Goring across the hall to what proved to be the library.

"Not at all. Langley enjoys showing off the house. Uncle Henry has made some vast changes and would want you to see it," Richard insisted.

Dominating the book-lined room were the Lely portraits of Restoration Bankses, and the keys to Corfe Castle which brave Dame Mary Banks had defended so valiantly during the Civil War.

After chocolate for Fabia and madeira for the captain, Langley escorted them through the drawing room, the saloon, and the dining room, pointing out the changes his master had made after a trip to Rome some years ago. Fabia was impressed by the statuary and pictures, but thought it much too elaborate a residence for comfort.

On their way back toward Wimborne Minster, after Captain Goring had delivered his mother's note to Langley, who would see that Mrs. Banks received it, she hesitated to make her views known.

"A bit overwhelming, don't you think, for a simple country squire," Goring suggested mildly, sensing Fabia's reaction.

"I would not be comfortable living there, although I certainly enjoyed seeing it, rather like a museum," Fabia admitted.

"Quite right. For a simple sailor, it's too elaborate. My own people have a rather plain Queen Anne manor house, comfortable but hardly grand," Goring explained. "You must visit it. But I warn you, it is nothing like Kingston Lacy."

"I don't think you are a simple sailor, Captain Goring."

"And why not, Miss Thurston, or may I call you Fabia?" he dared.

She chuckled. "Of course you may. I don't think *simple* is the adjective I would use to describe you. For one thing you are very young for such an exalted rank."

"I'm just lucky. And I went to sea very early. However, I do wonder what adjective you would use to describe me," he mused with a lift of his eyebrows.

"I shall not tell you, bad for your consequence," Fabia teased, delighted with this interchange. She found herself falling under the spell of the charming captain despite her best efforts to remain impervious.

"We will have to pursue this fascinating topic at another meeting. And may I hope there will be many more?" he asked, giving her a look whose meaning she could not help but find flattering.

In too short a time, they had returned to the Wetherell's house, where Fabia, thanking him for the treat, asked him to come inside.

"I would enjoy that; however, I must meet my friend, the one who cried off that meeting the other day at the Wimborne Arms. But I plan to come to the Assembly next Friday, and I intend to request several dances. I am sure your card will fill all too rapidly, so I must be well beforehand," he added.

"Of course, Captain, I would be delighted," Fabia answered, a small thrill of pleasure bringing a blush to her cheek.

"My name is Richard. And I will look forward to our next meeting, Fabia," he said, doffing his hat. As she entered the door, he ran down the steps with a cheerful grin. Miss Thurston would be seeing quite a bit of him, he promised himself. He found her devilishly attractive. And he wanted his parents to meet this new acquaintance. His mother was often urging him to marry, and now perhaps her patience would be rewarded, he thought, as he tooled his curricle into the main street. Fabia Thurston had hidden qualities he was determined to discover, and who knew where that might lead?

If Fabia's thoughts ran along parallel lines, she had no time to pursue them, for she was confronted by her cousin the moment she entered the house.

"Hollins tells me you went out with Captain Goring. I suppose he was vastly disappointed not to find me at home?" Petra said with annoying complacency.

"He may have been. He did not say," Fabia answered shortly, her momentary delight in the recent encounter dampened by her cousin's insistence that any right-thinking gentleman would prefer her company to that of her cousin's.

"Will he call again?" Petra pursued.

Possibly. You must arrange to be present next time," Fabia said curtly, and continued on her way upstairs, leaving Petra staring after her with a frown.

Three

Petra, left standing open-mouthed in the hall, stared after her cousin, more amazed than angered by the short shrift she had received. Could it be possible that Fabia hoped to annex the eligible captain for herself?

Petra had spent the morning pursuing information about Goring. Determined to learn all she could, she called upon her bosom bow, Mary Anstruther, a meek, toadying, rather mousey brunette who was grateful for whatever Petra offered. Mary Anstruther had one asset, though: she collected gossip like a magpie and knew about every respectable family within a fifty-mile radius of Wimborne.

"So, Mary, what do you know about the Gorings?" Petra asked over the chocolate cups in the Anstruther morning room.

"They are very reserved people, not at all eager to go into society. But they're very well-connected, received at Kingston Lacy, and well thought of in naval circles, from what I hear," Mary obliged.

"It's strange we have not met Captain Goring before this," Petra mused.

"Not really. He went to sea early and then has

been serving abroad for years. Spent very little time in Dorset, I believe."

"And of course, I was away at school," Petra agreed. Then she asked, "What do you know about their place? Is it very extensive?"

"Beechwood, it's called. They open it occasionally for church fetes and similar affairs. I went once to an orphans' relief sale a few years ago with Mother. You were away visiting, I think. Very nice, the house, although of course the sale was on the grounds, so we couldn't see much. Lady Goring was very starchy, I thought, and Sir Thomas rather austere. Are you sure the son is all that attractive?"

"Of course, and not at all starchy. He has lovely manners and seemed quite taken with me. Fortunate that Fabia had that slight accident in Market Street and had the sense to bring him home," she mused, her eyes narrowing as she considered possible schemes to attach the captain.

She never made any effort to hide her plans from Mary, who could not thwart them even if she wished. On the whole Mary only envied Petra's ability to go straight for her objective, which in almost every case was a man. But Mary had a streak of shrewdness, inherited from her merchant father, and she wondered sometimes why it was that Petra had no difficulty in gathering a train of beaux, but never managed to wring a proposal from any of them. Still, that might be because Petra had never really fallen in love, Mary argued grudgingly. She disliked giving up her romantic ideas, and Petra was the very image of a gothic heroine, but love did not appear to figure in Petra's assessment of a husband. But naturally, with her beauty, she should make the best match possible, and the options were limited in Wimborne where few exciting and eligible types made their appearance.

"You are interested in this Captain Goring, then?" she asked slyly.

"Well, I don't know. He might improve on acquaintance. He's here on leave and must be bored to death. Certainly if I were a man, I would not hang about in Dorset but travel posthaste to London and enjoy myself," Petra replied.

"Your brother seems to like it here," Mary said a bit tentatively. She admired Trevor Wetherell greatly, but thought Petra had not discovered this fact and wanted to keep her frustrated yearning a secret, sensibly feeling that Petra would make some use of it.

"Oh, Trevor. He's so stodgy, content to read his old moldy law books and never cut a dash." Petra dismissed her brother with a careless wave of her hand.

"Do you think Captain Goring will come to the Assembly next Friday?" Mary asked to distract Petra from any suspicion she had an interest in Trevor.

"Yes, I do, and what's more, I will let him have as many dances as he wants, and hang what those old chaperons say," Petra said insouciantly, knowing how shocking her statement was. No respectable girl danced more than twice with a gentleman unless they were formally engaged. To do so was to risk gaining a reputation of being fast, possible to ignore perhaps in London, but not in a conservative Dorset minster town.

Mary displayed the proper reaction to such a daring idea: "You wouldn't, Petra!"

"Yes, I would. Don't be such a goose, Mary. No man with any spirit wants some tame dreary girl who is constantly bleating about the proprieties. And I think I know the kind of girl Captain Goring admires," she preened. Then tiring of confidences and a bit annoyed at having betrayed so much to Mary, she took her leave.

However, Petra was soon to admit that she might have been mistaken in her insistence that she knew the kind of girl Captain Goring admired. Changing her tactics, she began to make an effort with Fabia, pretending an interest which did not deceive her cousin.

If Petra had behaved with even a lukewarm friendship toward Fabia when she had first settled into the Wetherell household, she might have welcomed these overtures, but Fabia distrusted her cousin. She was ashamed that she felt uncomfortable at Petra's attempts to alter their relationship, but she doubted her cousin's sincerity and suspected the reason for it.

Captain Goring had called one afternoon in response to the rector's invitation to tell him more of his naval experiences. He showed no inordinate interest in either of the cousins but confined most of his remarks to the rector, who bore him off to his library after tea for a discussion of these exploits. Petra, to her annoyance, could not tell whether he preferred her to her cousin, and Fabia herself made no real push to attract his interest. Still, Petra comforted herself with the thought that the Assembly was just two days off, and she knew that she appeared to best advantage on these occasions. It might be best to probe Fabia's intentions, though, and perhaps warn her off delicately. In this stratagem she encountered a cool rebuff.

"What are you planning to wear for the Assembly?" she asked Fabia in what she thought was a winning manner.

"I haven't given it much thought," Fabia replied, not raising her eyes from some delicate household mending. She was an accomplished seamstress and often lent her hand to repair torn sheets and tablecloths.

"Perhaps you have decided not to go," Petra offered, not quite able to mask her hopes that this might be true.

"Oh, no, I will attend. I have already been solicited for several dances and could not disappoint my partner," Fabia insisted a bit wickedly.

"And might I ask who this fortunate gentleman is?" Petra asked, biting her lip in vexation. Really, Fabia could be annoying.

"I think I will let it be a surprise. You are not the only girl in demand at these affairs, Petra," she answered sharply, becoming irritated by her cousin's ploys.

"Of course, I know that, Fabia. I did not intend to pry. I just thought you might confide in me," Petra retreated, sensing her cousin's affront at the question. She began to worry that the gentleman just might be Captain Goring, but how was she to discover that and what could she do to circumvent his dancing with Fabia? Petra's conceit could not contemplate that she had a serious rival in her cousin.

Fabia did not respond to her cousin's wistful suggestion of confidences. Petra, hiding her anger at such obstinacy, veered off in another direction.

"I believe I will wear my blue silk. I thought of the green, but it is rather a harsh color for blondes, don't you think?"

"Depends on the blonde," Fabia retorted, becoming weary of this fencing.

"Guy Fancher says I look best in blue. You have not met him yet, Fabia, but he really is quite entertaining. He's also a naval officer," she explained artfully.

"Really. I suppose with some of the fleet in Portland we will be seeing officers, although Wimborne is a bit distant for daily meetings."

"I do like the navy. Much more dashing than the army," Petra pressed. "Captain Goring is certainly unusual, don't you think?"

"I don't really know him that well. He seems most unexceptional."

"Oh, Fabia, you're so prim and proper. How will you ever get a husband if you don't try to attract one?" Petra fumed, frustrated by Fabia's laconic remarks.

"I'm not sure I want to make an all-out assault on the marriage mart. There are other options."

"A girl must marry unless she wants to spend the rest of her life sitting by the fire, mending her relatives' linen, and taking tea with old women like Mrs. Milford-Smythe." Having delivered this Parthian shot, Petra left Fabia to her sewing, having learned nothing to banish her doubts about her cousin's interest in Richard Goring.

That evening as she brushed her hair before retiring to bed, Fabia tried to examine her feelings about that disturbing young man. Disturbing because she was spending too much time thinking about him and disturbing, too, because she had no intention of entering the lists against her cousin in regards to Richard Goring, even though she did not think he cared tuppence for Petra. That young lady had determined to pursue him and would never be deterred by matters of propriety or accusations of immodesty. Fabia's own reactions to Captain Goring were a mixture of pleasure and hesitation. She did not want to chance her heart and be rebuffed. Not that it had yet come to that.

Lying in bed later, she sensibly decided she would take a day at a time. The captain might just be amusing himself, trying to attract her as an antidote to boredom during his shore leave. But she could not quite make herself believe that.

Since those first days when she had learned of her family's death aboard the ship carrying them back to Nevis, she had coped with the tragedy by trying to forget it. It was not always possible, but she had learned that she must try to put those dreadful days behind her. Her happy childhood had not prepared her for the blows that rained upon her, and it might be deemed fortunate that scarlet fever had dimmed the memory of those days following the death of Stella's betrothed. She had been protected then by her parents from much of the horror, but the subsequent death of her family

had changed her from a cheerful adventurous
schoolgirl into the sober young woman her cousin
Petra found so boring.

The Wetherells had, for the most part, proved to
be a kind refuge from loneliness, and she was grateful to them, even if she could not offer the warm
affection they deserved. Now she might have to
emerge from that long arid apathy to risk again the
hurt which giving one's heart demanded. Did she
want to abandon her defenses? And was Richard
Goring the man who would force her to emerge
from her detachment? Fabia, who had little patience
with self-pity or much experience in examining her
feelings, decided sensibly that she was borrowing
trouble. She admired the gallant captain and was
flattered by his attentions, but it need go no further
than a pleasant interlude. Having decided on that
course of action, she fell into a fitful sleep, dark-
ened by dreams of shadowy figures quarreling amid
the lush green sugar fields of her birthplace while
she stood by, helpless to alter events.

Fabia's Uncle Aubrey was also haunted by the
specters of that island tragedy. He had tried to follow the sensible advice of his son and banish all
suspicions that Richard Goring could have been involved in that grim affair. During his conversations
with Goring, he had learned that the young officer
had indeed visited Nevis during his tour of duty.
More worrisome was the fact that Goring seemed
strangely reluctant to discuss that episode in his career. He was most frank and open about his family
and his service with Nelson in the Mediterranean,
but whenever the rector tried to raise questions

about his West Indies service, he brushed aside the inquiries, implying that it was of little importance compared to later engagements.

Aubrey Wetherell was becoming convinced that Richard Goring had a past of which he was deeply ashamed, which might mean the young captain could be the man who had killed Stella Thurston's betrothed in that drunken duel. He did not appear to be a dissipated man, nor did the rector think that his career could have prospered so well if he had been that man, but doubts remained. The reverend greatly feared that Richard Goring was falling in love with his niece and before long would ask his permission to pay his addresses to her. Then what course should Fabia's guardian follow?

Aubrey Wetherell wrestled with the dilemma through many prayerful hours but could not come to a decision. His inclination to avoid precipitating a crisis might be cowardly, but inaction seemed his only choice. He dreaded having to remind Fabia of those days. And the irony of her coming to care for the man who had brought her sister such misery was intolerable. Worry would avail him little, but he could not entirely banish such a possibility. He must trust that God, who had never failed him, would solve this problem and show him the right direction.

Richard Goring, not unmindful that the rector had some maggot in his head about his eligibility, wondered what that estimable gentleman's objection could be to himself as a suitor for his niece. The only solution he could find was that the Reverend Mr. Wetherell preferred Richard as a son-in-law, the husband for his daughter. How was Richard to hint that lovely as Petra might be, it was her cousin he wanted for a bride? Only a very tolerant father could accept such a rejection of his daughter.

Richard had not been unaware of Petra's ploys to engage his interest, and he had done his best to stifle her intentions, but so convinced was the young lady of her charms that she would not accept his preference for her cousin, if indeed she even noticed it. Well, he would have to take positive steps to see that she understood the situation, a tricky maneuver that would call on all his skills as a tactician. But Richard Goring had decided that Fabia was the bride he wanted, and he had no hesitation in moving toward his goal. Of course, Fabia might refuse him, but he sensed she was coming to care for him, and he would do all in his power to secure her affections. He was not a man easily dissuaded from his course once he had decided to pursue it. But he did not dream of the malign fate that would soon overtake him.

Four

Wimborne Minster's Assembly, held on the second Friday of every month during the season, was a much more casual affair than similar gatherings in Bath's Pump Room or London's Almack's. The hall itself, a new Georgian brick building on Market Street, had little to recommend it beside its size. This Friday evening an unusually large number of the gentry crowded the stark paneled room, which could accommodate about thirty couples comfortably and perhaps a dozen more in a squeeze. Some of the neighborhood young gallants were dismayed to see an influx of naval officers, at least a half a dozen, who were casting them in the shade. Petra, looking radiant in her promised blue silk, her hair artfully arranged in tendrils, was in great demand, but Fabia, too, quickly filled her own card. She was wearing a simple French-embroidered muslin gown in apricot with long white gloves and a double strand of pearls. Richard had been prompt to claim his two dances, the opening quadrille and the supper dance. Courtesy demanded he ask Petra to be his partner as well, but to her disappointment he only scrawled his initials on one reel. She pouted at this omission and protested coyly.

"Oh, Captain Goring, I particularly saved the supper dance for you."

"How kind of you, Miss Wetherell, but I supposed a lady of your attractions would be besieged, and I made other arrangements," he answered smoothly.

"Well, of course I am," she said smugly, not willing to admit he had neatly turned down her offer. "As a matter of fact, I think I'm already promised to Guy Fancher." She indicated a fair-haired man standing in the circle about her, who stepped up closer when he saw that she was about to honor his request.

"Do you know Lieutenant Fancher, Captain Goring?" Petra asked. "You should, you know, as he is a naval officer, too."

Richard bowed and acknowledged the introduction a bit curtly. He did not like the look of Fancher: those pale blue eyes and thin lips hinted at obstinacy allied with a certain self-conceit.

Fancher, all affability, replied, "How fortuitous; we must compare notes, old man. Alas, I have not really seen much active service, but I am sure that will soon be remedied. I am waiting for a ship now."

"Do you live in the neighborhood?" Richard asked, as the two men separated a bit from the cluster about Petra. Fancher had secured the supper dance from her, although he did not like to acknowledge that he was second choice.

"I am visiting some relatives nearby. Very tedious this hanging about, and I must say the entertainment is limited. There are few beauties like Miss Wetherell, alas, but she is certainly a *Nonpareil*, don't you agree? We have formed quite a friendship," he said, implying that Richard was late in the field.

"Quite. Have you met her family?" Richard asked. Somehow he did not like the idea of this man being on intimate terms with the Wetherells. If he confined his intentions to Petra, that would be acceptable, but Richard did not want Fabia to meet him. He had to admit that at first glance Fancher was a handsome devil, but his manner had a touch of the mountebank about it. Far too fond of himself, also.

"Not yet, but Miss Wetherell has promised such a meeting will not be long delayed. We must get together and share a glass. I am sure you could give me some good advice," Fancher replied.

Annoyed that he had let the man get to him, Richard agreed and turned away to find Fabia, for the first dance was about to begin.

"What do you think of our local hall, Captain Goring? I suppose you have seen grander assemblies and might despise our rustic affair," Fabia asked as the movements of the dance brought them together.

"Not at all. I think it's quite cozy. I have attended some assemblies in Bath and London which were terrible crushes. Not at all to my taste. I really prefer the country to more sophisticated circles. London depresses me with its bustle, crowds, and poverty. Behind the smart facade there is an underworld full of pathetic men and women living in utmost squalor, and worse, every sort of depravity."

"I have always wanted to visit London. I passed through the city on my way to Cheltenham, to school, but I remember very little, except the noise

and confusion of the streets. It is disheartening to
hear there is so much destitution and vice when on
the surface there is so much wealth and style."
Fabia's opinion of Captain Goring had risen to new
heights when she heard sentiments that echoed her
own.

"If we finally defeat Napoleon, I want to retire
and live down here. My father needs help with the
estate, and I might even stand for Parliament. Dorset may have an idyllic situation, remote and un-
spoiled, but farm laborers lead lives of grinding toil
with little to mitigate their lot. There will be trouble
before long if the government does not come to
their aid in some way," Richard promised. Then he
shook his head in self-reproof. "What am I thinking
of with such gloomy talk. You know, Fabia, you have
an uncanny way of making me reveal my more serious side, not at all the thing when I should be
entertaining you with harmless gossip and compliments. I do apologize."

"Not at all. I am flattered. I, too, have a deep
concern over the plight of our agricultural workers.
I have talked to Uncle Aubrey about it, but his only
answer is prayer. Now Trevor, his son, is also sober
and serious but has more experience of the world.
You have not met Trevor, I believe."

"Trevor, no, I have not met him. Is he here tonight so I can remedy this omission?" Richard asked
as the figures of the dances concluded. He wondered if Trevor, Fabia's cousin, could possibly be a
rival. She spoke most favorably of him.

"Yes, just over there with the young lady in the

white sprigged gown, Mary Anstruther. We might join them at supper."

Although Richard had no intention of saying so to Fabia, he hoped that Trevor would prove to be more satisfying than the Wetherells he had already met. How unfortunate for Fabia that the relatives who offered her a home after her parents' death, although not unkind and certainly willing to accept a certain responsibility for her, had failed her in many ways. He could not imagine Honoria Wetherell comforting the bereft girl, nor her daughter Petra capable of a sincere friendship. He acquitted Aubrey Wetherell of indifference, but wondered what beyond the usual nostrums of a pastor he had used to comfort Fabia. No wonder she had developed an air of prim aloofness as a protection against further hurts.

But perhaps he was exaggerating the inadequacies of the Wetherells due to his own fervent desire to accept Fabia's comforts himself. Trevor Wetherell remained an unknown quantity. He looked forward to making the young man's acquaintance.

Having delivered Fabia to her aunt, where her next partner was awaiting her, he strolled onto the balcony which overlooked a small garden to the rear of the hall. The night remained warm, exceedingly so for April, and he felt the need of a respite, wondering how he was to proceed with the enigmatic Fabia. Every conversation with her strengthened his admiration and convinced him they shared a common outlook on life. He was not such a cold-blooded prig that he believed marriage consisted wholly of shared interests, respectable background, and certain worthwhile qualities. Fabia had first attracted him by her lack of artifice, her lovely figure, and green eyes which hinted not only of mystery but of passion beneath that facade of reserve. Not for Fabia the conventional flirtatious manners of her shallow cousin or the country belles who made up Wimborne society. Her uncle had informed Richard of the tragedy which had formed her character, exposed her to trials most girls her age would never experience. She had learned to cope with her loneliness of spirit with courage, but her vulnerability could not be hidden from one who cared enough to probe behind that curtain of reserve.

He had undertaken an arduous mission, to teach Fabia to trust him while persuading her of his love and belief that they could have a fulfilling life together. He must teach her to love him and not be afraid of the future, not an easy task since as a serving officer he might die on any tour while the country was at war. A rather daunting prospect, but not one beyond his powers, he felt. Of course, he could be deluding himself that Fabia cared a fig about him. Her rather polite, cool air might hide indifference if not actual dislike, but somehow he thought not. At any rate he had set his mind to securing her for his wife, and Captain Goring was not one to be easily turned from a challenge.

All these thoughts had run rapidly through his mind as he stood alone on the balcony of the Assembly Hall, unaware of the activity behind him. But social obligations could not be ignored. It was time for his dance with the arduous Petra. Shrugging off his distaste, he sought out his partner, who

was as usual surrounded by luckless importune
beaux who had not secured a dance with her.

"Miss Wetherell. I believe you are promised to
me for this dance." Richard bowed, not at all impressed by Petra's turning her back on the cluster
of gentlemen and pressing herself against him,
clinging to his arm.

The steps of the dance allowed them more opportunity to talk than Richard wished, and Petra
appeared determined to seize the chance to portray
herself in her best light, not suspecting the captain
only considered her a duty, not a delight.

"Oh, Captain Goring, I was so disappointed that
some other more fortunate girl secured you for the
supper dance. I wanted to have the chance to have
a *real* intimate conversation together. But it will have
to wait until a more opportune time. A ride in the
country, perhaps, now that the weather has turned
mild."

Repressing a shudder at the thought of being
trapped in his curricle with Petra for several hours,
exposed to her irritating brand of flirtation and attempts to lure him into a compromising position,
Richard merely smiled and said lightly, "I am sure,
Miss Wetherell, you have many more fascinating fellows begging you for your company. I am really the
dullest of sailors, unaccustomed to paying compliments and exchanging repartee with a fashionable
belle such as yourself."

Petra, angered by Richard's honeyed rejection,
gave up any pretense of coyness. "I know that Fabia
has thrust herself upon you, you poor man. I have
introduced her to several likely men, but she doesn't

seem to take, if you understand my meaning. I suppose meeting you in that rather surprising way, she could not be despised for taking advantage."

But Richard was not to be drawn, no matter how spiteful and immodest Petra's remarks struck him. Some expression must have revealed his distaste, for she quickly corrected her mistake, remembering too late that her mother had always warned her that men dislike girls running down their rivals. She must not leave him with the impression that she was a nasty cat.

"Of course, Fabia is the dearest girl, and we are the best of friends. But I do get impatient that she won't make more of an effort socially. For her own good, you understand." Petra swirled near him as the maneuvers of the dance brought them back together.

"Oh, quite," Richard replied laconically, understanding all too well what Petra meant.

At last the dance ended and Richard escorted Petra back to her mother and collected Fabia for the supper dance. This rather boisterous country dance did not allow for much conversation for which Richard was thankful. Petra's sly comments had left an unpleasant and worrying impression, not eased by that young lady's raised eyebrows when she saw that Richard's escort to supper was the cousin she had just damned with faint praise.

Panting a bit from the dance's spirited steps, Fabia laughed at Richard, whose breathing had hardly quickened. Richard enjoyed the sight, for he could not recall her appearing so carefree at their other meetings.

"You enjoyed that, I believe," he teased as they drifted toward the supper room to the left of the hall.

"Yes, indeed, but I realize I must take some more strenuous exercise if I am not to dwindle into one of those frail misses inclined to vapors."

"Nonsense. The weather has not encouraged such exertions lately. Do you ride, Fabia?" he asked.

"I used to, and as a child was never off my mare, but Wimborne Minster does not offer many opportunities."

"Well, we must arrange the opportunity. I have a rather nice mare in the stables that might suit you. We will plan an outing."

Pleased by Richard's reference to future meetings, Fabia entered the supper room, realizing that for the first time she was finding this Assembly to her taste. Noticing her cousin Trevor seated at a small table, she indicated she wished to join him and his companion, Mary Anstruther.

Trevor stood at their approach. Fabia introduced Richard to him and Mary.

"You look very cozy here. May we join you?" she asked.

"Please do. I see Petra entering on the arm of Guy Fancher, and you will kindly spare me a dose of that gentleman's company," Trevor replied.

"I have yet to meet the man, but he seems quite interested in your sister, Trevor. Do not be unkind," Fabia reproved, sitting down in the chair Richard was holding.

"If you will excuse me, I will search out the refreshments. What do you recommend, Wetherell?"

"Very little. The offering is rather sparse as usual, but avoid the ginger cake and concentrate on the creamed chicken patties. They are edible," Trevor advised.

Petra, undeterred by her brother's unwelcoming expression, whispered into Guy Fancher's ear an engaging plea, and the pair approached Trevor's table.

"Can we join you? If we crowd together a bit, I am sure there is room. Mary, just push closer to Trevor," Petra suggested wickedly, knowing her friend would be embarrassed by the idea. Guy Fancher quickly secured two chairs from a neighboring empty table, and when Richard returned with filled plates, he saw that their party had been augmented by the very pair he had hoped to avoid.

Sitting down beside Fabia, he noticed that the arrival of Petra and Fancher had cast a blight over the party. Fancher, having just met Fabia, Mary, and Trevor, was on his best behavior, flattering Trevor by asking his advice about a local tailor, but casting ingratiating smiles at the ladies. Petra had adopted a certain arch gaiety that Richard found grating, and ignoring her, he turned to the modest Mary Anstruther.

"It seems odd that we have never met before, Miss Anstruther, seeing we are both from Dorset families," Richard said kindly.

"Oh, Mary's father is a merchant, a very successful one, but I doubt if your parents would have come across him or his wife," Petra said, interrupting carelessly and bringing a blush of mortification to Mary's cheek and a frown from Trevor.

"Well, in a way, the Gorings are merchants, too.

What we sell is farm produce. Whatever the market calls for we can supply. I suppose that is why Napoleon calls us a nation of shopkeepers," Richard said, hoping to repress Petra.

"And a good thing, too," Trevor offered stoutly. "Where would our nation be without trade?"

"And without the navy to defend that trade," Fabia suggested.

"Yes, without gallant officers such as Guy here and Captain Goring, we might all be murdered in our beds," Petra said extravagantly, realizing that her efforts to put Mary in her place had only pushed her into the limelight.

"Hardly that, I think, Miss Wetherell," Richard argued in a blighting tone. Really, she was not only a most annoying girl, but a cruel, selfish one beside.

Trevor, not unmindful of his sister's gaffe, rushed into a discussion of Horatio Nelson, for whom he had a great admiration, as did both officers. His tactful digression kept the party fairly amicable until sounds of the orchestra tuning up called them back to the ballroom. As they prepared to join the other dancers, Trevor drew his sister to one side and warned her, "You will never get a husband if you continue to behave so shabbily to other girls, Petra. Keep your spiteful tongue to yourself." He turned away before Petra could reply.

Suitably chastened, because she realized she had behaved badly, she joined her next partner determined to show Trevor, Richard Goring, Guy, all of them, that she was still the reigning belle of Wimborne.

Richard lingered by Fabia's side as she waited for

her own partner. "I regret that propriety limits our dances to two. But I intend to hold you to your promise of riding now that spring has finally made some expeditions possible. And I want you to come to Beechwood and meet my parents."

A little breathless from the intensity of his gaze and the feeling that they were fast approaching a turning point in their relationship, Fabia hesitated, only to be disarmed by Richard's smile and explanation. "Sailors are always in a hurry. Who knows how long one's time on shore can be. So, now you see the reason I cannot afford a leisurely courtship." He bowed, leaving Fabia astonished but not displeased with this frank avowal, and her next partner, a portly young squire's son, was favored with such a blinding smile that he could not believe his good fortune.

Five

Having declared himself, Richard lost no time in carrying out his plan. A few days after the Assembly, Mrs. Wetherell received a letter from Lady Goring inviting the family for luncheon at a date convenient to them. A bit flustered, Mrs. Wetherell turned to her husband for advice. She took the unusual step of cornering him in his study, where he was supposed to be writing his sermon. In actuality he was gazing out the window at the brave show of daffodils and crocuses in his back garden.

"So sorry to interrupt, Aubrey, but I have just had this charming note from Lady Goring inviting us all to luncheon on a day of our choosing. I knew I must arrange it to your convenience. Do you think that young Richard is interested in our Petra and that is the reason for the invitation?" she asked, sinking a bit breathlessly into a chair beside her husband's desk.

"No, Honoria, it is not Petra he is interested in, but Fabia," the rector said shortly.

"Oh, how odd. Fabia is such a serious girl, but quite attractive. I would never have thought any man would prefer her to Petra." Honoria shook her head as if puzzled by the vagaries of men's tastes.

"You must rid yourself of the notion that every young man yearns for an empty-headed beauty with little notion of how to go on or how to talk sensibly. After the first fine rapture, such a companion can be a trial, and Petra, although she's a lovely looking girl, lacks the intellect required by a man such as young Goring."

Aubrey Wetherell was intelligent and honest enough to admit, if his wife was not, that Petra's charms would be ill-suited to a serving officer's life, and from the first he had sensed that Richard Goring found few appealing qualities in his daughter. Honoria might find that surprising, but her husband quite understood, although he had hesitated to explain Petra's faults to her mother. Privately the rector thought his wife had done little to repress the selfishness and shallowness of their daughter, and that her ambitions for the girl's fine marriage would not be fulfilled.

"I think you are most unkind and unfair to Petra, Aubrey. She is a beautiful girl and has always had a flock of beaux," Honoria insisted, with maternal pride.

"Yes, but I have not noticed that any of them wanted to marry her. At least they have not approached me to that end. Young Goring is an earnest suitor of Fabia. I will have to give serious consideration to his offer, if indeed he makes one."

"Well, of course you will consent. It would be a splendid match for her." Honoria looked surprised that her husband would have the least reluctance to agree.

"Yes, well, we will see." He was not yet prepared

to share with his wife his questions about Richard's connection to the Nevis tragedy.

"Trevor likes him," Honoria said more decisively than usual. She knew her son's opinion carried more weight with the rector than her own.

"Yes, I know, and so do I, but I have a responsibility to my sister. Fabia will come into a nice competence on her twenty-first birthday or her marriage. I must see that she is protected from fortune hunters," he explained, realizing how weak that excuse sounded. He had never feared that Richard Goring was a fortune hunter.

Honoria looked puzzled. She did not understand her husband's reluctance to endorse this splendid opportunity for Fabia. Although Mrs. Wetherell was not of a passionate temperament and took life placidly for the most part, she found it difficult to feel deep affection for her niece. If Fabia married Richard Goring, she would be relieved. Not only would her niece no longer be her responsibility, but Fabia's new position would allow Petra to be introduced into a wider, more elegant social circle.

"Well, of course, I will be guided by whatever you think best, Aubrey, but Fabia can be very determined underneath that aloof manner. She might insist on marrying this man whatever your objections."

"Perhaps, but we may be borrowing problems. This invitation may not be a portent of Goring's intentions but just a neighborly gesture since we have entertained him. Today is Wednesday. Suggest next Monday to Lady Goring, always a good day for me," the rector advised and put on his spectacles, signaling the interview was at an end.

Honoria gathered up Lady Goring's missive, nodded to her husband, and left the room, her mind scurrying about aimlessly, but coming back to the one impression she had received. For some reason, Aubrey was not enthusiastic about Richard Goring as a husband for Fabia.

Guy Fancher was also speculating about the relationship between Fabia and Richard Goring. A little judicious probing had revealed that Fabia had a more than tidy competence. In fact she was almost an heiress, according to the ubiquitous Mrs. Milford-Smythe, a bosom bow of his godmother's, with whom he was staying.

Over the teacups the lady had confided that Fabia had inherited a huge sugar plantation in Nevis from her late parents, and as her sister had also died, she was the sole legatee. If Guy marveled at Mrs. Milford-Smythe's sources, he was convinced her information was accurate as she had learned about Fabia from Honoria Wetherell, that lady being unable to resist Mrs. Milford-Smythe's prying. He also learned that Petra, who in some ways he preferred, had only a modest dowry.

Guy acknowledged he might have a rival in Captain Goring, but his own conceit dismissed his fellow officer as a threat to his own intentions. Guy badly needed money. He had run through the inheritance left him by his uncle, and his parents lived in genteel poverty in Shropshire, where he rarely visited them. Mrs. Milford-Smythe, her nose for rumor twitching, soon realized that this personable young

man with the charming manners was interested in
Fabia, and she wondered spitefully if Petra would
be abandoned for her cousin, an interesting situation, and one Guy did nothing to disabuse her of.

He knew he must act without delay if he hoped
to attract Fabia's interest, and he lost no time in
putting his plan into effect. The day after the tea
party, he called at the Wetherells hoping to lure
Fabia for a ride but was disappointed to learn she
was absent. He made do with Petra, who never
doubted for one moment that she was the object of
his call. Although he was not sure how to free Petra
from the idea that he would soon offer for her, he
knew that here was an excellent opportunity to quiz
her about her cousin, and so the pair set off, each
with different motives for the outing.

"And where is your cousin today? She's quite a
pretty girl. I wonder why I had not met her before
last Friday's Assembly," Guy said a bit maliciously,
knowing full well that Petra could not entertain the
thought that her cousin might appear attractive to
any man that she herself had decided to honor with
her attention.

"She's out riding with Captain Goring," Petra answered sharply. She had arisen late to learn that
Captain Goring had arrived with the promised mare
and that he and Fabia had left soon after breakfast
for a gallop. Petra decided she would have to abandon her usual practice of breakfasting in bed so as
to be on hand to prevent any further mishaps.

"He seems a nice chap," Guy offered, suspecting
that Petra would reveal the full details of the relationship between Richard and Fabia.

"Rather dull, even though he is quite handsome," Petra conceded, giving Guy a roguish glance which implied that he had equally appealing assets.

"Is it serious, the situation between your cousin and Goring?" Guy asked carelessly, as though it was of little interest to him.

"Oh, no, I don't think so. He's just bored, waiting for his ship, and ready to indulge in a little light flirtation."

"But I thought he was dull, and he seems, too, the epitome of propriety. Surely he would not lead your cousin to expect an offer when he has no intention of giving one."

"Of course not. But you gentlemen are all the most errant flirts. I don't trust any of you," Petra trilled, delighted with the chance to engage in a little harmless bandiage.

"I am wounded, Petra, that you suspect me of frivolous conduct."

"Nonsense. You are probably engaging in just such inconstancy this minute. You are a rake, Guy Fancher," she insisted, her tone suggesting that she found this quite fascinating.

"And you are a minx, Petra, but a stunner for all that. What's a poor fellow to do when you treat us all so carelessly?" he riposted, knowing that what she wanted to hear was a profession of undying devotion. Well, she would wait a long time for that.

The ride continued with neither party particularly satisfied.

* * *

Meanwhile Richard and Fabia were having a much easier and more companionable conversation.

"I am delighted you and your relatives can come to luncheon Monday week. I do want you to meet my parents," Richard said, his sincerity apparent.

"I am looking forward to it," Fabia replied, slowing her mare to a walk as they neared a rather dilapidated bridge. She patted her horse's neck appreciatively as the mare responded to Fabia's sure hand on the reins. Richard, following, admired her straight back and good seat. She had a gentle but firm hand, he decided.

"You do not seem to have lost any of your riding skill," he approved as they crossed the bridge and rode abreast.

"This is a darling mare. She has no nasty habits and has obviously been well-trained, so all I have to do is relax. I am quite enjoying this ride."

They continued silently for a while when Richard suggested they might dismount and sit on a convenient stone wall as the day was bright and sunny. Fabia agreed, and he handed her down and secured their horses before joining her.

"So difficult to talk when you are riding," he complained.

"But the object is exercise, not chatting," Fabia teased, quite content to follow his lead, but not entirely willing to let him have it all his way.

"Well, I haven't much time. My ship should be ready in a few weeks," Richard informed her with a wealth of meaning in his tone and glance.

"Time for what?" Fabia asked, deliberately misunderstanding, but not displeased at his hint.

"I want to impress upon you what a marvelous fellow I am before I sail away," Richard replied lightly, but his eyes belied the frivolity of his words.

"Are you a marvelous fellow?"

"I doubt it, but I would like you to think so." Then, surprising her, he leaned over and kissed her gently on the lips. Fabia found it not unpleasant, but she had a fleeting moment of doubt. Was he just flirting, passing the time until he sailed away as he had indicated?

Richard, as if reading her thoughts, said, "I am not a bounder, Fabia, and I want you to think well of me. I find you a completely attractive young woman: compassionate, sensible, and intelligent."

"That sounds like a very paragon, and not at all attractive. I would much rather you found me provocative, exciting, perhaps even unattainable." Fabia could not resist leading him on to further disclosure.

"I hope you are not the latter. You must know I am not just flirting with you, Fabia. I find you out of the ordinary, and just the kind of girl for a sailor." He wanted to pursue the idea, but he noticed her slight withdrawal. "I know it is too soon to make any commitment, but do not see our acquaintance, may I say friendship, as a light affair. I do not want to rush you, but I warn you now I have serious thoughts of you."

Fabia could not repress a shudder of delight at his frank expression of his feelings. His kiss had not shocked her, only left her with inchoate emotions she could not define, but certainly they did not include distaste. Richard Goring was a very appealing man, but she could not allow him to presume too much. She did not want him to think she reacted as her cousin might, wantonly and eagerly. She stood up and indicated they must resume their ride.

"You are not angry that I kissed you, are you, Fabia? Frankly, I want nothing more than to do it again," he said with an outrageous smile.

"If all sailors are as bold as you, Richard, I will have to be on my guard. No, I am not angry, only surprised."

"And perhaps just a bit pleased?" he asked, pressing his advantage.

"I will admit nothing," Fabia laughed as he helped her into the saddle.

"Not yet, but I am a determined chap and have not lost hope," Richard replied, settling her skirt with a pat and turning away before she could read his expression.

They rode on with the knowledge that a decisive point in their relationship had been reached, however delicately they had skirted over the implications. Fabia discovered that she anticipated future passages at arms with Richard Goring. She could not doubt his sincerity nor that he felt attracted to her as she did to him. The future looked very promising, indeed.

Six

The Wetherell party set off for Beechwood and the meeting with the Gorings with a variety of emotions. Mrs. Wetherell worried about the carriage. It was a matter of some chagrin to her that her husband refused to keep a vehicle, claiming there was little need for this expense. Honoria felt ashamed at his parsimony, believing it unwarranted. And what would the Gorings think of such a shabby economy? Her husband, much too concerned about the coming interview with Sir Thomas, gave no thought to their conveyance. He was determined to discover if Richard was the duelist who had shot Fabia's sister's betrothed and brought tragedy to the Thurston family.

Petra, pleased with her cerulean blue walking dress and the rather dashing flat-crowned gypsy bonnet trimmed in matching ribbon, could not entirely repress the disagreeable sense that she would not be the center of attention at this gathering. Her conceit notwithstanding, she had been forced to realize that Fabia, not herself, was the reason for this invitation, a circumstance that vexed her exceedingly. However, she still had hopes of retrieving the situation.

Only Trevor and Fabia appeared to be anticipating the day at Beechwood with relative pleasure. Trevor, because he, like his sister, sensed that the occasion was a prelude to Richard Goring asking for Fabia's hand in marriage. Trevor liked both Fabia and Richard, thought they were well-matched, and was pleased for his cousin, whose life had not been filled with much happiness. And he admitted to a certain gentle enjoyment at his sister's discomfort. Petra was too apt to consider herself a *Nonpareil*, and entitled to any proposals going.

Fabia, reluctant to examine her own hopes for this meeting and what it promised, could not help a certain surge of excitement. Richard had admitted he cared for her. She doubted that his parents' approval or disapproval of his choice would influence him greatly, but she certainly did not want them to take her in disgust. Really she was a ninny to imagine such a thing. She was sure that the Gorings were friendly well-disposed people who would welcome her and her relatives warmly and that the day would hold no pitfalls. She knew in her heart that Richard cared for her, and she, in turn, had finally admitted to herself, if not to him, that she loved him, too. What could possibly happen to darken that felicity?

In rather less than an hour the hired carriage covered the fifteen miles to Beechwood, and as they rolled up the long avenue, lined with beeches, Fabia glimpsed in the distance a square Queen Anne house of Portland stone, softened by Tuscan pilasters. A comfortable manor house, the Goring establishment was neither too lavish nor too plain; just right, she thought, looking with approval at the spare lines and well-spaced windows below the hipped roof. As their carriage approached the marble steps, Richard came out to welcome them.

"Good morning, sir, and Mrs. Wetherell. Trevor, Petra, so glad you could accompany your parents," he said warmly before turning to assist Fabia, giving her a speaking look, "I hope you will like my home, Fabia," he said simply.

Her only reply was a smile. He escorted them into a generous gray-slated hall, where a manservant relieved them of their outer garments, and then Richard shepherded them into the drawing room.

Fabia had a fleeting impression of the comfortable salon—spring flower bouquets, chintz-covered chairs, and pale green silk curtains—before her eye was drawn to the brown-haired woman rising to greet them. Lady Goring looked too young to have a grown son, with her trim figure, unlined creamy complexion, and luxurious brown hair skillfully arranged. She wore a garnet merino gown, simply trimmed with Michelin lace, and her dark eyes softened as she turned to Fabia after politely acknowledging Richard's introduction.

"We are so pleased to see you here, my dear. Richard has told me a great deal about you, and I look forward to a nice coze, just the two of us, after luncheon," Serena Goring said, leaving Fabia in little doubt that Richard had confided in his mother. And, well he might, she conceded, for Serena Goring suited her name, calm, secure, yet compassionate, with none of the country snobbery that Fabia had sometimes encountered.

Sir Thomas, an older edition of Richard, with his son's clear blue eyes and shock of dark hair, politely welcomed the Wetherells before turning to inspect the young members of the party. His rather fierce manner softened somewhat on meeting Fabia.

A shrewd judge of character, Sir Thomas looked over Petra and saw that the pretty minx was a bit out of sorts; she seemed the type who preferred to be the center of attention. Like his wife, deciding that Fabia would repay a closer examination later, he flattered Petra and had her quite believing that she had not lost her ability to charm any man, whatever his age or position. Soon the party had settled down for a chat about the fireplace, enjoying some refreshments before lunch, ratafia for the ladies, madeira for the gentlemen.

"Although we have met before, Wetherell, on county business, I am pleased to have this opportunity to extend our acquaintance. I know you must have many calls on your time, so we doubly appreciate your sparing us this day," Sir Thomas said smoothly. Trevor, listening to the conversation, thought that Sir Thomas must be quite an asset to the magistrate's bench. Experience, competence, and breeding were just a few of the qualities Sir Thomas displayed. Trevor decided he would not be an easy man to deceive, nor did it seem as though he would be influenced by wealth or position.

Aubrey Wetherell was having his usual second thoughts on a course of action already decided. He liked Sir Thomas, was impressed by his manner and his courtesy. How could he quiz this man, accuse his son of reckless and drunken conduct that had resulted in the death of a young man and plunged Fabia's family into grief?

Trevor, watching his father, read his reaction perfectly. If only he would hold his tongue, the young man thought. What good could come of bringing up that ancient tragedy?

Lady Goring, a tranquil and accomplished hostess, steered the conversation into easy channels, reminding Mrs. Wetherell of a previous meeting at a Bring and Buy sale, complimenting Petra on her appearance, and generally setting a relaxed tone. If Fabia had feared she would be on view, subject to searching questions about her background and suitability, she was soon disabused of that notion.

After about a half an hour, the company adjourned to the sunny dining room, where Sheraton chairs upholstered in a green- and cream-striped fabric were placed around a shining mahogany table. Sir Thomas discussed the weather, the possibility of a coming naval battle, and their pleasure at Richard's leave. They lunched on a pleasing fruit compote, then spring lamb and garden peas, followed by syllabub, and cheese for the gentlemen.

Fabia, having been slightly on guard, found herself flattered by Lady Goring's tolerance and warmth. Accustomed to yielding the limelight to Petra on social occasions, it was enjoyable to realize that she was the center of Lady Goring's interest. Occasionally Petra tried to interrupt but was thwarted, much to Fabia's amusement, by Lady Goring's firm control of the conversation. Somewhat awed by her hostess, Petra subsided, and so gentle was Lady Goring's touch that she felt neither ne-

glected nor unappreciated. It was clear to Fabia that
Richard had been brought up in a loving yet disci-
plined home where good manners and a concern
for others had been the rule. How fortunate he had
been, she thought, to enjoy the companionship of
such intelligent and caring parents.

At the end of the meal, Lady Goring removed
the ladies leaving the gentlemen to their port. After
escorting them to the upper chambers where they
could repair their toilettes, she gave them an amusing and gracious tour of the house. Obviously she
was proud of Beechwood but not vainglorious. She
explained the family portraits in the upper gallery,
admitting wryly that some of the past Gorings had
been rogues, but insisting that there had also been
some stalwart citizens and astute managers. At the
end of the gallery was a Gainsborough study of
Lady Goring herself and two very young boys, one
of whom was blond and sulky; the other Fabia recognized at once as Richard. Turning to her hostess
she exclaimed, "Have you two sons, Lady Goring?"

A shadow crossed Lady Goring's face and she
sighed. "Yes, Richard's older brother, Randal, died
quite young. A stupid tragedy brought about by
heedless behavior, I regret to say. Randal was gifted
in many ways, but he lacked self-control, and I am
afraid, surrendered to self-indulgence."

She paused, avoiding Fabia's sympathetic expression, then, as if despair must not be paraded, said
brightly, "But, of course, Richard is a far different
type, a very rewarding son and, as I understand, a
respected and clever commander. I sometimes wish
he had chosen not to go to sea, but from the time

he was a little boy that was all he wanted to do. We miss him, but he does come often on his leaves, and that is a cheerful prospect. We are fortunate that he likes his home and his parents. So many young men prefer London, with all its sophisticated entertainments, to the quiet countryside."

"I can quite understand why he does," Fabia answered, touched by Lady Goring's quiet explanation.

"Thank you, my dear. Do you prefer the country to town?" Lady Goring asked, anxious to return the conversation to more pleasant topics.

"Yes, I think so. I have had so little opportunity to visit London or any other large town, for that matter. I do not miss what I never had, I guess," she admitted, laughing a bit. "I was raised in the West Indies, where my father had a large sugar plantation," she explained.

"Richard had told me that you were orphaned quite young. So we share some experience of tragedy. But you seem happy with your aunt and uncle," Lady Goring said, and if her tone was questioning, it was of only the slightest trace.

"They have always been most kind," Fabia insisted, unwilling to go further.

Petra, overhearing the last remarks, determined to join the conversation. "Fabia has only been with us about a year. She was at school in Cheltenham," she explained, wanting to attract Lady Goring's interest and rather bored with the tour of the gallery. Still, she thought it was an impressive house, well-decorated and unobtrusively redolent of the necessary income. She would not mind being the chatelaine of such an establishment.

"And what about yourself, my dear? Were you at school, too?" Lady Goring asked, realizing that Fabia's cousin might feel a bit ignored and recalling herself to her hostess's duties. Mrs. Wetherell joined in the explanations, and the four women soon were chatting in a friendly manner as they entered the drawing room. Only Richard and Trevor greeted them.

"Father and Mr. Wetherell have adjourned to the library to look at a rare psalter, but I suspect to discuss naval battles. I have discovered that only sailors are averse to reconstructing engagements over the port. But it is a harmless indulgence, so we will leave them to it," Richard explained, looking at Fabia with impatience. He longed to get her to himself, but courtesy demanded he play the polite host.

Lady Goring, reading her son's expression, came to his rescue. "Why don't you take Fabia into the garden, Richard? Although not looking its best right now, it deserves a visit. The daffodils and hyacinths are making a lovely show, and the tulips are about to blossom."

But Petra was not to be ignored, relegated to old women's gossip in place of exhibiting her charms to the only eligible man around. "Oh, yes, let us go into the garden. A little recreation is just what we need after that delicious lunch. Come on, Trevor," she insisted, tugging at her brother's arm as Fabia and Richard made their way toward the French windows that led to the terrace and from there to the wide sweeping lawn beneath the north portico of the house.

Raising a disgusted eyebrow behind Petra's back,

Richard escorted his party outside, leaving Lady
Goring to entertain Mrs. Wetherell as best she could
while wondering just how her son would shake off
the persistent Petra. Perhaps she might insert some
gentle hints here to help her son's cause.

"Your daughter is so attractive, Mrs. Wetherell,
she must have legions of young men begging for
her favors," Lady Goring said.

"Yes, yes, indeed. Petra is quite the belle of Wimborne, but she cannot seem to settle on one for a
husband. It's worrying, for naturally a mother is
concerned about her daughter's choice," Mrs.
Wetherell confided.

"Certainly, and a mother of her son, too," Lady
Goring agreed, wondering how to persuade her
guest to further confidences without revealing her
own hopes.

Mrs. Wetherell brightened at this hint. Did Lady
Goring think that Richard might be interested in
Petra? Lady Goring, usually so astute, did not
dream that Fabia's aunt had ever entertained the
notion that her own daughter, not her niece, might
be Richard Goring's choice as a bride.

"Fabia has been a pleasing addition to your
household, I am sure, Mrs. Wetherell. How fortunate she was to have such obliging relations to support her when her parents died."

"Well, yes, but Fabia, although the nicest girl, is
difficult in some ways, so reserved, so, well, *secretive*,
I think. I make every allowance, but really I feel that
she does not really hold us in affection, and after all
we have done to make her feel at home. Then, she's
so different from Petra, who is so confiding, so eager

to tell us her every thought, and so popular with all the young people in Wimborne."

Lady Goring's assessment of Petra did not quite march with that of the young lady's mother, but her only reply was a slight nod and smile.

As Richard shepherded his guests into the garden, Petra had contrived to inch her way up to him and put a demanding arm within his.

"Let's allow Trevor and Fabia to make their own way about. That will give us a chance for a comfortable coze. I have been wanting to talk to you for ages, and I am sure you feel the same, but somehow Fabia always manages to force herself on us." Petra had decided that this might be her last attempt to wrest Richard from her cousin's grasp. She had persuaded herself that he had been pushed into a compromising position by Fabia and now would feel obliged to offer for her. Petra could not believe that if he had a choice he would not prefer her more obvious charms.

Richard, prepared to be polite, but not willing to abandon his intention of a quiet chat with Fabia, felt more than irritated. Petra was either so insensitive or so ambitious for a husband, she appeared willing to expose herself to the most humiliating set-downs. But Richard, casting a look back at Fabia, who was strolling with Trevor, noticed she did not seem to see his dilemma. Whatever the cost, he must rid Petra of her fanciful idea that he really admired and preferred her to Fabia.

"Come, Petra. I think it is time you and I had a

little chat, as you suggest. There is a nice bench just behind this yew border which will suit admirably." Richard steered her firmly in the direction indicated, leaving Trevor and Fabia to their own resources.

"My sister is making the most awful fool of herself," Trevor explained to Fabia. "She is frantically jealous of Goring's interest in you and believes if she points out her own assets he will see the error of his ways. He's not that much of a sap-skull. I have no doubt he will give her a monstrous setdown, and she deserves it. Tedious girl."

"Trevor, you are unkind," Fabia said mildly. "I am sure you really love your sister. It's just that you become occasionally annoyed at her antics. She is so lovely to look at that perhaps she does not believe other qualities are necessary."

"Like kindness, courtesy, respect for others," Trevor replied with some heat. "She is a vain, selfish, shallow girl, and I am ashamed of her, particularly the way she assumes that no man will look at you when she is about."

"Oh, Trevor, you are a doughty champion, and I thank you for your concern. But Petra's japes do not bother me. It is doubtful if we would ever be rivals. The men she admires I would not find to my taste."

"Like Guy Fancher, I suppose, a swarmy cove, I think. And you may be right about Petra's choices, except for Richard Goring, and it is not his character she admires, nor even his looks: it is his position and his rent roll. Much good it will do her," Trevor said, grimacing.

"I suspect all sisters and brothers are at odds with one another at times, but all will come about. You are fortunate to have each other," Fabia reproved him a bit sadly, remembering Stella, although she was honest enough to admit they had often fought and their characters had been most dissimilar.

"I simply don't like the way she treats you, or for that matter, Mary Anstruther, a nice girl too timid to defend herself against Petra's thrusts," Trevor explained. All was clear to Fabia now, and she was pleased. She thought Trevor the very man for Mary but had not realized her cousin had the sense to recognize Mary's worth under her somewhat reserved facade.

While Trevor and Fabia wandered about the Beechwood gardens exchanging confidences, Richard steeled himself to the task ahead.

"I am so happy to have this chance to confide in you, Petra. Your advice and help would be a real boon to me. You may have noticed that I have been spending a good deal of time with Fabia. You have often mentioned it, so it should come as no surprise to you that I am deeply devoted to her and hope she will accept my proposal of marriage. I know I can count on your cooperation," Richard said, as ingenuously as he could muster.

Petra flushed, then paled, anger barely restrained. She had to bite her lip not to scream. Richard, watching her guilelessly, had difficulty in suppressing a grin. He had certainly spiked her guns. What could she do but assent unless she wanted to be judged a harpy and a mean-minded jade?

"Well, I shouldn't think you will suit, but Fabia

would be a fool to refuse you," Petra said tightly, trying to regain her composure, but at a loss to understand how this situation had come about. Still, she would waste no more time on this misguided man. He would regret his choice. Standing, she shook out her skirts and prepared to return to the house.

"It's becoming a bit chilly here, I think. Mother will be wondering what has happened to me. Shall we return, Captain Goring?" she suggested frigidly. Richard, his face grave, but secretly relieved and amused, agreed with polite alacrity.

Collecting Trevor and Fabia from their admiration of a bed of jonquils, Richard signaled that he wished to speak to Fabia and that Trevor might follow Petra into the house. Grinning at his furious sister's back as she flounced away, the young Wetherell agreed, leaving Fabia and Richard alone. He had no doubt what Richard meant to say to his cousin.

"I have been trying all day to get you alone, and now before Petra or someone else interrupts, I am going to speak my piece," Richard said, determined to put his proposal to Fabia. "You must know that I love you and want you to be my wife. I wish I had the address to present my offer with the flourish of a poet, but you will just have to believe that I have never been so sincere in my life, or so scared, not even when the French guns were booming in the Med," he insisted with a grin. But Fabia knew that his words hid a deep emotion; his eyes deepened with feeling and his cheeks flushed.

"I would be honored to marry you, Richard. I love you," she accepted simply.

Richard, who had been holding his breath, afraid of rejection, gave a great sigh and took her in his arms. The kiss that followed gave evidence of all the passion he had repressed before, and Fabia returned it, her heart pounding and an incredible glow of happiness warming her whole body as his warm lips and roving hands evoked a deep response. Finally she broke away to look at him with tender eyes.

"We shouldn't be behaving in such an abandoned fashion in your parents' garden when you haven't even spoken to Uncle Aubrey yet," she said, her reproof not meant to be taken too seriously.

"I had to be sure of you first, my dear girl. And I had to sort out Petra. I was afraid she might cause trouble. But the silly wench knows where she stands now," Richard informed Fabia, who tried to look stern but could not keep back a smile.

"Poor Petra. She will hate it that I have attached a husband, and such an eligible one, before her," Fabia teased, knowing she was behaving in a shocking manner but unable to help herself.

"She's a minx, and no man in his right mind would look at her when you were in the same room. But don't concern yourself with her. I will speak to your uncle immediately, although even if he bans me from his house, I will not be deterred. We will gallop away to Gretna Green."

"How dashing. I had no idea you were such a romantic. But really, Richard, there is no impediment to our marriage. Uncle Aubrey will gladly consent."

"Wants you off his hands, eh?" Richard riposted,

so overcome with joy that he took refuge in humor.
"But come, we must join the family or they will
have all sorts of lascivious ideas. I have a few myself."

Laughing, the pair walked into the drawing room,
where Lady Goring took one look at their faces and
knew that Richard had won his bride. Trevor, too,
realized that his cousin had accepted Richard. Only
Petra and her mother looked a bit disgruntled, but
that was to be expected. As Fabia and Richard hesitated, wondering whether to announce their news,
the drawing-room door opened and Mr. Wetherell
and Sir Thomas joined the party.

Seven

Fabia, completely filled with happiness, failed to notice her uncle's unhappy expression, but Trevor had more perception. Caught between Fabia and Richard's obvious delight and his father's concern, he understood immediately that Aubrey Wetherell had questioned Sir Thomas about his son and the resulting explanation had not eased his mind. Richard, eager to gain Fabia's guardian's permission for the marriage, would have rushed up to the rector and dragged him off that moment to secure the necessary endorsement. But Fabia, rather shy before the company who all seemed to be watching her, wanted a little time to savor what had happened. Under the cover of Sir Thomas's courteous excuses for their absence, Fabia murmured in Richard's ear, "Say nothing now, but come to see Uncle Aubrey tomorrow. I want to keep this lovely secret to ourselves for a day or two," she insisted.

Richard, eager to satisfy his love in every way, agreed reluctantly, and the two separated to do their social duty. Mrs. Wetherell, like Lady Goring, suspected that a great deal more than a view of the early jonquils had taken place in the garden. She had not really thought Petra had a chance to annex young

Goring, but she knew that her daughter would not take kindly to her cousin stealing a march on her in the marriage stakes, to put it crudely. And Mrs. Wetherell sighed as she contemplated the sulks and tantrums which would be their domestic fate in the weeks to come. If only Petra would make a push to attach one of the several eligible young men who buzzed about her. As a fond mother, Honoria Wetherell would not admit that although her daughter's dance card was always full, somehow her success at the Assembly did not translate into more lasting tokens of affection. Still, she must not let her concern over that state of affairs cloud this gratifying party. The Gorings had been so hospitable, so kind, she would be rag-mannered not to repay their attention with gratitude.

After tea, the Wetherell party returned to town, Richard having only a moment to murmur to Fabia that he would call tomorrow and settle matters with her uncle. She gave him an uncertain smile that for some reason left him feeling uneasy. Was she regretting her decision already? Richard, practical, efficient, and clever with regard to his naval responsibilities, was prey to all the silly fancies that worry a man in love. He felt unworthy and triumphant all at the same time, and impatient to put matters on a proper footing. As the Wetherell carriage rode off down the Beechwood driveway, Richard decided that if he could not speak to Aubrey Wetherell now, he could, at least, tell his parents of his decision to marry Fabia and her agreement.

"Father, Mother, I have something to tell you," he said as he joined his parents in the drawing room where Lady Goring had repaired for a restorative cup of tea. She thought the meeting had gone rather well except for Petra's sulks, and she was eager to hear that Richard had made his offer and been accepted. Looking up at her son with a twinkle in her eye, she smiled happily and said, "I think I know what you want to say, and I am pleased. Your Fabia is a delightful girl."

"Oh, Mother, you are a wonder. No point in trying to hide any secrets from you. I am going to see Mr. Wetherell tomorrow and settle the whole business. I don't want a long engagement. Who knows when I will be called back to sea, what with that Corsican on the rampage again. The only deterrent to his landing at Dover is the Navy, I am convinced. He does not seem to fear our soldiers, so it is up to us to do the job."

Richard, although always restless on land, now had every reason to hope a renewal of hostilities would be delayed. Lady Goring knew that he never imagined harm coming to him in sea battles, for the young rarely considered their own mortality. Much as she would like Richard to leave the service and come back to Beechwood to help his father in running the estate, she would never suggest such a course. Perhaps a bride would be more persuasive, but she doubted Fabia would make that kind of demand on him. Well, she could not have everything, and the possibility of grandchildren was very cheering. In her pleasure at Richard's news and her daydreaming about the future, she had not noticed her husband's silence. Now she looked up to see Richard frowning at his father.

"Come, Father, surely you have no objection to Fabia as a daughter-in-law?" he asked rather angrily.

"Not at all, Richard. She's a lovely girl, and what's more, a sensible one, I think. It's her uncle. I am afraid he may have some objection to you as a husband for his niece," Sir Thomas said gravely, pacing back and forth before the fireplace, his hands behind his back, a pose Richard knew he adopted when he was troubled.

"But why, Thomas, should Aubrey Wetherell object to Richard? He should be relieved that Fabia will marry such an upstanding, attractive young man," she insisted with a mother's fierce pride.

"I don't believe it's Richard himself he dislikes. It's the family connection. I had to tell him, when he asked about Randal," Sir Thomas explained, unable to meet his son's eyes. The behavior of his elder son had always been a source of great grief to Sir Thomas, whose own moral values and respectability had never wavered from the strictest standards. Randal's rejection of the Goring values and expectations had been a bitter blow to both Sir Thomas and Lady Goring, only partially mitigated by Richard's far different character and career.

"Was it necessary to tell Mr. Wetherell about Randal?" Richard asked, knowing how painful the subject was to his father.

"Yes, it was. He asked and now knows that Randal is the young man who shot Fabia's sister's betrothed in a drunken duel. If that is the case, your offer for her will not meet with any enthusiasm, I am afraid," Sir Thomas said baldly. He did not want to forecast unhappiness for his son, but he always

believed in taking his fences straight and not avoiding trouble when it must be faced.

"Oh, no, Thomas, what pernicious fate could
make Randal the instrument of Fabia's tragedy?"
Lady Goring wailed, tears welling in her eyes.

"Well, I will not let that stop me. I intend to
marry Fabia, and soon," Richard insisted stoutly.
His father, who saw grim shoals ahead, was reluctant to warn his son of the dangers. Even if Mr.
Wetherell consented to the marriage, Fabia would
have to be told of Richard's relationship to the man
who had shot her sister's betrothed. That Randal
Goring had died some days later of Paul Beaumont's returning fire would not ease Fabia's horror
of aligning herself to the family which had produced the man she must consider responsible for
all the subsequent tragedy.

Sir Thomas hesitated, then blurted out what he
thought to be the truth, "I hope for your sake you
are right. Fabia was a mere child. Perhaps she does
not remember much about the affair, but there is
no denying that if Randal, in a drunken burst of
temper, had not challenged young Beaumont, Stella
Thurston would have married her groom the next
day, and they would have lived happily in Nevis.
Certainly there is every reason to suppose Fabia's
sister and parents would not have been lost at sea.
So you see, she might believe, that save for Randal's
intemperate challenge at the wedding dinner, she
would be living in the midst of her family today."

"And I would never have met her," Richard conceded, thinking of the turn of fate which had
brought him Fabia and damning his brother, not

for the first time, for all the agony he had brought not only to his parents but now to strangers who had turned out to be the family of the girl he loved.

Lady Goring, hating to see her men worried and unhappy, went over to Richard and laid a hand on his arm. "Try not to look on the dark side of this dreadful reminder of the past. Fabia must love you or she would not have accepted you. She will not have given her love lightly. You must trust in that, my boy."

"Yes, but what girl could contemplate marrying the man whose brother was responsible for all that pain! That is what she will think—anybody would. Randal was my brother, and I know I should view him with charity, but he caused such havoc alive, and now dead he is continuing to influence us all."

Normally Richard would not have spoken so harshly, knowing how painful such reminders were to his parents, but his whole happiness was at stake. Why should Randal, from beyond the grave, cast a shadow over that happiness, even prevent Richard's marriage? He had already ruined Fabia's family's life, and now Randal might be the instrument of Richard's misery. For if he could not marry Fabia, he would be inconsolable. Richard had no doubts about his love for her. She would not be easily forgotten, or forgiven, if she failed him now. At the core of Richard's tolerance and compassion was an implacable streak which his parents had long ago recognized. He would not allow unkind fate to rob him of his bride, and if Fabia resisted him, who knew what he would do?

Richard, sensing his parent's concern and not

wanting them to worry, decided it would be best to end the conversation, but his mother was not easily distracted from the matter.

"Then you will approach Mr. Wetherell tomorrow, Richard?" she asked.

"First hour it's respectable," he promised with a grin. Then, determined to close the subject: "Whatever happens, I must be up to London before the end of the week. I have notice to report to the Admiralty."

"Then that was the message that came for you Saturday? In all the excitement of our visitors, I forgot to ask you about it," Sir Thomas said, then not wishing to appear prying, "Not that it is anyone's business but yours, my boy."

Unlike my marital chances, Richard thought to himself, but realizing how much his father yearned to know about his career, he volunteered, "I don't think my ship is ready yet, so perhaps they have another job for me, even another ship. Affairs are coming to a climax, and a big battle with the combined French and Spanish fleets cannot be postponed much longer. Nelson has been waiting in the Caribbean for a decent wind to follow Villeneuve across the Atlantic. He suspects Napoleon has some devious plan for a battle which will destroy us and enable him to invade England from Boulogne," Richard explained, knowing his father followed the maneuvers of the fleet with great interest, heightened by Richard's own involvement. His mother, always fearing for his safety, did not like to think her only son would be in danger again, and cared little for the naval strategy Richard was outlining.

"If you two are going to discuss the possibility of a battle, I will leave you to it. I have a few matters to take up with Cook," she explained and left the room.

There was a short, not uncompanionable silence after her departure. Richard and his father understood each other very well.

"Your mother cannot grasp the larger picture. It's your life, your ship, your movements that concern her, not the fate of England, Spain, or even Admiral Nelson, much as she admires him," Sir Thomas explained lightly, happy to abandon personal problems for the international ones.

"Yes, I understand that, but I know I can confide in you, Father, and I think this summons from the Admiralty might be related to some disturbing rumors I have heard around the harbor at Portland."

"What rumors?" Sir Thomas asked, a bit startled.

"Well, you remember I have told you how vulnerable our fleet is while in Channel ports. And it is a simple matter for Napoleon's agents to infiltrate the ports and pick up news about ship sailings, fleet movements, armaments, all information vital to French hopes of a Naval victory."

"Spies? You mean there is a nest of spies in Portland?" Sir Thomas growled with all the distaste of a patriotic Englishman.

Richard smiled a bit grimly at his father's reaction. "Armies and navies have to have intelligence, Father, and the best way to get it is the nasty business of spying. Many men are patriots and take on a dangerous and unrewarding job for love of country, but I fear many others do it for money, and

Napoleon has proved to be very generous to turn-coats in the past."

"Englishmen betraying their country to that blasted Corsican. Nonsense, I don't believe it," Sir Thomas protested. But he was neither naive nor stupid, and he realized that it was entirely possible, having had some experience of the fallibility of his fellows.

"I have a nasty suspicion that the Admiralty will give me some very unpalatable orders. They think that since I am on the spot, less than an hour's ride away from Poole and little more to Portland, I might investigate. After all, it is a waste of resources to have an officer idling about without his ship. They will put me to work," he quipped. Despite his jocular tone, Richard was not sanguine about conditions at the Channel ports. Too many loose and drunken tongues, as well as paid informers, and Fouche's agents gathered a budget of news that affected the fate of English ships from the Caribbean to the Mediterranean, from Gibraltar to Plymouth. Still he doubted he could be of much use.

After a dinner during which the Gorings, by tacit consent, did not discuss Richard's coming interview with Fabia's uncle, he and his father played a game of billiards, and then retired. If Sir Thomas and Lady Goring passed a troubled night, Richard, with youth's optimism and a serving officer's ability to sleep on whatever watch assigned him, had no difficulty in dropping into a deep sleep, but his dreams were haunted by shadowy visions of figures facing each other across a greensward and exchanging fatal shots.

Waking unrefreshed but determined, he made a careful toilette before descending to breakfast. He may have decided to ignore the upcoming interview until the hour was upon him, but he had to confess privately that he dreaded facing Fabia when she learned that it was his brother who was the instrument of her family's tragedy. That Randal Goring had brought unhappiness to his own family did not mitigate the Thurstons' grief. The Gorings had tried to put Randal's behavior behind them, but it remained an abiding pain. And now the whole miserable affair would be resurrected. Sir Thomas and Lady Goring sent their son on his way to Wimborne with cheering words, but in their hearts they feared that once again their late dissolute elder son would bring even more sorrow to their family.

Eight

Fabia, unknowing of what lay in store, greeted the morning with a feeling of excitement and expectation. Even the rather gloomy gray day failed to depress her spirits, and she bade her aunt Honoria a cheerful good morning at the breakfast table. Petra was still abed, and Trevor and Mr. Wetherell had breakfasted early, the rector wanting to avoid his niece until after his interview with Richard, to which he was not looking forward. His indecision and concern had impelled him, rashly, to confide in his wife. If he had hoped to find comfort from her advice, he was doomed to disappointment. Honoria Wetherell was not an unkind woman, but Petra's disillusion and rage that Richard preferred Fabia to herself had made her mother champion her daughter. Petra's jealousy had infected her mother, and looking at her niece who appeared at the table aglow with pleasurable anticipation aggravated her feeling of injustice.

"I suppose you are in a fever over Richard Goring's promised interview with your uncle. You expect he will make you an offer, I suppose," she said a bit tartly, watching Fabia eating a hearty meal of ham and shirred eggs.

"He has already made me an offer, Aunt. He has
to secure Uncle Aubrey's consent, that is all," Fabia
said, not understanding her aunt's tone. She might
have realized if she had not been so distracted by
her own anticipation that her aunt seemed unusually
somber. Not normally unperceptive she assumed her
relatives would be pleased with her good fortune in
marrying such an upstanding and well-endowed
young man. Only Trevor had been whole-hearted in
his good wishes, and so enthusiastic had he been that
Fabia had hardly heeded Petra's pique and her uncle's abstraction. That Honoria found her niece's an-
nexation of one of the county's most eligible young
men an affront to her hopes for Petra, Fabia could
not conceive. She was soon to discover her mistake.

"When you know the truth about Richard Goring,
you might not be so eager to join your life to his,"
Honoria said roughly.

"What do you mean, Aunt? Surely there can be
no objection to Richard. He is a most respectable
young man. I have not been attracted just by his
handsome appearance, you know. I am convinced
we share many interests both of outlook and values," Fabia returned, a bit puzzled.

"Your uncle is too much of a coward to tell you,
but I believe you should know that Richard's
brother, Randal, is the man who challenged Paul
Beaumont to a duel, and then killed him. His
brother was the instrument of your sister's terrible
loss," Honoria explained, priding herself on her
honesty. Fabia certainly was entitled to know the
whole story. If Honoria had any compunction at the

revelation, she concealed the guilty pang beneath a facade of righteous indignation.

"Richard's brother was that man? I don't believe it!" Fabia gasped, appalled at this attack.

"Well, he was. I cannot think why you did not notice the similarity of the name. Surely your illness did not efface all remembrance of that dreadful night and morning?" Honoria insisted, wanting to transfer some of the responsibility for this grave situation to her niece.

"If I ever knew his name, I do not remember it. I only remember the horror of the morning, Stella's screams, the wedding finery abandoned, my parents in distress. It is all so shadowy, so distant. I don't believe I ever knew who the young man was, except he was a drunkard and a ne'er-do-well. He should never have been invited to the dinner," Fabia said dully, a vague memory of that ill-starred party returning.

"Well, Richard's brother was the villain. How you can contemplate joining your life to that family, I cannot understand," her aunt said coldly, trying to ignore Fabia's pale face, her dull eyes, her rigid expression. She looked up in alarm as Fabia rose, and as if sleepwalking, moved to the door.

"Wait, Fabia, where are you going?" her aunt cried, now thoroughly alarmed. She had not really believed that her niece would react so badly, if she had thought at all. Her own resentment that Richard had chosen Fabia over Petra had overcome all prudence. She half-rose in her seat as if to follow Fabia, then subsided limply. What more could she say? And Fabia would rebuff any offer of comfort.

Who could blame her? Honoria Wetherell began to regret her impulsive words, wished now that she had held her tongue, but it was too late. What would Aubrey say to her?

Distraught and horrified by her aunt's disclosure, Fabia's first thought was to escape the confines of the house before Richard's arrival. She could not face him until she had time to think of what this ghastly coincidence meant. How could she have suspected that Richard and his kind parents could have any relationship to the reckless drunken young man who had killed Paul Beaumont?

Grabbing her shawl, she ran from her bedroom into the garden behind the house, where she knew she would not be disturbed. Gray and lowering as the day was, in the walled garden the flowers were just beginning to blossom; hyacinths, daffodils, primroses, forsythia made a brave display. But Fabia scarcely noticed them. Throwing herself down on a stone bench, she huddled in her misery, racked by memories that had until today been buried deep.

Richard, unaware that Fabia had been apprised of the situation, rode up to the Wetherell house in the best of spirits. He had no apprehension of the interview with Aubrey Wetherell; his thoughts were completely occupied with the image of an early wedding before he put out to sea. His only concern was whether his desire to marry Fabia so quickly might not be considered selfish, for he had little doubt that a big battle with the French forces loomed in the next few months. Well, he would put it to her, and if he had read his loved one correctly, she would not hesitate to agree despite the danger that he would be facing.

Tethering his horse, he ran lightly up the steps and pounded on the knocker, to be admitted almost immediately by a grave Hollins. With the stoicism of his kind, Hollins showed none of the disquiet he felt, for although he had not been present in the breakfast room, he knew some trouble had erupted there. He had watched Fabia run white-faced from the dining room to her bedroom and then come down almost immediately and flee to the garden. The mistress ringing a peal over her because young Goring preferred Miss Fabia to Miss Petra was his guess. And a good thing, too, he thought, for Petra had never been a favorite in the servant's hall.

Richard, surrendering his hat and gloves to the butler, asked for Mr. Wetherell, his impatience obvious. But he could not forbear inquiring after his beloved.

"Miss Fabia is here, is she not, Hollins?"

"Yes, sir, I believe she is in the garden," the butler said solemnly. Just then Petra strolled languidly down the stairs, stopping for a brief moment as she saw Richard talking to the butler.

"Ah, the gallant suitor," she mocked, continuing her descent and greeting Richard with a curt nod.

"Good morning, Petra," he said, thinking how tiresome she was for a girl who had so many assets. After a few hours exposed to her particular archness and witless, self-absorbed conversation, a man could easily discount her beauty. That kind of attraction faded in an intimate domestic environment, and then what was left but a vapid companion with little warmth or sensitivity. A depressing picture. Richard had been neither flattered nor attracted by Petra's efforts to attach him, and he gave only a passing wonder to what man would finally be lured into her net.

Hollins, seeing Petra's nose was out of joint, as he put it later to Mrs. Brewer, directed Richard with little ceremony to the library, leaving Petra looking after him with a scornful smile, still unwilling to admit that he could choose Fabia over herself. Really, the man was prosy and stupid. She was well rid of him, despite his rugged looks, tidy income, and certain inheritance of Beechwood. She would like to hear what her father would say to him, but with Hollins guarding the hall, she had no choice but to wander into the morning room balked of her intention to eavesdrop.

Aubrey Wetherell rose at Richard's entrance and regarded him with a grave stare, as if he were a sinful penitent.

"Good morning, Captain. I believe I know the purpose of your visit at such an early hour," he said, implying that somehow Richard had been maladroit in rushing from Beechwood to secure his bride.

But Richard ignored the rector's admonitory attitude, and proceeded to the reason for his call.

"I am sorry, sir, if the hour is inconvenient, but I am anxious to settle this matter. You must have suspected that I have developed a *tendresse* for your niece Fabia, and I am happy to say she seems to return my love. I want to marry her as soon as possible, since I will be putting to sea before many weeks. Can there be any impediment to your consent to this wedding?"

"I understand your impatience, Richard," Aubrey Wetherell said, his natural kindness overcoming his concern. "But you should know that your father informed me that your late brother was the miscreant responsible for Fabia's sister losing her bridegroom, and therefore somewhat responsible for the death of her family later. They would not have come to England, I suspect, if the tragedy had not taken place and hence might not have suffered that shipwreck in which they lost their lives. Fabia knows nothing of Randal's part in that tragedy which robbed her sister of her fondest hopes, and I do not know how she will accept the news."

"Surely, sir, the past, no matter how hateful, must be forgotten. It has little to do with Fabia and myself now. I was not responsible for Randal's actions—indeed, I deplore them as much as you do. He caused my parents great pain and anguish when he was alive. I can only hope his shadow will not darken the present," Richard argued, a horrid fear overtaking his optimism.

"I hope so, too, my boy, for under other circumstances there is no man I would rather welcome into our family as Fabia's husband. I have prayed mightily about this problem, and I must confess I have behaved, perhaps, in a cowardly fashion. Fabia does not know of your relationship to Randal. I thought you should be the one to tell her. In her happiness with your proposal, she might not consider it important, since obviously you share none of your brother's distressing characteristics."

"I am relieved to hear you say that, sir. I will, of course, tell her, since there should be no secrets between us." Richard hesitated, then pressed on. "I have your permission to speak to her?"

"Yes, of course. And you have my blessing, for whatever that is worth," Aubrey said with a sigh. Captain Goring was undoubtedly a brave and competent officer of many sterling qualities, but he wondered if the young man was sensitive enough to realize Fabia's dilemma. Having brushed through this meeting, if not happily at least honestly, Aubrey rang for Hollins, eager to distance himself from whatever would happen. His one wish was to depart the house for the sanctuary of the minster, where he might seek solace in prayer and confess his ineptitudes to a compassionate God.

"Hollins, please ask Miss Fabia to come to the morning room. Captain Goring has my permission to see her alone," the rector ordered when the butler appeared.

"Miss Fabia is in the garden, sir. If you will come this way, I will direct you," Hollins requested, ushering Richard from the library, sensing that the young officer was about to make Fabia an offer. He thoroughly approved, for he thought Fabia had a difficult role in this household and deserved a ménage of her own with a man who would care for her and protect her. Not that the Wetherells were unkind, Hollins believed, but rather indifferent, with all the mistress's attention centered on her daughter.

At first Richard, upon emerging from the French doors of the dining room onto the small terrace,

did not see Fabia, huddled on the seat near the far
brick wall. One look at her bowed shoulders and
glazed eyes as he approached told him she had already learned of his brother's part in that island
tragedy.

"Fabia, my dear," he said softly, putting a consoling hand on her shoulder. "I see you have heard
the distressing tale of my brother's role in your family sorrow."

Fabia looked up dully, as if barely recognizing the
stalwart figure before her. "Richard," she finally
muttered, then drew back as if his hand had
scorched her.

Paying her no heed, he sat down on the seat next
to her and grasped her cold hands in his warm
ones. "I cannot tell you how I regret this unlooked-
for misfortune. I know it must be a dreadful shock
to you, especially since you had lost most memory
of that painful occasion, but it can make no differ-
ence to us, to our future together. I am not my
brother, and I feel nothing but abhorrence of his
wicked behavior in Nevis." He spoke with both sincerity and passion, noticing that she seemed unable
to absorb his explanation.

Seeing that she was not really listening to him,
he tightened his hands and said more forcefully, "I
love you, Fabia, and think you care for me. Do not
throw away our chance of happiness, marriage, a
home, children, a worthwhile life of shared values
and affection, for some scruple over your debt to
your family, long gone."

Suddenly Fabia raised her head, and her eyes
flashed furiously. "Some scruple. How can you say

that and relegate the past as if it were a mere foible? If I married you, I would feel I have betrayed all I hold dear. I would be a monster."

His own anger rising at this unjust accusation, Richard felt his control slipping. "You would not be so mad as to deny our love, our future, just because I had a brother who behaved recklessly in a drunken temper," he accused her as if she was acting in a vaporish gothic fashion.

"How can you make those specious excuses? And for all I know, those same traits might be buried deep behind your facade of a respectable, outstanding naval officer. When would they surface to dominate me? I would be at your mercy, the mercy of the brother of a murderer," she blurted out, hardly knowing what she was saying in her misery, swamped as she was by the memory of her sister's screams and the darkness which had fallen over the once-glowing plantation, which now seemed like a halcyon dream buried in a romantic past.

"You are being ridiculous. Stop this morbid fancying at once," Richard insisted, showing in his frustration and unhappiness all the outward signs which Fabia confessed she feared.

Gaining some control of herself and wishing only to end this painful encounter, Fabia rose to her feet, Richard rising with her. "I will not marry you, Richard, and that is all there is to say." She turned away as if rejecting any further pleas or arguments.

"No, that is not all. You will regret this, my girl, and when you want to whistle me back, it will be too late. Since you are so disgusted with me now, it little matters what I do. I will give you a real disgust," he growled, and dragging her into his arms, he pressed passionate, brutal kisses on her lips, his hands compelling her to respond.

Despite her anger and what she thought of as repulsion, Fabia could not deny her blood rose to meet his demands, and her heart quickened under his caresses. Ashamed, she felt her resistance weakening, knowing that Richard could have his way with her and that she would be powerless to prevent it. Just when it seemed she would surrender, he threw her from him, his face dark with revulsion.

"Don't expect me to apologize. You deserved that and more. But I will leave you to wallow in your martyrdom. You will not be bothered by me again," he said with a cold bitterness which brooked no appeal. Then, turning on his heel, he left her, abandoned in the garden.

Nine

The days following Fabia's rejection of Richard created an atmosphere in the Wetherell household that involved not only Fabia but her uncle, aunt, and cousins. Trevor was quietly understanding and supportive, although he privately believed Fabia had behaved foolishly. He applauded her loyalty to her sister but thought she should not have sacrificed her own happiness to her sister's tragedy. Petra, as might be expected, delighted in her cousin's refusal of one of the most eligible gentlemen in the neighborhood, although she, too, thought Fabia foolish, but she masked her pleasure with spurious sympathy and casual comfort. Mrs. Wetherell, both confused and irritated at the events, had little to say. Fabia's white face and stoicism repelled any attempts at consolation. Only the Reverend Mr. Wetherell tried to give his niece some assurance that he understood her actions and hoped her future would offer the happiness her decision denied her now. Whatever Fabia thought, regret or misery, she kept to herself, going about her usual duties in a calm manner, unwilling to discuss the matter.

Affairs were not much better in the Goring home, where Richard had returned, obviously in a rage of disappointment and disgust. All he told his parents were the bare facts that Fabia had refused him because she did not want to be allied to the family whose one son had killed her sister's betrothed. In order to discourage his parents' efforts at comfort, he left immediately for London, claiming the press of Admiralty business. Lady Goring, grieving for her son, debated a course of action she knew her husband would not encourage. She determined to see Fabia herself and plead Richard's case. She knew neither Sir Thomas nor Richard would countenance such interference, but she felt she must do something to bring the lovers back together.

Using the time-worn excuse of shopping, she ordered the carriage and informed her husband she had vital commissions in Wimborne. Richard had been from home several days when she arrived at the Wetherell rectory, braced for a difficult interview. She suspected Fabia would not be welcoming. In this she was correct, although Fabia was all politeness when she met Lady Goring in the drawing room, accompanied by her aunt. Sensing that Honoria would be of little assistance in her attempt to change Fabia's mind, she gently asked her hostess if she would mind leaving them. A bit offended, Honoria Wetherell withdrew, her curiosity aroused, but too timid to deny Lady Goring, who could be imposing when she wished.

Appalled at Fabia's pale face and dark-ringed eyes, Lady Goring realized that this had not been an easy decision for the girl she had hoped to welcome as a daughter-in-law. Sitting down next to the tense figure, she took one of Fabia's cold hands and said softly, "This has been a horrid time for you, my dear, and I quite understand how you feel. I can offer little mitigation of Randal's intemperate challenge to Paul Beaumont and the dreadful result of his action. Unfortunately Randal was always a problem, self-indulgent, conceited, uncaring of others, and arrogant. Perhaps the fault was ours, for not exerting more discipline, although we tried, heaven knows. But Richard is not like his brother. Can you not find it in your heart to separate him from the tragedy that scarred your family?"

"No," Fabia said briefly, then realizing that she must explain, although she hated to hurt this kindly woman whom she respected, she continued levelly. "He behaved brutally when I told him that marriage between us was unthinkable."

"Brutally!" Lady Goring exclaimed, surprised. "That does not sound like Richard."

Loath as she was to discuss the disastrous interview she had experienced with Richard, Fabia's natural courtesy and her sincere liking for Lady Goring forced her to further explanations.

"He told me I was a martyr and ridiculous. He showed no sympathy for my natural revulsion for his brother. And he made it quite plain that he had lost all regard for me. Even if I changed my mind, he said, he would not be whistled back," Fabia said wearily. She could not tell Richard's mother of that ruthless kiss which still haunted her.

"I am sure he did not mean it, Fabia, just as I am sure he cares deeply for you. He was speaking from disappointment and frustration at the denial of his fondest dream, to marry you. When he left the house that morning, he was so happy, so certain in his anticipation. Certainly you can understand we all say things that we later regret under the pressure of shock."

"He meant it," Fabia said firmly. "I know your action in coming here rose from the kindest motives and your concern for Richard, but believe me, Lady Goring, there is no hope that we will ever be reconciled." Fabia was finding this interview painful in the extreme, and only wished Lady Goring would leave.

Serena Goring, much troubled and disturbed, felt perhaps she had done more harm than good, and she had no recourse but to accept Fabia's decision, painful as it was. Deciding that further pleading would only worsen affairs, she rose reluctantly.

"I am very sorry, Fabia. You and Richard are so well-suited. He is not responsible for his brother's behavior and deplores it, as we all do. If you should think differently about him, I hope you will have the courage to tell him. Richard is not vindictive, only miserable. And I will intercede if that is what you wish."

"Thank you, Lady Goring. I appreciate your efforts, but matters can never be put right between us. Richard behaved in a way which only reinforces my decision that we would not suit. He has more of his brother in him than perhaps you realize." Fabia spoke harshly, hating to traduce Richard to his mother but determined that she would suffer no further pleas to change her mind.

Puzzled and aghast at Fabia's description of her son, she knew it was useless to persist, so Lady Goring took her leave, only saying as she left, "Sir

Thomas and I regret this exceedingly, and if you should need our help in anything, please look upon us as your friends." She made her farewell with dignity, hiding her dismay that she had accomplished so little.

Left alone, Fabia felt the tears rising and ruthlessly choked them down. She had hated denying Lady Goring, realizing that Richard's mother had come to see her with only the best intentions, not wanting to cast judgment or try to excuse her other son. But Fabia had not been able to tell her how much Richard's behavior had shocked and disgusted her. Denied his triumph, he had acted in a manner that had both frightened and repelled her. She could not forget that last brutal kiss nor his hateful words. They both would not easily banish the memory of that encounter. She would just have to put the halcyon period of his courtship behind her and get on with her life, but it would not be easy.

Fabia was to be reminded that evening of how difficult it would be to resume normal life. Petra, upon hearing from her mother that Lady Goring had called, could not resist quizzing her cousin about the visit. Despite warning frowns from her father and brother, she boldly asked what Lady Goring had wanted.

"I suppose Lady Goring wanted to know why you had refused Richard, if you did. Or did he decide after all that he did not want to marry you?" Petra asked spitefully, tired of playing the comforter.

"Fabia's affairs are no concern of yours, my dear," Aubrey Wetherell objected mildly.

"Well, we all have to live with her frozen face and

grim manner. I think she could at least tell us what happened," Petra persisted.

"Don't be a mushroom, Petra," Trevor reproved angrily, seeing Fabia's set expression. "You really are the most annoying chit."

"You should not speak to your sister like that," Honoria Wetherell protested weakly.

"Well, she should learn to behave and repress her envy and jealousy, for that is what it is," Trevor insisted, not at all reprimanded by his mother's words.

"Oh, please, stop it. I don't want to be the center of a family dispute. I am not going to marry Richard, and that's the end of it," Fabia said, alarmed by the family rancor.

She rose and rushed from the room, leaving behind a satisfied Petra, who felt she had scored over her cousin, and a troubled Trevor and his father. Mrs. Wetherell, always eager to avoid any appearance of dissension, tried to soothe her children, who appeared on the verge of a nasty quarrel. "It is so difficult. One does not know what to say, but really, Trevor, how can you speak so rudely to your sister? She is only expressing the concern we all feel."

"Concern? It sounds more like spiteful satisfaction to me. And what you will do, Petra, and you, too, Mother, is drive the poor girl from the only relatives she has. Surely Fabia has had enough tragedy in her life without you adding to it," Trevor said firmly. Making his own excuses, he left behind a smirking sister, a troubled father, and a mother who wondered if what he had said might be true. She would not be sorry to see the back of Fabia.

The undercurrents and outright animosity in the Wetherell household convinced Fabia that she could not recover her spirits and put the business of Richard Goring behind her if she stayed with her relatives. She decided, therefore, to accept an invitation from a schoolfriend to visit her in Weymouth. She wrote off to Anne Meynell and within days received an enthusiastic answer, pressing Fabia to come immediately and stay as long as she liked. Fabia was explaining her plans to her uncle, who protested, but saw the sense of her plan, when Hollins announced she had a caller. For a moment a wild hope sprang up in Fabia's mind, soon quenched by the butler saying the gentleman was Guy Fancher.

Mr. Wetherell protested, "Miss Fabia is not seeing callers, Hollins."

The butler, well-aware of the tension in the household and the reason for Fabia's sad demeanor, nodded as if in agreement. Privately he thought Guy Fancher might offer a distraction and at the same time show that little minx, Miss Petra, that she was not as fascinating as she thought. Petra's barely concealed satisfaction at the failure of Fabia's engagement had not gone unnoticed in the servant's hall. Both Hollins and Mrs. Brewer knew the reason for the estrangement between Miss Fabia and Richard Goring, and deplored it. Now it seemed Guy Fancher might prove to be just the tonic Miss Fabia needed to put the unpleasant affair in the past. And a good thing, too.

Fabia herself must have secretly agreed with Hollins, for she said, "That's all right, Uncle. I will see Mr. Fancher." She had not taken to the naval officer when she first met him, but as events had proved, she was not a particularly astute judge of men. He would certainly distract her from the thoughts which burdened her. Leaving her uncle with a weak smile, she followed Hollins out of the room.

Guy Fancher, having heard from Petra of the quarrel between Richard and Fabia, and of his rival's departure forthwith to London, had decided to grasp the opportunity to attach Fabia. On greeting her in the drawing room, he was all affability, and wisely made no reference to the affair.

"It's such a lovely day I thought you might consent to ride out with me, Miss Thurston," he said, giving her his most winning smile.

Grateful for his tact, Fabia agreed a bit reluctantly, but then defiantly. Why should she sit in the rectory and mope? If Guy Fancher was not her choice of an escort, at least he was an antidote to her unhappiness.

To her surprise she rather enjoyed herself. Fancher was amusing, entertaining her with gossip about Mrs. Milford-Smythe and other ladies of the parish. She laughed heartily at his tale of Mrs. Milford-Smythe's rout by her own gardener, who refused to cut his prize roses for her Altar Society and threatened to leave if she persisted. His mimicry of the redoubtable matron and her brusque servant was most apt, and he was rewarded with an appreciative chuckle. Having paved the way, Fancher did not lose the opportunity to persuade Fabia that he had been *bouleversé* by her charms, a flattering sop to her bruised feelings.

"You know, Miss Thurston, I never expected to find a girl of your quality rusticating in this backwater. Wimborne is such a stuffy provincial town. Why have you not been tempted to visit London, where you would certainly be appreciated?"

"I suppose because it was just easier to join my uncle's household. I know few people in London, and no one to chaperon me. But I have decided to spread my wings a bit. I am going to Weymouth at the end of the week," she confided.

"How fortunate. I will be there myself on naval business," Fancher answered, deciding on the spur of the moment that his efforts to attach Miss Thurston might well succeed once she was away from Wimborne. Also he wanted to escape the attentions of Petra, who might become an obstacle to his plans. "I do hope you will let me see something of you there. You must give me your direction."

Politeness demanded that Fabia tell him her friend's address, although she really did not want to pursue the acquaintance. Still, it might be sensible to have an escort when she went out on the town. Agreeing to meet in the seaside town, they parted amicably, and Fabia decided that the outing had been an agreeable distraction.

She was quite prepared for some caustic words from Petra about her eagerness to accept Guy Fancher's overtures, but for once that miss held her tongue. Petra had received quite a set-down from her father, which was so rare an event as to convince her she had best try to hide her dislike and envy of her cousin. After all, Petra said to herself peevishly, Fabia would be leaving soon, and then

Guy Fancher and the other eligible men of Wimborne would flock back to court her. Why any man would prefer the prim Fabia to herself she could never fathom, but she soothed her vanity with the belief that Fabia's comfortable circumstances were the cause.

So Fabia left the Wetherell household bound for Weymouth in a hired carriage with her maid, leaving behind a family who could only be relieved at her absence, she decided.

If Fabia thought a change of scene would help put Richard out of her mind, he, too, had hoped that London would banish some of the anger and disappointment he had felt after that last agonizing interview. He posted up to London and spent his first few days in the traditional manner, drowning his unhappiness with the bottle and several nights of debauchery in the company of a fellow officer, Benji Bentham.

Benji, who aboard his ship was an industrious and courageous sailor, ashore abandoned all caution and behaved in a reckless and wayward fashion, intent on enjoying all the delights of the town. Richard said nothing of his feeling for Fabia, and Benji cooperated fully in Richard's intention to sample the fleshpots.

On the third day of his visit, Richard awoke with a bad hangover and the realization that his efforts to banish Fabia from his mind were unavailing. The only solution was to put to sea as soon as possible, and he hoped today's interview at the Admiralty would solve his most pressing problem: escape.

He groaned when he remembered his brutal behavior at that last searing encounter with Fabia. He had thoroughly lost his temper and acted badly, he admitted. What chance had he now to persuade her to see him as an indulgent and loving husband? He must have been mad to attack her thus when she was still suffering from shock. He should have responded with kind forbearance and tried to assure her that although his brother Randal was despicable, he shared none of his brother's tendencies to drunken profligacy and temper.

Well, his only hope was to let her anger and disgust have time to mellow, and perhaps she would look upon him with more sympathy. His first reaction, to try to forget her in an orgy of drinking and wenching, not at all his style, now appeared foolish and futile. He had best put and end to it and concentrate on his naval duties for a spell, he decided with his usual good sense.

Time was a great healer, the pundits insisted, and perhaps Fabia would see the senseless sacrifice she had made was to the detriment of both their futures. Not that Richard had any great belief that he was such a desirable catch, but he was convinced that he and Fabia shared a real affinity and that they could be happy together. He truly felt he would never find a girl to match her, and he only prayed that she would come around to a similar decision. So, dressing in his well-pressed uniform, he rode to the Admiralty to see what they wanted of him.

In Whitehall he was received, to his delight and

surprise, by his godfather, Admiral Sir Samuel Hood, just returned from a foray against the French fleet in the Caribbean.

"Well, Richard, you are looking a bit fine drawn. Shore leave getting you down, I suspect," Admiral Hood said with a twinkle in his eye. He had no doubt that Richard was indulging in the usual pastimes of a sailor ashore. "How are your parents?"

"Fine, sir. Happy to see the back of me, I am sure, although Father pretends he needs my help with the estate," Richard replied.

"I know you are anxious to rejoin your ship, and I suspect a big battle is looming with the French, but in the meantime there is a little commission for you in Portland. We are quite sure that naval plans and strategies, ship sailing dates, and other pertinent matter is finding its way into the hands of the French from Portland. Being a Dorset man and on the scene, we thought you might be just the one to discover the miscreants for us, although I know Intelligence is a far cry from commanding a ship of the line."

"This is appalling, sir," Richard said. "I had no idea French spies were infesting the port. Of course, I will do what I can, but I have no experience in ferreting out spies, you know."

"Well, you can hardly do worse than the people we have sent there. I sense that the villain is not a Frenchman but some disgruntled Navy man, revolting as the idea may be. He must have access to the yards, to serving officers, and of course to the taverns where idle seamen congregate. It's very worrying. Villeneuve seems to know our every move.

We want to send Nelson after him, but if Villeneuve has learned in advance of the fleet's rendezvous, it will rob us of any element of surprise. We have to catch his informers."

"I can see that, sir. And since I expect to join Nelson as soon as the *Andromeda* is ready to sail, I can certainly agree with your concerns. I'm not keen to be shot out of the water by Villeneuve's cannon," he added dryly. "But I am afraid my talents as a cloak-and-dagger type are not too promising."

"Nonsense, my boy. You are a keen observer, know men and ships. I have every faith in you. And it will be a real fillip to your career if you are successful," Admiral Hood insisted staunchly.

"A certain inducement," Richard agreed ironically. He did not like the idea that his future in the Navy was contingent upon unmasking spies. That was not what he had been trained to do. Still, he could not deny his godfather, to whom he thought he owed a great deal of his preferment in the Navy, modestly discounting his own success as a commander.

"You will take on the job, then," Admiral Hood said, grinning. Then sobering, he reminded Richard, "It will not be without danger, and needless to say, you must confide in no one, not even that scamp Benji Bentham."

"Surely you do not distrust Benji. Whatever his faults, he is a good commander and a brilliant sailor," Richard protested.

"And also apt to have a loose tongue when in his cups. No, I don't suspect Bentham of any chicanery, just that, for your own safety, it would be best to say nothing. I suppose he knows you are here today. Tell him you had a little chat with me about the *Andromeda* and that's all,'' Admiral Hood said sternly.

"Of course, sir," Richard agreed, a little surprised at his godfather's vehemence. Sir Samuel must be truly worried, and he only hoped he could find the source of the information leakage. It obviously was extremely serious. After a few more instructions, Admiral Hood relaxed a bit, chatting about Richard's leave and, as a Dorset man himself, trying to gauge the temper of the county. But Richard was convinced that the admiral wanted him to waste no time in leaving for Portland, and he promised to be on his way on the morrow. With mutual expressions of goodwill, Richard took his leave. Walking out of Whitehall he wondered how he was to go about his assignment but had little doubt of the importance of his mission. For the moment Admiral Hood's request had driven all thoughts of Fabia from his mind.

Ten

If Richard was able to relegate Fabia to the back of his mind under the pressure of his new assignment, she was not so fortunate. However, Weymouth and the Meynells did their best to distract her. Mr. Meynell, a wealthy merchant who owned a large red-brick house several blocks from the sea, traded in sugar and wool, and presided over a happy household consisting of a pleasant pretty wife, two charming daughters and two sons, one in business with his father, the other a serving army officer now in India. Anne and her brother Henry were the only ones at home as her sister Catherine attended the Cheltenham Seminary at which both Fabia and Anne had been enrolled. Henry, Anne, and their parents appeared to regard each other with respect and affection, which Fabia found reassuring after her experience in the Wetherell rectory.

"We are so delighted you could come on a visit, which we hope will be a long one. Anne has told me so much about you," Mrs. Meynell said, welcoming her over the tea table on her arrival.

"Oh, dear, that sounds ominous," Fabia said with a smile. "As I remember it, we got up to some shocking japes in school."

"Instigated by me, I fear," admitted Anne, a slight girl with titian curls and a merry face which was not beautiful but fetching. "You were always the serious one, restraining me from outrageous actions. Really, Mother, it is entirely due to Fabia I was not expelled from that stuffy academy."

"Then accept my heartfelt thanks, Fabia, and I hope you will continue to exert a beneficent influence on my wayward daughter," Mrs. Meynell said with a laugh.

"Alas, I am a sore trial to Mother. She would like to see me married off as soon as possible," Anne admitted.

"And is there any chance of that?" Fabia asked, certain that her former schoolmate had shoals of beaux, she was so exuberant and winning in her ways.

"Well, yes, as a matter of fact. But enough of that. You must tell us all your news and how you are going on in Wimborne," Anne probed. Despite her insouciant air she was a sensitive girl who had realized that her friend had come to Weymouth seeking refuge from some problem. She determined to have it out of her and do her best to restore Fabia's spirits, although she knew that wringing confidences from her friend would not be easy.

After giving them a brief budget of news, not including the quarrel with Richard, and enjoying her tea, Fabia was swept off by Anne to the bedroom given to her during her visit, a light airy room overlooking the gardens behind the house.

"What a delightful room. I know I will be most comfortable here, and I do like your mother, Anne.

Of course I knew I should as I remember her from her visits to you at school," Fabia said in all sincerity, then added a bit wistfully, "You are so fortunate to have such a nice warm family."

Anne, who knew a bit about Fabia's tragedy, having been a comforter when the news arrived at their seminary, agreed briskly, then turning to her friend, asked, "I know you accepted my invitation because something was troubling you at Wimborne. If you don't want to tell me, of course I will respect your reticence, but if I can help in any way, do please call upon me." Warm and generous with the benefit of a supportive home, Anne had the sense to realize that her friend shared none of these circumstances. She hoped she could ease some of Fabia's unhappiness.

"Oh, Anne, I don't know what to say. How can I explain without sounding like a complaining shrew? It's just that the rectory is not a pleasant place for me right now, and I admit I leapt at the chance to escape."

Fabia turned away from the window, where she had been looking at the garden, undecided whether she should tell the whole tale to Anne. Not that she doubted that Anne would respect her confidence, but she did not want to be the object of pity or scorn. Richard had said her notions were ridiculous. Perhaps Anne would feel the same, but she had to talk to someone, and Anne's sympathetic expression broke down her resistance. Also Anne had a wise head on her shoulders, despite her merry spirits.

"Of course you did. I only met your cousin Petra once, but frankly I did not take to her. I suspect she has a lot to do with your problem," Anne surmised shrewdly.

"Not really, although she has been a trial. I can see you will not rest until you have the whole story." Fabia smiled, relieved to have such a kind and caring confidante with whom she need make no excuses and whose advice she thought would be honest and sensible. The two girls sat down on the window seat, Anne expectant but a bit worried, as she felt Fabia's unhappiness was no trifling affair. No doubt a man was somewhere in the picture, she thought wisely, although Fabia was not the kind to become involved with a rake.

Fabia could not resist Anne's unspoken sympathy and within moments had spilled out the whole story of her romance with Richard and a little of that last hateful interview. Anne sat quietly making no comment, letting Fabia explain her feelings without interrupting. She was not unmindful that her normally reserved friend must be in a desperate state to so easily let down her guard and wanted to say nothing to upset her further. She noticed that tears had risen to her friend's eyes, hastily blinked away, and Anne was in no doubt that Fabia deeply regretted the outcome of her decision. That did not mean she would retract it, Anne knew. Fabia had always been single-minded with strong principles. How could she be dissuaded from the path Anne privately thought ill-considered?

After Fabia finished, there was a moment of silence. Then Anne said, "Of course I understand your revulsion at having the whole unsavory business of your sister's aborted wedding arising in such

an unexpected way. But I do think you are a bit
unfair to conclude that your Richard shares his
brother's odious characteristics. I know in the shock
of finding out the connection I might have behaved
just as you did, but now that you have had time to
think about it, are you sure there is no hope of a
reconciliation?"

Having omitted telling Anne of Richard's behavior at the end of their meeting, Fabia hesitated. She
could not share that experience, even with Anne.
"I just think he may have more of his brother in
him than I realized at first, not a good omen for
domestic bliss," she explained cautiously.

"You must not judge too harshly. I am sure he
was vastly disappointed when you rejected him,"
Anne argued.

"He was eager to escape. I thought he really
cared for me, but would any man behave so ruthlessly if he did? He told me if I changed my mind
I could not whistle him back," Fabia admitted. "He
was very angry."

"Yes, but that was in the heat of the moment. I
believe you will find he may think differently once
he has had a chance to consider things. After all,
it was a distinct shock to you, and he will make
allowances. But have you changed your mind?"

Fabia frowned, undecided. "That's just it. I don't
know whether I have. It's true that when my aunt
so callously told me the truth I was repelled and
aghast. I still am. But when Richard's mother, a
warm, lovely woman, tried to change my mind, I
wavered. She was so convincing—her disappointment
in her older son, her pride in Richard, her insis-

tence that he was nothing like his brother. . . . But how could I live with a man who was related to that odious cad? How can I be sure that Richard does not share some of his brother's habits and reactions?"

"You can't," Anne said baldly, "but a woman always chances her fate when she decides to marry a man. Men all appear in the best light during courtship, then with marriage their true characters often emerge."

"You sound as if you have experience," Fabia replied, sensing that her friend had a problem herself.

"Not really, but I have formed an attachment to an officer here, and I really know little about him. Then my parents favor a childhood friend and neighbor, Charles Cartwright, of whom I am also very fond. It's a dilemma," Anne admitted, reluctant to foist her own affairs upon Fabia, who had enough to concern her.

Having confided in Anne, Fabia felt her spirits revive, and she gave a feeble laugh. "We are a pair. Serve us right if our gentlemen abandoned us both. You are a dear, Anne, and telling you my sad tale has cheered me immensely. Also escaping from the confines of the rectory has restored my common sense. I am very grateful to you."

"Nonsense. I love having you. I have some friends here, of course, but no one who is a real bosom bow and with whom I can exchange confidences. You are doing me a great favor by your visit. And it's no wonder you feel better. I suspect living with Petra is quite a challenge, and your aunt is little help."

"Yes, and I did not realize how Petra's spite had

infected me, nor how much Aunt Honoria resents me. I was becoming a morose silly goose. I now feel much happier, and due entirely to you. We will have a famous time and try to forget these troublesome men. Women are at a disadvantage, always worrying about men, who can forget us easily under the press of their responsibilities. But tell me about your officer."

And so the two friends had a delightful coze. And if Fabia had persuaded herself for the moment that she could put the distressing affair of Richard in the past, she sensed that for all her brave words it would not be that simple.

However, in the following days she realized how fortunate she was to have found such a refuge. Mrs. Meynell was a sensible parent, never intrusive but always available for counsel and interested in her children's affairs without prying. She created a relaxed and secure environment for her family and enthusiastically widened her circle to include Fabia, treating her as another daughter. The Meynells' son, Henry, had inherited his mother's warmth as well as his father's acumen and appeared quite taken with Fabia. He reminded her of Trevor, teasing her with brotherly candor and eager to escort the girls about Weymouth. Her days now lay along pleasant lines, and Fabia was grateful. She determined to banish all thoughts of Richard and was mainly successful except during the darker reaches of the night.

She had been settled in the Meynell ménage for about a week when Guy Fancher called, anxious to join the Meynell circle. Although he was accommodating and polite to the whole family, Fabia sensed that both Anne and her mother had reservations about him. Influenced by their reaction, she was cautious in her reception of him, although she could find little in his manner that was objectionable. He often made a foursome with Lieutenant Alan Chalmers, Anne's officer, whom Fabia found an amusing companion. They escorted the girls to the Assembly and on picnics and rambles about the countryside, enjoying the fine weather along the seaside.

Since George III and his court had made Weymouth a popular resort, many of his subjects had followed him to enjoy the town. Now, alas, the poor monarch was too ill to make his seasonal pilgrimage, but Weymouth had become a holiday destination for those who could afford it. And with the great fleet gathering at Portland, Weymouth attracted naval officers waiting their ships, bored and restless, searching for entertainment. Anne Meynell had met Lieutenant Chalmers at an informal party, and he had pursued the acquaintance. He seemed genuinely attached to Anne, but Fabia, influenced by her own recent disappointment, thought her friend would be wise to temper her enthusiasm for the officer. No doubt the glamour of the uniform swayed her, and Charles Cartwright, in his father's law office, appeared a poor rival. Fabia thought Charles's chief drawbacks were his obvious devotion to Anne and his familiarity. The Meynells and the Cartwrights were longtime friends, and both sets of parents favored the match.

Despite the Meynells hospitality and Guy Fancher's

determined efforts to entertain her, Fabia often
found herself reluctantly thinking of Richard, wondering if he had heard of her absence or if he had
made enquiries. She knew that his ship was refitting
at Portland, and sometimes at night she would stare
across the harbor, watching the high-masted ships'
rigging casting reflections under the moonlit sky, and
wonder if he had joined his ship and had sailed away,
abandoning any attempt to alter affairs between
them. Had he really loved her? Or was his offer inspired by his parents' approval and the desire to wed,
to produce an heir. Somehow she could not believe
she had been so deceived. But he had certainly not
tried to reverse her decision, and he might have realized that she could have been persuaded in time to
see that Richard shared none of the proclivities of
his brother. That ruthless kiss could have been the
result of his frustration and disappointment. But he
had made no attempt to plead his case in the days
that followed. Where was he and what was he thinking now? she asked herself, brooding by the window
of her pleasant room and regarding the dark night.

In his room at the Crown and Anchor, less than
a mile from the Meynell house, on the Weymouth
waterfront, Richard, too, was staring out his window
at Portland Harbor, reflected in the lighthouse's
shadowy beam. Scores of ships, their masts bobbing
as a quickening breeze blew across the harbor,
looked particularly vulnerable to Richard's sailor's
eye. The brooding mass of Portland Castle, built by
Henry VIII to protect the Channel port, empha-
sized how vital the Navy was to England's protection. Not that Richard needed reminding, but

tonight, just hours after his arrival, his mission to discover the enemies who jeopardized that safety appeared overwhelming.

Surely the culprits would not be obvious, nor would they be the seedy hardened veterans found lounging about the port. According to Admiral Hood, the organizer of this network possessed both a crafty intelligence and access at the higher level of command. That meant an officer, without doubt, no matter how distasteful that idea was. That an officer of His Majesty's Navy could traffic with the French was inconceivable to Richard, whose own loyalties and love of country were the lodestars of his life. Admiral Hood had warned him not to reveal his task to anyone, not even the admiral commanding Portland.

Richard knew that Nelson, aboard the *Victory,* was in the West Indies, but so far had not crossed the Atlantic. Napoleon yearned to force the English out of the Channel ports, for their blockade of Cadiz and the northern French cities was becoming a severe strain on supplies. If Napoleon and his commanders had reliable reports on Nelson's movements, or that of the general fleet, it would enable them to deploy their ships to telling effect. Secrecy was vital and now in danger of being breached. Richard sensed that time was not on his side and that he must unmask the traitor within a few weeks.

Sighing, he turned away from the window. Later, when he lay sleepless, he thought not of the French spy but of Fabia, miles away in Wimborne, as he thought, and he wondered if she, too, was having difficulty sleeping, haunted by the past and the legacy that had forced her to end their romance.

Anne Meynell, eager to show off the sights of Weymouth to her visitor, had organized several exhaustive tours of the neighboring villages and vistas. On this particular promising June day, she had scheduled a picnic to the Chesil Banks, with stops along the way to view some noted prehistoric burial mounds. Fabia would have been content with a quiet few hours pottering about the town but recognized that Anne was doing her best to distract her from what she saw as her blighted romance, and Fabia felt she must accede to Anne's strenuous efforts.

Lieutenant Chalmers, invited to join the expedition, had refused due to his duties, so Charles Cartwright had been pressed into service. Guy Fancher did not appear to be burdened with responsibilities, and he happily accepted the plan to picnic at the Chesil Banks.

Fabia wondered about Charles Cartwright, for she had not been persuaded from her limited exposure to Lieutenant Chalmers that the officer was worthy of her friend. She welcomed the chance to get to know Cartwright better. At their first meeting she had found him affable, of a resolute nature, and not unattractive with his shock of heavy chestnut hair, candid blue eyes, and sturdy build. Not a man of romantic fancy but sincere and decent, she sensed. And there was no doubt of his devotion and affection for Anne. Fabia could understand Anne's attraction to the more witty Lieutenant Chalmers, who embodied all that was novel and exciting, a dangerous challenge. Still, Fabia believed that Charles Cartwright possessed the more reliable qualities so necessary in a husband. But, then, she was probably not a good judge, she conceded, thinking of her own situation.

The quartet set off in Charles's barouche, driving along the waterfront out of town. Guy Fancher, with his facile and accommodating manners made every effort to win the approval of Charles Cartwright, who regarded him with a pleasant yet aloof air, as if not quite prepared to give him his seal of approval yet not inclined to dismiss him as unworthy. Fabia thought Cartwright's attitude understandable and was rather amused at Guy's attempts to ingratiate himself with Charles.

Fabia exerted herself to behave in a lighthearted fashion, determined to put her problems out of mind for the day. And she was looking most appealing in a light silk navy riding dress faced with cream and a matching straw bonnet tied in cream ribbons trimmed with a sprig of cherries. Anne, who usually favored green to complement her russet hair, was equally fashionably dressed in a redingote of emerald sarcenet. A dashing hussar's hat perched jauntily on her head looked quite fetching. She basked in Charles's obvious admiration.

As they passed the Crown and Anchor on their way out of town, Fabia, looking idly about her, bit back a gasp of surprise. Surely that tall man striding from the inn's door bore a striking resemblance to Richard. His back was turned from the barouche, so she could not be sure. She hoped she was not foolish enough to be so obsessed with her memories of him that she saw in a stranger the aspect of her former lover. Shaking off her suspicion, she resolutely turned to Guy and questioned him about some of the ships in the harbor. She would not allow her fancies to spoil this glorious day. Richard was probably miles away, and she was a ninny to even dream of him.

Richard, who had paused at the street corner, turned, thinking someone had hailed him, and noticed the barouche receding as he admired the matched grays driven by a skilled hand on the ribbons. For a moment he thought one of the ladies sitting straight-backed on the forward seat had a look of Fabia, but that was impossible. He chided himself for allowing her to cast a shadow over his pressing duty. His job was to discover a spy, not allow every passing woman to remind him of his lost happiness.

Eleven

Chesil Banks, a shingled shore, stretched from Weymouth to Bridport along the sea, with unequaled views across the Channel.

As the barouche ambled along the road which had existed since Roman times, they glimpsed the prehistoric barrows that marked much of the landscape. Anne insisted they stop now and then to examine these strange features of the area and pointed out their attractions. About ten miles from town, they discovered a charming cove where they decided to alight and enjoy the vista while they had their picnic. After a delectable meal of cold chicken, fruit, and cheese, washed down with lager for the men and lemonade for the ladies, they idled in the sun admiring the scenery.

Guy Fancher, although he found Charles Cartwright a dull dog and was conscious that his host had not fallen completely under his practiced charm, decided he would win Charles by allowing him a tête-à-tête with Anne. Also, he believed this might be his best chance to further his ends with Fabia.

For her part, Anne might have preferred Lieutenant Chalmers as an escort, but long familiarity with Charles, of whom she was genuinely fond, made for a relaxed atmosphere. She watched with a wicked enjoyment Guy Fancher's attempts to attach Fabia. She was not convinced that her friend found the engaging officer as admirable as he thought. He was a trifle complacent, but she could not fault his manners. Fabia seemed to enjoy his company but did not give any indication that she found him irresistible.

After some desultory chatting Guy suggested to Fabia that they explore along the beach, thinking that Charles would thank him for his tact. Fabia agreed, and they strolled off, leaving Charles to entertain Anne.

Experienced in handling women, Guy found Fabia's polite acceptance of his compliments rather rankling, but he was not entirely discouraged. As they widened the distance from their companions, he endeavored to put her at her ease. "How are you finding your visit with the Meynells, Fabia?"

"Very soothing. I needed a holiday. The countryside here is charming, and I certainly understand how His Royal Highness enjoyed his time here. Alas, the poor man can no longer make the journey."

Not wanting to become involved in a political discussion, Guy cleverly turned the conversation to a more personal note. "I am delighted to have this opportunity to further our friendship, Fabia. I feel you might think your cousin Petra has a prior claim on my affections, and I want to assure you that is not the case," he said with every appearance of sincerity.

"Petra is a lovely girl, so pretty, and attracts scores

of beaux. She must have difficulty in deciding which among you she will honor with her favors," Fabia suggested, understanding Guy's implication.

"Well, although I agree that she is exceedingly pretty, that is not always the deciding factor when one is looking for a wife," he hinted boldly.

"And are you hanging out for a wife, Guy?" Fabia teased.

"A sailor's life is a lonely one. It must be rewarding to return from sea to the center of domestic tranquillity," he argued glibly.

"Perhaps, but sailors are rumored to have a girl in every port. Not the best inducement to accept one as a husband," Fabia suggested with a glint in her eye.

"Such a harsh judgment. We are not all tarred with the same brush, I hope."

"I have not the experience to say, but there is little doubt that a man of Charles Cartwright's sterling qualities seems a better risk than Lieutenant Chalmers, for example," Fabia insisted.

"Perhaps, but I was not thinking of Miss Meynell, but of my friendship with you."

"Do we have a friendship? I thought we were the merest of acquaintances," Fabia said quellingly. She did not like the direction of the conversation and turned, as if eager to return to their companions.

"A set-down, indeed. How wounding," Guy answered wryly, hiding his irritation. Surely the girl understood he was within an ames-ace of making a declaration.

"Not at all. I scarcely know you, Guy, and I am not hanging out for a husband, you know."

"Certainly not. I am sure your standards are very high. However, I want you to know I admire you exceedingly and can only hope that our acquaintance will deepen into a more lasting relationship," he explained, mustering all his charm and smiling at her with every evidence of candor while inwardly cursing her indifference to his avowals.

"That's very flattering, and now I think we should rejoin Charles and Anne," Fabia said, dismissing him summarily, a bit embarrassed by his words as well as distressed. She did not need another suitor, although Guy's admiration was soothing to her *amour-propre*. Since she had begun to walk back toward the picnic site Guy had perforce to follow her, not entirely displeased with their chat. Even if he had suspected that although she found him a pleasant distraction, he could in no way ever satisfy her ideal of a serious contender for her hand, he would not have accepted her decision as a permanent one. Whatever the outcome of her relationship with Goring, Guy Fancher had too much conceit to consider any other man a serious rival when he himself was in the running. Still, Fabia was an unusual girl, her reticence and reserved demeanor a challenge he intended to meet. And he believed he had made a promising start. Following her as they walked quickly back, he told himself that he had other rewarding prospects beside the wooing of the starchy Miss Thurston, and he would not be tardy in pursuing them.

The foursome was quiet on their return journey, each of them occupied with their thoughts. Fabia had no intention of encouraging Guy, and he would have to realize it in time. As for Charles and Anne, despite Cartwright's efforts to win her, she remained obstinate, if kind, in her rejection, and he was determined to wait for his happiness.

Finally having delivered the girls to their door, the gentlemen departed with assurances of a meeting in the near future. If Fabia had known of Guy's rendezvous with a woman of dubious reputation, she would have been neither surprised nor disgusted. She sensed that Guy's appetites might be more worldly than he would want her to suspect, but as his attention was of no moment to her, she forgot him as soon as he made his farewells.

Agreeing that the picnic had been an enjoyable interlude, Anne and Fabia repaired to their bedrooms to dress for dinner and the theater. They did not exchange confidences about the merits of their escorts, Anne respecting Fabia's silence, and Fabia, in turn, realizing that despite Charles Cartwright's efforts to change her mind, Anne had not altered in her determination to refuse him.

The Meynells, always thoughtful hosts, had planned the visit to the small Weymouth house as a special treat for their guest, for it was not often that a traveling troupe entertained at the resort. A farce and a melodrama was on the bill, and Fabia looked forward to the evening. Mr. Meynell had secured a box for them and had prevailed upon Henry to join the party. It was in an expectant, festive mood that the company settled into their seats. The theater was crowded, and as Fabia observed the house, she noticed a large group of officers in the stalls. The Navy's presence in Weymouth was pervasive, and she thought the men must often be bored by the slow pace of life in the town as they waited for their ships. Tonight's crowd was a raucous one, shouting encouragement to the actors and roaring at the rather banal lines. After a bit her attention wandered, and she amused herself watching the antics of the customers.

Then she lowered her eyes, her heart racing. Surely that was Richard a few rows back from the stage in the company of several enthusiastic companions. He seemed to be intent on the performance and did not spare a glance at the box to the right of the proscenium, but Fabia drew back, hiding behind her program. So it had been Richard she had glimpsed earlier. Had he followed her here? No, she could not believe that. He must be about to join his ship, to sail away, out of her orbit, their brief romance relegated to the past. Somehow this idea depressed her beyond measure. Thoughts of that final scene between them rose up to bedevil her. Had she behaved foolishly, abandoning all hopes of happiness with her first violent reaction? Would she come to regret her rejection of him. Did she regret it already, seeing him again? Was she allowing her loyalty to Stella to lead her to false conclusions? Aware of her dismay and confusion, her emotions tried, she had the greatest difficulty in remaining quiet, not calling attention to her malaise. All she wanted to do was to escape, run from the theater, leaving behind her despair and Richard himself.

Getting a firm grip on herself, she managed to quiet the racing of her heart and her overset nerves.

When the curtain fell, she managed to get the group to leave quickly, claiming a megrim. Despite herself she had not been able to tear her eyes from him during the performance. It was impossible to see his expression, but she thought he was enjoying himself, far from brooding. Obviously her rejection of him had not left any lasting scars. This realization disturbed her greatly. She was suffering and the object of her unhappiness appeared unmoved.

She was wrong, however. While his investigations filled his days, his nights were spent thinking of Fabia. After several nights of meditation on her, he realized he must win her back for both their sakes. Just how he was to accomplish this, he had not decided, and his doubts were reinforced by his hasty words and violent actions at their last meeting. Certainly Fabia would not easily excuse his ruthless kiss or his vow that he would not be whistled back. Why had he spoken so intemperately? He groaned whenever he thought of that last encounter. Well, at least here in Weymouth he would have time to plan his strategy when next they met, as he was determined they would do.

Fabia and Anne emerged from Weymouth's most fashionable draper's shop the morning after the theater party and ran right into Richard, who was walking from the Crown and Anchor to the harbor. Fabia, somewhat prepared, wondered for a moment if Richard would snub her, but she had not made allowance for his natural courtesy.

If he was surprised, he hid it well. "Good morning, Miss Thurston," he greeted her, a bit austerely but politely. "What a surprise to see you here."

"Yes," Fabia countered weakly, not knowing exactly how to proceed, but remembering Anne, all agog at her side, she introduced the pair. "This is my friend, Anne Meynell, with whom I am visiting. Anne, this is Captain Richard Goring."

Anne, feeling the tension between the two, realized that Richard must be the gentleman who had caused Fabia so much heartache, but she evidenced no sign of this and greeted him cheerfully. After a few moments of casual chat, which hid the surging feelings of both Fabia and Richard, Anne took pity on them. "Do call, Captain Goring, if your duties permit. Our house is on High Street, just some blocks away."

"Thank you, Miss Meynell, I would enjoy that," Richard said civilly and, lifting his hat, made his adieux.

The girls walked toward home for several minutes in silence. Then Anne, always irrepressible, could not restrain herself.

"What an attractive man. Where did you meet him?" she asked with a wicked glint in her eye.

"In Wimborne. His family lives near there," Fabia answered tersely, knowing that Anne, awake on every suit, had identified Richard as her former suitor.

Although fascinated by this romantic imbroglio, Anne was a compassionate girl. She wanted to help this star-crossed pair sort out their problem. "Are you regretting how you parted, Fabia? Captain Goring seems quite charming. Perhaps you have judged him too hastily."

Fabia sighed and admitted, "Perhaps I have, but

it is too late to make an apology, and he did not behave charmingly at our final meeting."

"Not your final meeting. He will call, I am sure, and then you can try to mend affairs," Anne advised cheerfully.

"Oh, Anne, you are such a tonic. How boring my tangled problems must appear to you. I can't imagine you ever behaving in my gothic fashion."

"Don't be too sure. You are not the only one to make mistakes, you know. I am in such a quandary over Lieutenant Chalmers, and then there is Charles. We women are such gudgeons, getting ourselves into a state about the men in our lives," she complained with a wry grimace.

Eager to dismiss more talk of Richard, Fabia asked, "Why are you in a quandary over Lieutenant Chalmers? He seems most *épris.*"

"Do you think so? I have a suspicious nature, I guess. It's no secret that I will have a tidy marriage settlement and that Father is a warm man. Despite my myriad attractions, I fear that Father's comfortable income is a deciding factor with some of my suitors, and Lieutenant Chalmers can be no exception. I really know so little about his own situation, and my expectations must be alluring," she conceded honestly. "I don't want to be married for my money. You, too, should be alive to this possibility. That sugar plantation must bring in a considerable amount of money."

"Neither Richard Goring nor Charles Cartwright need be guilty of courting us for that reason. I am not so convinced that our Alan Chalmers and Guy

Fancher have the same motives," Fabia insisted candidly.

"Oh, has Guy Fancher proposed? When did that happen? On the picnic, I suspect. He seemed quite set down on the way home, I thought. Did you refuse him?" Anne asked avidly.

"He didn't actually offer, just hinted at the possibility, and I had to depress his intentions firmly. There is something about Guy I find disturbing. Well, let us forget them both and enjoy ourselves. After all, we can hardly ask them if they are attracted to us for our money."

"Alas, we poor frail creatures are at the mercy of our affections," Anne agreed dolefully.

"Nonsense, you are not a poor creature, and I have every faith you will make a wise and happy choice," Fabia insisted, wondering if she herself would have Anne's good sense. "Then, too, you are fortunate in having such warm and caring parents to assist you. I envy you that, Anne."

"Yes, I am blessed with a wonderful family," Anne said, unwilling to discuss Fabia's orphaned state, knowing how painful such memories must be.

Turning the conversation to their plans for the week, the young ladies continued home.

Richard, striding rapidly along the waterfront to a meeting with a sailor who had been a member of his crew on past voyages, was hardly conscious of his destination. He had hid his anguish well, but the sight of Fabia had stirred up a yearning in his heart to gather her up in his arms and run away with her. The past days without her had made him realize that he was deeply in love with Fabia. He wondered hopelessly if there was a chance now to repair that earlier damage. She had not demurred when her friend had invited him to call.

Suddenly Richard realized he had passed the tavern where he was to meet his crewman. In his turmoil he had almost forgotten his reason for being in Weymouth. This would not do. He must concentrate on his mission, although he was frustrated by his lack of progress. He could not disappoint his godfather. Personal affairs must wait on his duty.

The Black Dog, on the Weymouth waterfront, catered to a far different clientele than the Crown and Anchor. Dark and stained with soot, its low beams barely clearing Richard's head, the tavern did a brisk trade with the common seamen off the ships in Portland Harbor. At this time of day, few customers gathered at the scarred tables and ale-sodden bar. Richard found Aaron Potts drinking from a mug in the far corner of the tavern and motioned to the man to resume his seat, for Potts had stood up in deference to his former commander.

"How are you, Potts, behaving yourself?" Richard greeted. He remembered Potts had a quick temper and a fearsome reputation for brawls, although in a fight he faced the enemy with that same pugnacious stance, among the first of a boarding crew over the side.

"Can't do else, Captain, with my pockets to let ashore," the man reported gloomily. His clear blue eyes looked directly at Richard in an honest appraisal. Short and broadly built, Potts's hefty arms were browned and ropey with muscles. A tough man but one whose word Richard knew he could rely upon.

"Waiting for a berth, are you? Well, so am I. Let's hope the *Andromeda* will be fitted soon and we can put to sea. We sailors are apt to get into trouble ashore," Richard said cheerfully, sitting across the table from Potts.

"How long will it be, Captain?" the man asked, slamming his mug down with an expression of disgust.

"Just a few more weeks, I understand."

"Then it's off after the Frenchies. Will we be meeting up with the little admiral?" he asked, referring to Nelson.

"Who knows? I hope so. But I have a shore job for which I need your help, Potts, and it may put a few coppers in your pocket. I need some information, and you may be able to nose about and come up with some answers. It's important, and it may be dangerous," Richard warned.

"Aye," Potts grunted, looking interested and eager, not at all put off by the warning.

Richard gave him an edited version of the problem and his assignment. Potts showed every sign of disgust at the idea that it might be an English officer who was betraying him and his companions to the enemy. He agreed to accept the task Richard outlined, and they parted with mutual expressions of esteem and determination.

As Richard walked from the Black Dog, he hoped that he had not been injudicious in confiding in Potts, but he had to have an ally who haunted the waterfront. Whoever was spying on the fleet must be

able to relay his messages to a contact. There would
be a system of codes or surreptitious meetings, and
a seaman like Potts might be able to keep an eye on
the harbor more easily than Richard himself. But
somehow he sensed that his foe operated on a higher
level, in the wardrooms of the very ships he wanted
to destroy, rubbing shoulders with officers. A goodly
number of these officers gathered nightly at the
Crown and Anchor, where drink often loosened their
lips. Was this where the spy learned the movements
of ships? Somehow Richard believed it was more
complicated and organized than this. And any
Frenchman would be hard-pressed to hide his identity among the types in either the Crown and Anchor
or the Black Dog. Potts's task was to nose about the
wharves and try to discover if any foreigners were
asking questions or behaving in an odd way, flush
with coppers and bragging of their newfound wealth.
Many of the shorebound sailors were working on re-
fittings. They could learn the destination of the ships
and the sailing dates. Then to whom did they purvey
these facts? The man had to be a clever dissembler
and inventive. Brave, too, for spying was nasty work,
only undertaken by a dedicated patriot or a greedy
man with a taste for gold.

Time was pressing, and Richard felt a deep frustration that the intriguer might elude his efforts.
He must outwit the fellow before he was recalled
to his ship. His own life might depend on his success.

Twelve

The evening after Fabia's encounter with Richard on the street, she dressed for the local Assembly in a far from anticipatory mood. The thought of exchanging witticisms with her partners, of stifling Guy Fancher's advances, and of appearing light-hearted and entertaining depressed her. She would have preferred to spend a quiet evening thinking about Richard and what their meeting might mean. Did he intend to call despite his harsh words when she had rejected him? He had seemed reserved and almost indifferent when they met so unexpectedly. Was he just being polite before Anne, or did he really want to mend matters between them? And could she bear to discuss his brother and what Randal Goring had done? Discuss it and dismiss it? And did Richard share any of his brother's vile traits? She really did not think he was a monster, but could she marry a man, even if he would have her, with such a brother?

Barely aware of donning her gown, an attractive cream gauze and shot silk with a ruched flounce, she looked at her pale face and shadowed eyes in the mirror, impatient with her abigail's attempts to arrange her hair. Finally the girl was done, and

Fabia dismissed her with an absent smile of thanks. If she had stayed in Wimborne, she would not be facing her current dilemma. Did Richard think for a moment she had followed him here to try to win him back? How lowering. Especially if he had lost all regard for her. And she could not blame him. Well, she must just put on the best face possible and hope that the Meynells would not sense her disquiet. It would hardly be fair to spoil Anne's evening because she was prey to vague fancies and disgust at her own behavior.

Anne might not have been deceived by Fabia's efforts to join with enthusiasm into the evening's entertainment, but she kept silent. She had her own problems to consider. So both girls, chaperoned by Mrs. Meynell and escorted by Henry, set off for the Assembly Hall hoping to find distraction from their troubled thoughts.

On arrival at the Hall, a much more imposing building than the one at Wimborne, the girls were immediately surrounded by men, mostly naval officers, requesting their hands in dances. Guy Fancher managed adroitly to elbow out most of the supplicants and secure Fabia for the opening quadrille, but Fabia had promised the supper dance to Henry, much to Guy's annoyance. As they took their places on the floor, he complained, "I really think you might have saved the supper dance for me, Fabia. I know the Meynells are your hosts, but you do not really want to encourage their son to think you favor him."

Fabia, annoyed at Guy's proprietorial air, said firmly, "Henry is a very entertaining man, and a dear, besides."

"Surely you do not think of him as an eligible *parti,*" Guy protested rashly.

"I am not looking for an eligible *parti,* Guy, but if I were, I could do much worse than Henry. I will not have him traduced. He has been very kind to me," she said quellingly.

Guy, realizing that perhaps he had gone too far, grimaced and hurried to retrieve his mistake. "Of course, you are quite right. I guess I am jealous of any chap you honor with your attention."

Fabia gave him a speaking look but did not reply, and the movements of the dance drew them apart, to her relief. At first she had been flattered by Guy's interest, a soothing sop to her vanity, but seeing Richard had made her realize that Guy was but a poor substitute for the man she really wanted.

Determined not to let her preoccupation with Richard cloud the evening, Fabia pushed disturbing thoughts of the captain from her mind and chatted easily to her succeeding partners, but not without an effort. She noticed that Anne appeared somewhat subdued, and she wondered if that was because Lieutenant Chalmers was absent. She knew her friend had hoped to see the young officer that evening and had dressed with special care in an attractive white patterned muslin gown which set off her figure to advantage.

After a particularly exhausting country reel, Fabia and Anne retired to the chaperons' corner for a rest, under the approving eye of Mrs. Meynell. Anne whispered to Fabia, "I saved the supper dance for Alan Chalmers, and he has not turned up. I wonder why?"

"I suppose his duties must have claimed him. But you need not worry. I see Charles Cartwright has just arrived. No doubt he will prove an equally enjoyable partner."

And as if he had heard Fabia's words, Charles, accompanied by Henry, walked across the room to them. Thinking not for the first time what a nice husband Henry would make for some fortunate girl, Fabia smiled with enthusiasm at him as he suggested they join Anne and Charles for some supper. With his usual courtesy he asked his mother if she would not like some chicken patties, her favorite viand, and was assured that Mrs. Meynell had made an arrangement with some of her friends for supper. Charles took the opportunity to draw Anne aside and request that he escort her to supper. Somewhat reluctantly she agreed, and the four set off to find a table. As they entered the room, Fabia noticed Lieutenant Chalmers had entered the hall and was in close conversation with Guy Fancher.

She wondered idly if the young men had become friends. But she was more annoyed that the lieutenant had forgotten his arrangement with Anne. If her friend noticed his defection, she did not mention it, chatting brightly with Charles about a suggested outing to Dorchester.

At ease with one another, the quartet ate heartily and laughed at Henry's tales about some of the dowagers who were chaperoning the evening. One mature lady in an outrageous magenta satin gown with an imposing turban received a special mention, and Henry told them she was a former butcher's daughter who had married above herself and preened and postured over her good fortune. They were laughing at his story of how Mrs. Ryder insisted that her father had been a man of substance, not a storekeeper, and her attempts to get her husband, a worthy farmer accepted into the gentry, when Richard appeared at the door of the supper room, his gaze wandering over the company.

Seeing Fabia in a festive mood, he frowned in annoyance. He had hesitated before accepting the invitation of a fellow officer to attend the Assembly, not prepared to face Fabia until he had sorted out his feelings and decided his next move. It was apparent that she was not pining, he saw, but he would not be deterred. Crossing the room, he approached the table and greeted them. Anne hurriedly introduced Charles and her brother.

After acknowledging the two men and lady pleasantly, Richard turned to Fabia and asked a bit cautiously, "Could you spare me a dance later, Fabia, or are you all booked?"

"I'm afraid so, Richard," she said, a bit startled by his sudden appearance, but reluctant to have him think she wanted to avoid him.

"Perhaps one of these gentlemen would be kind enough to relinquish his claim?" Richard suggested, looking insistently at Charles and Henry. The latter, always obliging, agreed.

"I have the next dance with Fabia, but if she is willing, I will bow out, Captain, although not without reluctance," he offered, aware that there was some underlying tension between the pair. Could they have quarreled and now the captain was hoping to mend matters? Henry was not unperceptive.

"Really, Henry, you seem very eager to abandon me," Fabia said lightly, not wanting Richard to know how much she wanted to be alone with him.

"Not at all. But I have an unfair advantage over the captain since you are our guest. There will be other occasions for you to honor me," Henry said gallantly.

"Thank you, Meynell. You are a Trojan." Richard smiled gratefully and extended his arm to Fabia. "I believe the music is beginning."

Since she had little choice, Fabia rose and accompanied him, hoping he did not know how her heart was racing and that the flush which deepened her cheeks might be put down to the heat of the room.

"There is a small retiring room off here to the left. If you would not mind, can we ignore this next set and sit it out? I have something to say to you," Richard said firmly.

Fabia acceded weakly, wondering at her supine agreement but unable to help herself.

He settled her on a sofa in the small room, which happened to be untenanted, and sat down next to her, increasing her perturbation.

"I wanted to see you, Fabia, to apologize for my behavior at our last meeting. But I was afraid if I called at the Meynells, you would not receive me."

"Oh, no, Richard, I would not be so impolite."

"It's not politeness I want from you, Fabia, but understanding. I behaved like a boor and can only hope you know it was because I was so disappointed."

"I spoke intemperately, too. It was such a shock, discovering your relationship to the duelist," she said simply. Then, thinking that a further explanation was needed, she hurriedly continued, "After all, you were not responsible for your brother's actions. Your mother very kindly called on me and tried to mend matters. I am afraid I was not too receptive. But I have had time to reconsider.

"Only recently have I examined my memories about the shooting. It made an indelible impression and I was so young, then my family's tragic accident and my illness—all of it is a dark chapter I wanted never to open."

"I quite see why you reacted as you did," Richard said gravely. "I had hoped to tell you myself. I never intended to hide my relationship to Randal, but your aunt anticipated me, and I feel, perhaps, did not put the case as sympathetically as she might have."

"Quite right. I see now that she does not really like me. She fears I am competition for Petra, which is ridiculous."

"Not ridiculous, only realistic. Petra is a vapid piece, and I pity the man who wins her." Richard smiled, aware that affairs were marching along more happily than he could have imagined.

Eager to abandon that topic, Fabia asked, "And why are you in Weymouth? Is your ship ready?"

"No, alas." He hesitated, then, thinking there must be no more secrets between them, said, "I know I can trust you, Fabia. The Admiralty has sent me here on an intelligence assignment, and a nasty business it is as well as being unproductive so far."

"Is there danger?" Fabia asked, suddenly filled with anxiety.

"I like having you worried about me, Fabia, but

I must confess that so far all I have done is laze about the town, discovering nothing. But if I hadn't come, I would not have met you so soon. I had every intention of returning to Wimborne when I finished my job here, to try to repair our relationship," he said earnestly.

"Of course, I will say nothing about your mission here. I do wish I could help."

"Thank you, my dear. You have cheered me immensely, but I doubt there is anything you could do. It's a thorny problem involving espionage. But I will say no more. Can I now assume I will be welcome if I call at the Meynells?"

"Yes, certainly. They are a delightful family, and you will enjoy them, I am sure. Anne has been so supportive during this troubling time. My uncle and Trevor were most sympathetic, but it was not comfortable enduring Petra and my aunt's comments while in Wimborne. I am fortunate to have found a haven at the Meynells."

"If they have comforted you, I am in their debt," Richard said, reaching across to take her hands in his warm clasp. "I promise not to rush you into any avowal, Fabia, but let me have some hope you have not turned me off forever."

"Oh, Richard, I am so confused about my feelings. Please don't be disgusted or impatient. I will try to come to an acceptance of this whole unfortunate affair. That's all I can promise."

"That is enough, Fabia. And I promise not to badger you, but my future depends on your decision," he said, seeing that this was the most he could expect and grateful for that.

"Shall we return to the ballroom?" Fabia asked. "I am sure I have cut my next dance, such shabby behavior, and I do not want Mrs. Meynell to think I am rag-mannered." She wanted to think over Richard's offer of a reconciliation.

He still desired her as a wife, that she knew now, and such fidelity warmed her heart. And certainly she had met no other man who embodied all she wanted in a husband. Still, there was the question of his brother. If they were to argue, and all married couples lost their tempers at times, would his brother's infamous conduct arise again between them? Fabia's divided loyalties weighed heavily, although her every instinct was to accept Richard. She tried to compose her expression. This was neither the time nor the place to examine her conscience.

Richard, seeing her distress, stood up and offered his arm. "Come, Fabia. I have no wish to cause you anguish. Let us just see how matters proceed. You might decide after all that I am a dreadful ogre with whom you would be miserable. I am not without faults, I know," he conceded whimsically, trying to lighten the atmosphere.

Fabia, taking his arm, felt comforted, and then remembering what Richard had said about his mission in Weymouth, insisted with a touching gravity, "You must not allow me to distract you from your work. That is more important than our private affairs."

Although he was not sure he could agree, he nodded, and they entered the ballroom, where immediately Fabia was met by Guy Fancher. He gave a hard look at Richard, but beyond a civil nod said nothing to his rival.

"Ah, here you are, Fabia. I did not believe you would cut our dance," he said, assuming a look of patient endurance at her shabby treatment.

"Of course not, Guy. You remember Captain Goring, of course. He was just bringing me news of Wimborne," she said soothingly.

"Well, the orchestra is tuning up. We had best take our places. Good evening, Captain," Guy said dismissively.

Richard, amused by Guy's conceit and not at all worried that Fabia could be seriously interested in this poseur, made his adieux. Fabia noticed that he crossed the room to Anne's side, where she was sitting by her mother. No doubt he was securing an introduction and an invitation from the hospitable Mrs. Meynell. Richard's manners could not be faulted. But her musings about Richard were interrupted by Guy, who, as they came together in the steps of the dance, said reproachfully, "I do hope Goring's reappearance does not mean you have decided to abandon me, Fabia."

"Of course not, Guy. I am always pleased to see my friends," she explained cautiously. She did hope Guy would not continue this role of embittered suitor. She had never given him the right to think he had any claim upon her.

After the dance, as he was escorting her to the chaperons' corner, she asked him idly, "Will you be in Weymouth for some time, Guy?"

"I have just been appointed flag lieutenant to Admiral Parkinson, who is in charge of shore operations here, so I should be settled in Weymouth for some time," he reported smugly, eager to boast of his preferment.

"Congratulations. I am sure your duties will keep you occupied," Fabia replied noncommitally.

A shore assignment would keep him out of the fighting and still place him in a position to gain the promotion he probably thought he deserved, she reasoned. Placing himself in danger aboard a fighting ship would not be at all to his taste. How different was Richard's outlook, but she should not compare the two. It was not at all fair to Guy, who, whatever his faults, had always behaved in a most gentlemanly way to her. He could never win her heart, however, even if she had never met Richard.

Having made his bow to Mrs. Meynell and danced once with Anne, Richard left the Assembly. And if Fabia thought the evening had lost its luster after his departure, she showed little sign of it, for she danced until the final set with every evidence of a young lady enjoying the evening.

On arriving back at the Meynells soon after one, Fabia quickly prepared to retire. In some ways the evening had exhausted and confused her, and she wanted time alone to ponder over events. She was not so selfish and concerned with her own affairs that she ignored Richard's confidence about his intelligence task. Appalled at the idea that spies were moving in their midst, prepared to put the lives of hundreds of men in jeopardy for their own greedy purposes, she wondered how Richard would unmask the miscreants. Would Richard himself meet peril as he went about his distasteful duty?

Before she could settle herself for sleep, there

came a light tap at the door. Anne then stuck her head around the door. "Oh, good, you are not asleep. I think the best fun of a party is to discuss it with someone afterwards. I hope you are not too tired."

If she was, Fabia was too kind to say so. "Of course not. Do come in and we will have a late-night coze."

Anne perched on Fabia's bed, looking far from her usual merry self. Obviously she wanted to talk about Alan Chalmers, and Fabia could not deny her friend, who in her turn had been so comforting and understanding of Fabia's problems.

"Alan explained that he had been delayed by his duties and that it was too late to send me word when he knew," she threw out carelessly, but seemed braced for criticism.

"I suppose we should not be gudgeons enough to think these officers are in Weymouth just for our entertainment. I am happy he made his apologies," Fabia said warmly, but reserving her opinion. She was quite worried that her friend was falling deeply in love with Lieutenant Chalmers and she wondered if that would bring Anne happiness. But it would be churlish of her to state her objections and vex Anne, perhaps even cause a rift between them.

"He is so charming, so dashing, not at all like Charles," Anne confided as if expecting an argument.

"I like Charles greatly, and the poor man is at such a disadvantage: no handsome uniform and tales of derring-do. But really a man of solid worth and deep devotion," she offered, then wondered if that endorsement would make Cartwright seem prosy and dull. Unfortunately virtue rarely triumphed over meretricious gallantry.

"Your Richard seems to have all the most admirable qualities: a fine naval record, respectability, wealth, and his own brand of charm. His only drawback is his brother, and that does not seem insurmountable," Anne said, a question in her voice.

"I know. I am behaving like a goose. But I promised him I would give a great deal of thought to our relationship and try to overcome my doubts and my loyalties to Stella," Fabia explained with a depth of sincerity that impressed Anne.

"Then Guy Fancher is no rival?" Anne asked.

"Not at all. There is some quality in Guy that disturbs me. I don't believe he is trustworthy."

"Like Alan, I suppose," Anne conceded, looking sad.

"I must be fair, but yes, I think both those gentlemen are looking out for themselves, eager to grasp any opportunity to further their fortunes. We should be on our guard," Fabia admitted, unwilling to suggest that Anne would be making a dreadful mistake if she favored Alan Chalmers.

"You are so sensible, Fabia. I have a feeling of foreboding and only hope I will not be a victim."

"Nonsense. I have every faith in your ultimate good judgment. You will not be lured into indiscretion by a handsome face and winning ways. No, enough of this. We had agreed not to let these gentlemen consume our every thought. Let us sleep on it and take one day at a time," Fabia advised cheerfully, hiding whatever unease she felt at Anne's prescient words.

"I agree. Oh, Fabia, I am so happy you are here. You must stay a long time."

"Thank you, Anne. I am vastly comforted by you and your family, and I promise you will be burdened with me for a long time yet. Now, good night."

Anne bent over and gave Fabia a warm hug and walked jauntily out of the room, but Fabia was far from convinced that her friend saw Alan Chalmers for what he was. Blowing out her candle, she settled to sleep, anticipating a troubled night. Tired from her evening, however, she fell immediately into slumber, with no dreams this night to haunt her.

Thirteen

Along the waterfront Aaron Potts, emerging from the Black Dog after a night of heavy drinking, shook off the drowsiness caused by so much indulgence. Richard's coins had been long spent, for Potts had been strictly rationed by his straitened circumstances and the chance to spend his blunt on tippling had been too much for him.

But even in his cups, Potts kept a strict guard on his tongue, and he had listened to the careless gossip of his mates with close attention. Not that he had learned much to help the captain. But he was not discouraged. Most of the men who drank in the Black Dog were disgruntled toughs who were bored ashore. Often if left without a berth for long, they wandered off looking for trouble. Life aboard ship was hard and lonely. Many of the crews were enlisted from the stews of the city, some impressed, for the Navy was hard put to find men to man the ships. There were few of Aaron Potts's stamp who really enjoyed putting to sea.

He would not be surprised if among his mates there were some who would be tempted by French gold to betray their country. But the average sailor was not in a position to discover much of value to the enemy. He admired Captain Goring, who took good care of his men, served passable food, and used the lash sparingly. Sailing under his command was a vast improvement over most officers, who usually treated their crews like the scum they often were. Potts respected the captain and shared his view that this pesky war with the French was dangerous enough without the risk of betrayal by one's shipmates. He would keep his eyes and ears open, and try to stay sober. As he ambled along the waterfront, he heard the muffled sound of bells, striking the half-hour after midnight, a change of watch aboard one of the ships riding at anchor.

The night was warm and still, and above he saw Orion winking in the stygian sky, but surely that was another kind of light flickering just above the horizon, far out at sea, beyond the Portland Harbor. Shaking his head to clear it, he thought he might be imagining it. He had some knowledge of signals, and it seemed to him that the light was sending a message, intermittent flashes. What could be the meaning of it? Was a fishing ketch in trouble? But even that frail craft could not need rescuing in this calm sea.

Sobering as he watched, his addled wits slowly settling, he kept walking. If the light was a signal, there must be someone receiving the messages. Surely no one would be abroad at this hour without some dubious purpose. Excited now, Aaron hurried farther along the harbor, searching for the hidden presence, but he could see nothing. He stood quietly beneath a convenient bollard, his seaman's eyes trying to solve the mystery.

After a quarter of an hour, the strange flashes ceased. Whatever the message, it must have been received and acknowledged, but he could not discover the source. The land was flat along the front, no convenient cliffs offering a vantage point. Could he have been mistaken? Should he report this odd occurrence to the captain, or was it all a hum, a figment of his blurred senses?

Well, he would be abroad tomorrow at the same time and in a better condition to nose about. Striding along more briskly, he walked several miles from the waterfront before abandoning his search. If there had been a receiver, he was well-concealed. And what could be the end of such strange goings-on? Surely no enemy vessel would be foolhardy enough to try and penetrate the Portland Harbor, risking discovery. Other men, taking the watch, could have seen this peculiar flashing. Potts sighed. It made no sense to him, and only the memory of Richard's warning caused him to think villains could be behind the business.

Turning away in disgust, Potts walked toward his lodgings, a sailors' rooming house on the waterfront. He must give this some thought before he decided his next move. A man accustomed to obeying orders, not initiating action, his reasoning was slow but shrewd. He was not easily gulled. If some havey-cavey business was afoot, he would get to the bottom of it. Richard had chosen his man well. Having made up his mind that there was dirty work afoot, Aaron Potts would not turn away. As he settled into sleep, he believed he had some evidence for which the captain would be grateful, and giving a satisfied sigh, he dropped into a heavy slumber.

Out at sea the ketch, its task accomplished, sailed slowly across the Channel on a quickening wind.

Unlike Potts Richard Goring found sleep elusive. Fabia had not repulsed his advances. There was a chance she could be persuaded to change her mind about accepting him, but he could not banish his doubts so easily. Guy Fancher had turned up too providentially. Could he be a serious rival for her affections? Was that the reason that Richard distrusted him? On the surface he appeared to be a personable chap, and Richard's dislike might spring from his concern that Fabia found the other officer attractive. He must find out more about Fancher.

Tossing restlessly, Richard wondered just how he was to go about such a task. He could hardly ask the man for references. He would nose about and perhaps learn from his fellow officers just what Fancher was doing in Weymouth. He had seemed, in Wimborne, to be just another officer waiting for a ship. Had he come here only because he had learned of Fabia's visit and hoped to take advantage of her anger with Richard?

Well, if so, he was in for a rude rebuttal. Goring could not conceive of Fabia rushing into an attachment to Fancher. She was no flighty belle, basking in the regard of a bevy of men. Once she gave her heart, she would not suddenly reclaim it and fall into the arms of the first fellow who offered for her. Richard might not win her himself, but surely Guy Fancher was not in the running.

If Guy Fancher was disturbed by Richard's appearance in Weymouth, he showed little signs of it. He continued to call on Fabia but made no effort to press his earlier avowals of devotion.

Richard, so occupied with his task of spy-hunting, spared as much time as possible to court Fabia in the approved fashion, sending her flowers, driving her about the town, and joining the Meynells whenever he was invited. Both Mrs. Meynell and Anne were amused by the wary rivalry between the two men, but Fabia gave small evidence that she preferred one over the other.

While Anne found Fabia's suitors entertaining, she was not so charmed by Alan Chalmers's attentions. If he indeed intended to offer for her, he was not rushing into a proposal. If this disappointed Anne, her mother did not share her feeling. Mrs. Meynell continued to hope that Charles Cartwright would prevail and win her daughter. Somehow she distrusted Alan Chalmers, although he was the embodiment of charm and courtesy when he called at the Meynells.

Finally, Mrs. Meynell could no longer restrain her unease and cornered Fabia for a frank chat. "Do you think Anne is seriously interested in Lieutenant Chalmers, Fabia?" she asked one morning when Anne had been sent on a convenient errand.

"She enjoys his company, I know, but she does not think he is being completely open with her," Fabia said cautiously.

"And what is your opinion of the gentleman?" Mrs. Meynell asked.

"He's somewhat of a mystery. He does appear to have good prospects, aide to an Admiral. The Navy must think well of him," Fabia insisted, wanting to be fair.

"But we know nothing of his family, his background. I would not want you to accuse me of being an ambitious mother, looking out for the main chance, and I have to confess I wish Anne favored Charles, but chiefly I want her to be happy. Somehow I doubt that Alan Chalmers would be a considerate or faithful husband. Still, I could be needlessly borrowing trouble."

"Anne is very fortunate in her parents, Mrs. Meynell. I envy her in that respect. She would do well to be guided by you. I wish I had the same security," Fabia said wistfully.

"My dear, if I can advise you in any way, I wish you would confide in me. Your circumstances are sad, orphaned so young and with relatives who have not offered you all the assurance and comfort they might have. I do not wish to pry, but I sense you, too, are vacillating between two suitors. We consider you as close as another daughter and want you to make a wise choice."

"Thank you so much, Mrs. Meynell. That is very heartening. Your household is such a happy intimate one. I am privileged to be accepted by you all. It means a great deal to me. And you are right, I am troubled by my future."

"Both Captain Goring and Lieutenant Fancher

seem estimable men," Mrs. Meynell conceded, but there was uncertainty in her tone.

"There is no question of my accepting Guy as a husband. My problem is Richard. You know that he is the brother of the man who killed my sister's betrothed."

"But Captain Goring is not responsible for his brother's behavior. I cannot imagine him acting in any but the most honorable way. He seems a personable and thoroughly upright young man. You are haunted by your past, but do not let it influence you so that you lose your chance at happiness," Mrs. Meynell insisted kindly.

"I shouldn't, I know, but it is difficult not to remember those dreadful days. And marrying Richard might be a constant reminder. I suppose I am a foolish ninny to be so unsure. But I have told Richard of my doubts, and he is very understanding and patient. I do care for him," Fabia confided, comforted by Mrs. Meynell's opinion, for she respected that lady immensely.

"And time is not on your side. This horrid war and the possibility that all these young men will be sailing into danger before too long is a factor, I fear." Mrs. Meynell wondered if Fabia had taken that prospect into account.

"I know. I cannot bear the thought of Richard in danger," Fabia said, remembering his current mission.

"Mr. Meynell and I are both so fond of you, Fabia. Please rely on us for any advice, although I think you are a sensible girl and will make a wise decision, as I hope Anne will."

That evening while Fabia and Anne were preparing for a small gathering at some neighbors, Aaron Potts was making his own plans of a far different sort. For several nights now he had watched for that strange signaling off the Chesil Banks, only to be disappointed. However, the weather had been stormy, not suitable for small ships at sea. If the fishing ketch had entered Portland Harbor for a rendezvous or to flash another message, it had not been successful.

Potts had decided that he could not contact Captain Goring until he had some definite news to confide, and so far he had not discovered any further evidence either from his night-time vigils or from conversation in the Black Dog. But tonight was clear and calm. If any mischief was afoot, he would be alert. He wished he understood more of the art of signaling. The captain would know and might decipher the messages being relayed from the fishing ketch, if that was what it was.

For now, however, his job was to uncover the site and the man awaiting the message. With his seaman's eye he had reconnoitered the possible places of concealment, and he now had an idea of the best vantage point. Tonight he would be successful, he felt. A man of sturdy common sense, he had a tested belief in his own ability to handle any villain who challenged him. He had little fear that he was placing himself in danger. All he wanted to do was to justify his captain's faith in him.

Just before midnight Richard escorted Fabia home from the party they had attended. Despite the successful evening, and Fabia's obvious enjoyment of his company, he felt uneasy. She could not distract him from the feeling that he had made a mistake in asking Aaron Potts to investigate matters on the waterfront. He liked the doughty little seaman and would hate to think he had pushed him into danger.

It had been four days since he had set Potts on the path of the spies, and he had heard nothing from the sailor. Preoccupied with Fabia and their relationship, which appeared to be improving, he had neglected to follow up on the man. After bidding good night to Fabia, he decided he must seek Potts out at the Black Dog.

His presence at the tavern excited some comment, but the customers were too intent on their drinking and brawling to pay much attention after the first few minutes. There was no sign of Potts, and Richard tried to discover where he might find the man. All the bartender could tell him was that Aaron lodged somewhere nearby but could not give Richard the direction. Tipping the man, Richard left uneasy and disappointed, intending to make further enquiries elsewhere.

He wandered up and down the waterfront, quiet now, and looked out over the still water. The soft lap of waves against the bulkheads only increased his disquiet. After several abortive calls at some seedy lodgings where he was not received kindly, he abandoned his search for Potts and returned to his own hostelry, a nagging guilt accompanying him. He did not fall asleep till near dawn and awoke depressed and logy to a sparkling sunny day. Morose over his lack of progress in ferreting out the spy, he decided a foray along the Chesil Banks might banish some of his disgust and satisfy his need for action. Calling for his curricle, he thought it would relieve his anxiety if he asked Fabia to ride out with him. On arrival at the Meynell house, he found Fabia happy to accept his invitation, which raised his spirits, and they rode out of town, both determined to enjoy themselves.

The day seemed designed to cheer even the most disheartened, sunny with a mild breeze quickening along the front. Fabia was looking most enticing, Richard thought, in a sea green silk spencer over a cream flounced riding dress. Her straw poke bonnet tied with matching green ribbons framed a contented face, and she carried a silk parasol to protect her from the sun. As they tooled quickly from the outskirts of Weymouth, Fabia turned to Richard and said, "This was a splendid idea. I was afraid I might be housebound on such a lovely day as Anne and her mother had to attend an Altar Society meeting and I felt disinclined to join them, although they invited me."

"You seem far more content at the Meynells than you were in Wimborne," Richard answered with a smile, pleased she was responding so happily. Perhaps she was at last abandoning her aversion to his relationship with Randal and seeing him in his own right.

"Yes, I am. They are so kind. I really am grateful for their including me in their family circle."

They did not talk much during most of the ride, content to be together, and Fabia sensed that Richard was mulling over his problem with the spy. She hesitated to broach the matter, not wanting to spoil the day, but she wondered if he had made any progress.

As if he read her thoughts, Richard finally said, "I'm worried, Fabia. I sent a former crew member to try to gather some information, and he seems to have disappeared," he confided, hoping for some comfort.

"You have been given a near-impossible task. I know you are expending every effort." Fabia was reluctant to voice her own fears for his safety.

"Well, so far it has been impossible. And today I heard from the Admiralty urging action. Still, let us not ruin the afternoon with such a depressing topic. I find the seashore soothing, especially on a day like today. We are coming up on a sheltered cove. Why don't we tether the horses and walk a bit," he suggested.

"Yes, indeed," Fabia agreed, eager to cooperate with anything that would cheer him. Richard helped her down from the curricle and tied the horses firmly to a skeleton of a tree, much buffeted by sea gales, but today standing lifeless and quiet. Then he took her arm, and they strolled down a rather steep incline to the banks. Here the wind was fresher, and Fabia furled her parasol, grateful for the warmth of the sun. They walked along companionably, saying little, but in perfect accord. Fabia felt much of her confusion and depression melting away under the halcyon clouds and realized, not for the first time, how much she had missed Richard and how unhappy their previous disagreement had made her. But that was now in the past, and she would forget it, if she could.

The shingled shore was smooth, the stones evened by countless tides, and Fabia looked with interest at the scene. To their right was a sandy cove, overhung with some rocks, and she noticed a bundle of rags stretched out at the very back, hidden somewhat by the overhang.

"What can that be, Richard? Has someone left their garments there, perhaps to bathe?" she asked, pointing out her discovery.

Richard, who had been staring out to sea, turned to investigate. "Wait here, I will see. There is a treacherous current here, and only the foolhardy or careless man would challenge it."

Motioning her to stay back, he walked a few yards and only with great difficulty bit back a gasp. The bundle was a man, lying facedown on the sand, his hands clenched and the back of his head a fearful sight. Bending, Richard turned the man over gingerly and discovered to his horror that he was looking into the sightless eyes and grimacing face of Aaron Potts. Fabia must not see this, but ignoring his order, she had joined him by the man's side.

"Oh, how dreadful, the poor man. He has suffered a terrible accident," she cried.

"Not an accident, I fear. Please, Fabia, this is no sight for you," Richard insisted, appalled and wondering how he was to cope with this situation. He must have help. Potts's body must be removed to a more suitable place and the authorities alerted. This was murder, and a foul one at that. Richard had a sinking feeling that Aaron had met his death doing his, Richard's, job, and he vowed to seek reprisal for the seaman's murder.

"Don't be ridiculous, Richard. I am not going to faint or have the vapors, you know. I have seen dead men before," she protested.

"Good girl, but I regret exceedingly that you should have to endure this nasty scene. And I am in somewhat of a dilemma. I hesitate to ask it of you . . ." His voice wandered off. He must report Potts's death, but how could he leave Fabia?

"Nonsense. You will leave me here and ride posthaste to town to bring help. It's obvious that the poor man is beyond our aid, but we cannot abandon him. The tide is coming in, and he will be washed to sea eventually," she said with calm good sense.

"You are quite amazing, Fabia. Most girls would be wailing and having hysterics at such a sight, and you show an unusual grasp of the situation. But I dislike leaving you to watch over Potts while I go for assistance."

"I doubt I am in any danger. Obviously he has been dead for some time. His assassin could not be lurking in the neighborhood still." She shrugged, looking about.

"No, I think he was attacked during the night. But perhaps the villains intend to return to recover any evidence of their heinous murder. The poor man was only trying to follow my instructions, and I feel guilty that it cost him his life." Richard frowned.

"Then this is the seaman you engaged to make enquiries for you. Obviously he discovered something and was apprehended before he could escape.

How foolish of him to try to handle the affair by himself."

"Potts was a brave man, and quite devoted to me. He probably wanted to bring me the news of his discovery and thought he could handle any interference. But I will find the men responsible for this and revenge poor Potts if it's the last thing I do," Richard promised, his face set.

"I know," she answered gently. "But you must hurry to town now. I will be perfectly all right."

"I wish we had brought Anne or Charles Cartwright with us. I hate leaving you alone."

"You have no choice. Now be about your business," Fabia ordered. If she felt any apprehension, she hid it well.

Richard took her in his arms, and she hid her face in his shoulder, comforted and reassured. He raised her chin and kissed her lightly. "I love you, Fabia. You are a remarkable girl, and someday, if I behave myself, I hope you might return that love."

Fabia did not answer him, only disengaged herself with a weak smile. "Hurry now," she said, and he turned away reluctantly, dragging his feet, then quickening his stride until he was running rapidly toward his horses and curricle.

Once he was out of sight, Fabia, who had been deliberately averting her eyes from Potts, looked at the man stretched out on the sand, his face still wearing a startled look beneath the grimace of pain that his fatal injuries had brought. From one of his clenched hands a piece of material peeked. Fabia, steeling herself, bent down and tugged at it, finally releasing it from Potts's death grip. Amazed, she looked at the small object in her hand. It was a patch of gorget, obviously torn from a uniform. That could only mean that Potts's assailant was a naval man, an officer. How horrible. He was probably the spy that Richard sought.

Putting the evidence carefully in the reticule which was tied at her waist, she drew away from the body and sat down on the shingle, prepared to wait for Richard's return, her horror somewhat mitigated by the news she would have for Richard. It was proof of a sort, but how could it help him in his efforts to unmask the traitor? The whole affair was assuming grave undertones and quite banished any of her personal concerns. That any officer of His Majesty's Navy could commit such a crime was incomprehensible, but it must be so, and now Richard must redouble his efforts to catch him, no matter what the cost.

Fourteen

Although the wait seemed interminable to Fabia, actually Richard returned within an hour, accompanied by a company of men. A young lieutenant of the dragoons with three troopers, an officer from the Custom and Excise department, and a police constable representing the civil government were all prepared to explain the death of Aaron Potts. Both the dragoon lieutenant and the Customs officer argued that Potts had no doubt been involved in smuggling and been killed by his confederates. Richard protested that the man was known to him, a former member of his crew, and insisted that was not possible. It looked very much as though there would be a wrangle over who had responsibility for poor Aaron's body, for the constable, a stout, self-important man with ruddy cheeks and small piercing eyes, held that the crime came under his jurisdiction.

Finally, Richard, accustomed to command and impatient with the confused arguing, suggested in firm tones that Potts be conveyed back to Weymouth without delay. Matters could better be sorted out there, and he wanted to remove Fabia from the scene.

Aside from Richard, none of the authorities inspired confidence in Fabia, and she did not mention the torn gorget. That was evidence better placed before Richard in a more opportune place and time.

Under Richard's direction one of the dragoons hoisted Potts's corpse over his saddle, and the company departed, the constable still protesting that he alone was responsible for the investigation of this death. Richard eyed the men glumly but allowed them to leave without further suggestion, promising to come to town and give a statement about the discovery of the body. Bidding the men a curt farewell, he shepherded Fabia gently into the curricle, and allowing the macabre party a good start, they trotted back toward Weymouth.

"The fools, believing Aaron Potts was a smuggler. Not that the dragoon officer was capable of reasoned thought. They are all so preoccupied by smuggling that they forget other products beside silk and cognac can be landed here. My understanding is that the French encourage smuggling in order to infiltrate their agents, who are of far more danger to the realm than a few casks of brandy or bolts of silk. But to imply that Potts is part of the trade infuriates me."

Fabia, who had not been impressed by the Customs man or the officer, tended to agree. "What will you do now, Richard?"

"That's the painful part, Fabia. I don't know. If only Potts had told me of his suspicions, I would have accompanied him on his search. And what aroused his interest in that cove?"

"He must have seen something or learned something along the waterfront that aroused his curiosity, and the poor man wanted to win your regard by checking it out and then coming to you with the *fait accompli*."

"And all he won for his pains was death. What could he have discovered?"

"Perhaps the secret rendezvous of the spies," Fabia offered. Then deciding she could keep her secret no longer, she blurted out, "There is a small clue. I know it was wrong of me, but after you left, I noticed that he had a scrap of cloth clutched in his hand. It appears to be part of a gorget from an officer's uniform, I think."

"My God, Fabia, don't tell me you touched him?" Richard was appalled at her daring. What other woman would have attempted such a gruesome task?

"Well, he could not harm me, and I thought it might be of importance. I have it safely wrapped in my reticule," she announced with a certain bravado.

"You realize what this means. All our suspicions are confirmed. The traitor is a naval officer." Richard groaned.

"But which one? You can hardly go about Weymouth and Portland asking every officer to show you their uniforms?"

"No, but now that I am sure it is an officer, I might be able to approach the affair from a different angle. There are more than a dozen ships at Portland, but not a full complement of officers, for most of them are on leave while awaiting orders. It should be a simple matter to get from their various commanders a list of those that are here. I will set about the task right away," he said distractedly, his eyes narrowing as he considered his options.

Fabia was silent. Now that this affair had assumed such proportions, she feared more than ever that Richard was exposing himself to peril. His could be the next body found on Chesil Banks. Despite herself she blurted out, "You will take care, Richard."

"Of course, of course," he said absently, then remembering that Fabia had endured a grim ordeal, he smiled at her. "You are a clever puss to have noticed the gorget. You will make a splendid officer's wife.

"Do you think so? My bump of curiosity might prove to be a disadvantage. I guess I am a very noticing sort," Fabia replied whimsically, but relieved that Richard had taken her into his confidence.

"You could never appear to a disadvantage in my eyes, Fabia. But you must keep silent about this business. You could be exposing yourself to danger. I am a serving officer under orders, but you should have no place in this distressing affair. Promise me you will not behave foolishly," he insisted, his concern warming Fabia's heart.

"I will try," she agreed, secretly resolved to pursue her own investigations.

"I understand that Guy Fancher has invited you and the Meynells aboard his ship for a tour of inspection and a reception. See to it that you remain circumspect and don't exercise that curiosity of yours," he ordered.

"Aye, aye, sir. But it is a pity. What an opportunity," Fabia teased.

"I mean it, Fabia. These people are ruthless. They have so much at stake, and are prodigal of lives, including their own. I cannot understand why any Englishman would be inclined to betray his country, but we know they do. Unfortunately too many have fallen victim to French gold. This is not an isolated case. Our intelligence service does the best job it can, but as soon as one nest of traitors is uncovered, another springs up."

"I suppose some do it for other motives, an admiration for Napoleon, a desire to be on the winning side," Fabia said.

"No hope of that. France could never invade England, despite its threats, and Napoleon, like all despots, will eventually be brought down. I have little doubt of that. But enough of this. You have had a wearying and ghastly experience. You must try to put it from your mind," he said firmly.

Fabia murmured an agreement, although she had decided to do no such thing. Still, there was little point in arguing with Richard, and as they drew up before the Meynell residence, she assured him that she would easily recover from the discovery of Potts's body. Before they said their farewells, she entrusted to him the torn gorget which he pocketed thoughtfully. She realized as he bid her a rather brusque farewell that for the moment he was occupied with various stratagems and she had been relegated to the back of his mind. She could not fault him for that. His first duty was to find the man responsible for Potts's death. Their private affairs could wait.

With so much to concern her, she was relieved

to discover that neither Anne nor her mother were home when she arrived, and she ran quickly to her room, where she tried to compose herself and think. Richard was convinced that the traitor was an officer, and he might well be, but he could not be acting alone. What had Potts discovered? He would not have been in that dangerous position late at night if he were not following someone or something that had aroused his suspicions. Sitting down on her window seat and looking out on the Meynell garden, now in its late spring glory, she tried to organize her thoughts.

Potts must have been looking out to sea when he was attacked. Did that mean that there was some activity out there that attracted him, a strange craft or even some attempt to land some agents? What else could it have been? Shaking off a feeling of real danger, she determined to make another trip to Chesil Banks and look over the land. Richard would be too busy in the next few days to escort her, and she hesitated to involve the Meynells.

There was no other recourse. She would have to make use of Guy Fancher, an unattractive prospect as she did not want to encourage him. Well, tomorrow night was the reception aboard his ship to which he had invited them all. She might be able to pursue her investigation there.

If she wondered why she was so determined to aid Richard in his mission, she did not question her motives. She was both worried over Richard's safety and concerned for her country. If any danger lay in her own position, she ignored it. She might be of some small use, and that comforted her. For the first time in a long while, Richard's relationship to Randal Goring seemed unimportant. More critical events had driven that tragedy to the past.

That evening the Meynells insisted that Fabia accompany them to a concert in Weymouth Hall to benefit sailors' comforts, a charity dear to Mrs. Meynell's heart. Although Fabia felt little enthusiasm for the entertainment, she agreed, unwilling to repay her hosts' hospitality with unkindness. The Cartwrights accompanied them with Charles.

Fabia found the elder Cartwrights a charming couple, warm and friendly, obviously of some importance in Weymouth, but not the least bit high in the instep. They showed great partiality for Anne and were inclined to include Fabia in their close circle. The hall was well-filled when their party arrived, but seats had been saved for them in the first few rows, a tribute to Mrs. Meynell's efforts for the charity.

The first offerings, a group of country airs by a local chorus and a rather tedious reading by a bespectacled gray-haired man (Mrs. Meynell informed her in a whisper that he was their resident poet) may have lacked polish but had a certain endearing innocence. At the interval Henry suggested that he and Fabia join Charles and Anne for a stroll outside, for the night was close and the hall suffocating. As they walked up the aisle, Fabia, looking idly about, thought for a moment she glimpsed a familiar blond head, but then dismissed it as the crowd came between them.

"Rather a paltry affair," Henry complained as they gained the courtyard before the hall and breathed the cooler air gratefully.

"Oh, I don't know. I think it was quite brave of the local talent to perform for charity," Anne demurred.

"The treat of the evening will come next. It's to be a piano recital by a French émigré, Roger Puissant, who I understand is a brilliant performer," Charles informed them.

"A French émigré?" Fabia questioned in some surprise.

"He has been here for several years, and I think the poor fellow is having a thin time making ends meet. He takes pupils and manages to eke out a living of sorts," Charles explained.

"I hear London is flooded with émigrés. Some came over during the Terror, and many since then, all escaping Napoleon and leaving behind their worldly possessions. Poor folk. It must be dreadful being forced from your home," Anne responded.

"Some of them are not all they seem, I fear, but most of them gravitate to London, where a colony of dispossessed Frenchmen have established themselves. I think Puissant is the only one in Weymouth. The French are not drawn to rural delights," Henry said with a certain astuteness.

"I have talked to him. He appears a harmless soul, cursing what has befallen his home country and a great supporter of his adopted country," Charles maintained.

Fabia wondered, but held her tongue. This was a fascinating development. She would like to meet M. Puissant. "What was his situation before the Revolution?" she asked.

"I'm not sure, but I think his patron was the Duc

de Romchauld," Henry said. "And, of course, that
made him suspect in the Republic. He managed to
escape just before being arrested, I understand."

"Well, I anticipate hearing him play and perhaps
meeting him," Fabia said, intrigued.

"Ah, these Latins. The ladies prefer Gallic charm
to solid English worth, I fear," Henry teased.

As the interval came to a close, the subject was
dropped, and the quartet filed dutifully back to
their seats.

Puissant was indeed a talented performer, delight-
ing the hall with his rendition of a Mozart work
and a Beethoven sonata. The audience was thrilled,
and not just because of his musical skills. Mr. Puissant was an attractive man with a shock of black
hair and melting dark eyes. When he took his bows,
several young ladies sighed gustily, enraptured by
his appeal. Perhaps a poseur, Fabia thought, but she
was not immune to his charm. He appeared very
grateful for his enthusiastic reception and smiled
winningly. Mrs. Meynell whispered that they would
meet him later at a gathering for some of the pa-
trons and performers.

Henry and Charles thought the girls' applause
overly effusive and growled a bit at the prospect of
meeting the Frenchman, but they all trooped on to
the reception hosted by the mayor in the Town Hall.

Mr. Puissant was immediately surrounded by ad-
mirers when he made, Fabia thought, an overly dramatic entrance into the hall. After partaking of the
rather Spartan refreshments, dry cake and a sweet
punch, Mrs. Meynell volunteered to introduce her
party to the star of the evening.

"Ah, mademoiselles, how kind. *Enchanté*," Puissant gushed as he bowed over their hands with practiced skill, an action that brought frowns from Henry and Charles.

"It's unusual to find such a talented performer in this seaside town," Fabia said, hoping he would be forthcoming.

"Weymouth is so hospitable, so, how do you say, so *fortifiant*, so bracing. And *les citoyens*, so kind," he said with a sweeping gesture.

"But you must miss your homeland, *votre patrie*," Fabia insisted.

"Alas, it is all gone, swept away by those *mauvais chiens*, those peasants. *Je suis très fortuné maintenant*," he insisted, then grimaced. "I do not *parle*, speak, English very well, I fear."

"You do quite well," Fabia argued a bit tartly. She thought his gestures exaggerated and his attempts to converse somewhat of a pose. He might indeed be a much-pitied émigré, but he had not explained how he had come to Weymouth. And was he what he seemed? He appeared a caricature of a Frenchman to her.

On leaving the reception, Mrs. Meynell did not share Fabia's doubts. "I do think M. Puissant is so charming, and the poor man has had a dreadful time. His patron, the duc, I understand, went to the guillotine with his entire family, children and all, as well as several servants. M. Puissant was indeed lucky to escape."

"I wonder," Fabia mused, but did not voice her disagreement. This was yet another development to report to Richard, who should check M. Puissant's credentials forthwith, she believed. She was inclined to agree with Henry, who scorned the pianist's affectations.

"Really, Henry, how can you be so harsh?" his mother argued, as they discussed the concern over some heartier refreshments at home. "Think what the poor man has suffered. And so clever. He played at court, I hear."

"Well, he may have, but he goes to great pains to let us know it. Not at all the thing," Henry objected.

His father joined him with a typical Englishman's disgust at a Frenchman's histrionic behavior. "Never trust these émigrés. Often they are charlatans, battening on us."

"But where else could they go?" Mrs. Meynell insisted, not prepared to abandon M. Puissant.

"Into the army. No wonder the Capets were dethroned. The fellows spent all their time in Paris instead of in the countryside, attending to their rightful business," her husband replied gruffly.

Fabia bit back a laugh, although she tended to agree with bluff Mr. Meynell and thought his words apt.

Later that evening before bed she wondered if she were behaving like a ninny, seeing French spies behind every door. M. Puissant was probably all he claimed, a dispossessed émigré, having a difficult time of it in an alien environment, but her doubts would not be stilled. England was facing a desperate enemy who would go to every length to see her downfall and in the process cause the death of fine young men like Richard.

Fifteen

Fabia realized that Richard was busily pursuing the clue of the torn gorget. She did not expect him to dance attendance on her or to spare time to acquaint her of the latest developments, but she could barely contain her curiosity about the outcome of his investigations. Restless and impatient, she found it difficult to read, sew, or arrange flowers, tasks all suitable for her station. She wished, not for the first time, that she could pursue some meaningful occupation, but that was denied to her because she was a woman. Chiding herself for such self-pity, she determined not to sit brooding in her room. Straightening her hair and giving a tug to her dress, she went in search of Mrs. Meynell, hoping that busy lady had some chore for her.

"If you would not mind, I wish you and Anne would take a basket to Minnie Sales, our old cook. She lives in a cottage down by the waterfront. That would give me the morning to check the linen, a tiresome task, but I have delayed doing it for too long," Mrs. Meynell said gratefully.

"Of course, Mrs. Meynell. I would be happy to visit your old cook. I need to get out and stretch my legs. I will just get my bonnet and see what Anne is doing," Fabia agreed.

Privately Fabia thought Anne had seemed a bit morose and quiet these last few days and wondered if she was unhappy over the absence of Lieutenant Chalmers. That young man had not been as assiduous in his calls lately. Fabia felt guilty that with her concern about Richard's investigation and her own doubts about their future together, she had rather neglected her friend, and after all Anne had done for her. Knocking on Anne's bedroom door, she heard a soft "Enter," and swept in, determined to put on a cheerful air whatever her friend's mood.

"Come, Anne, it's much too nice a day to sit in your room. Your mother has asked us to take a basket to your old cook, and we would benefit from the exercise and the knowledge we were doing a good deed."

Anne gave Fabia a weak smile, rising from her chair, where she had been looking out the window. "Of course, Fabia. You are quite right. I have been behaving badly, so selfish, not considering your entertainment—although a visit to Minnie Sales is hardly that. The old dear suffers from myriad aches and pains, all of which she describes in great detail, but I know she looks forward to our visits. How kind of you to accept Mother's burden." Anne shook out her skirts with resolution, as if deciding to rid herself of whatever unhappy thoughts had been worrying her, and fetched her bonnet.

Within a few moments the girls were walking through the town, having refused the escort of a maid. As they walked briskly along, Fabia hesitated, then broached her concern. "I think you are brooding over Alan Chalmers, Anne. Does that mean that you care for him deeply?" she asked with a forthrightness that would not be denied.

"I'm afraid so, and I feel such a silly goose, for obviously he does not share my feelings, or why else has he ignored me these past few days?"

"Perhaps his duties are occupying him," Fabia suggested.

"And what of Richard?" Anne asked rather tentatively.

"Oh, Richard is still pressing me to accept him, but he, too, is very occupied right now, and I am still indecisive."

"You must not hesitate too long or you will lose him. I sometimes think how much easier it would be to act the light skirt, taking men for the moment and not becoming too involved. They seem to have a thrilling time of it and never are concerned about the future." Anne spoke bitterly, and Fabia sensed that she believed she had been supplanted by such a one in Alan Chalmers's affections.

"Perhaps, but their futures must be grim after they have lost their looks and youth. I really believe the best option is a good faithful husband with whom one can share troubles and joy, and the blessings of a family life. And anyway, we have little choice. I don't think either of us would enjoy being a *demi mondaine*," she decided cheerfully.

"Men are rarely faithful, but I suppose children do compensate," Anne said.

Thinking that Anne had accurately assessed Alan Chalmers's inclinations and that she was not prepared to accept them, Fabia acquiesced. Oddly she had no such doubts about Richard, although that might be foolish dreaming.

"Here we are at Minnie's cottage. Brace yourself for a rigid inquisition," Anne warned, eager to turn the conversation. She wanted to forget Alan for the moment, and Minnie would prove to be a definite distraction.

Mrs. Sales was a round rosy woman, who greeted them effusively, asking in some detail about the whole Meynell family.

"And, Miss Anne, you have a visitor, an old schoolmate. How nice for you," she said after being introduced. Then she shepherded the girls to basket chairs on either side of a blazing fire. Despite the warmth of the day, the cottage was closed tight against the elements, oppressively hot and muggy, although sparkling clean. She pressed tea and cakes on the girls, and they accepted, not wanting to hurt her feelings.

After detailed enquiries into the Meynells' affairs and an equal curiosity about Fabia, Minnie Sales took this rare opportunity to describe her ailments at length. Still, she seemed a cheerful body, not at all oppressed by her aches and pains. The girls listened dutifully and consoled her as best they might, indicating that Mrs. Meynell had sent Minnie her favorite cordial, which might help her health.

They stayed an hour and only succeeded in making their farewells with difficulty. Despite Mrs. Sales's recitations of her woes, Fabia found the visit cheering. They set off to walk home through the High Street, both feeling buoyed by their good deed.

Anne abandoned her malaise and talked enthusiastically about the reception aboard Guy Fancher's ship that evening. She asked Fabia's advice about what she should wear, and as they passed a draper, she stopped and peered in the bowed window. "Oh look, Fabia, Mr. Nichols has some new ribbons. They must have just arrived, probably smuggled but worth examining. What do you think?" she said, indicating a bountiful display of silks.

Fabia smiled and consented, but as Anne continued to regard the ribbons, Fabia turned away, looking across the street, attracted by a familiar figure reflected in the window. Yes, she was right. That was Charles Cartwright and surely the man he was talking to was M. Puissant, the pianist they had heard last evening. Now what could those two have to discuss so seriously?

Anne tugged at her arm. "Come on, Fabia, let us have a look," she urged, and Fabia perforce had to follow her friend into the draper's. But as Anne gleefully sorted out the silk ribbons, selecting several, Fabia looked out the window, watching the two men. What was Charles Cartwright's business with M. Puissant? A dreadful suspicion came to Fabia's mind. Could they be conspirators? Surely not, chatting on the High Street for all to see. She was behaving like a pea goose, seeing spies everywhere. Still, it was odd. As she watched, the two men parted, and she abandoned her speculation to join her friend in an examination of the ribbons, but the witnessed encounter remained bothering.

The reception that evening aboard Guy Fancher's ship proved to be a glittering affair. Many of Weymouth's gentry had been invited and were impressed with the company, the neat vessel which had been scoured and refitted for sea duty, and the officers, all in uniform.

Guy greeted Fabia effusively, intent on letting her see how his recent promotion had given him new status. He was wearing a well-tailored, obviously new uniform, all glitter and gold, and Fabia could not help but wonder if his old one had a missing gorget. Somehow Guy fitted the portrait in her mind of a master spy. His surface charm and handsome looks might easily hide a devious, calculating, and ambitious character, not above sacrificing patriotism and morality for selfish gain.

Still, she had use for Guy, so she could not afford to antagonize him, but she had no intention of playing the simpering admirer.

"We have not seen much of you lately, Guy, but I suppose that your naval duties take up much of your time," Fabia said.

"And you have missed me. That is encouraging," Guy returned, flattered by her words.

"I always miss my friends when they are absent," Fabia returned a bit curtly. Really, the man had an overwhelming ego.

Guy laughed, not at all displeased. "That's what I admire about you, Fabia. You are so forthright and never play games. And may I say you look especially lovely this evening. You have done the H.M.S. *Pegasus* proud."

Fabia had dressed with some care, choosing a light yellow muslin accented with simple ruching about the neck and sleeves, and carrying a matching

silk shawl to ward off the sea breezes. She was a
little annoyed that Guy might think she had dressed
particularly to please him, but she only smiled.
"You are looking very smart yourself. That must be
a new uniform," she queried, unable to repress her
curiosity.

Guy looked smug and agreed, and then offered
his arm, suggesting they make a tour of the ship.
And since that was the purpose of the evening,
Fabia agreed. But she had not finished quizzing
Guy. As they perambulated around the top deck,
Guy pointing out the new armaments destined to
make the *Pegasus* formidable in battle, she asked
him if he expected to put to sea shortly.

"Not for a few months," he replied. "Nelson is
chasing the French about the Caribbean and seems
unable to force them into a fight. For all his
vaunted reputation, I am not impressed with his
current exploits. He yearns to return to Lady Hamilton and the sybaritic life of Naples, I think, rather
than face the French. And this time he might find
them more formidable."

With this criticism he had earned Fabia's scorn,
although she did not reveal it. She thought Nelson a
savior and a brilliant admiral, but it would not be
wise to antagonize Guy when she wanted more information. "Do you really think the French plan to invade England?" she asked with just the right amount
of awe, implying Guy was an expert in the matter.
She wanted to know where his sympathies lay.

"I think they might and so does the Admiralty.
They're massing a fleet in the Channel."

"Well, the French won't succeed," Fabia championed stoutly.

"Perhaps not, but Napoleon is a brilliant strategist. Don't dismiss him lightly."

Fabia nodded, angered by Guy's casual dismissal of the navy in which he served. Did his incautious words mean he had ties to the French command or was it just an idle remark? For the rest of the evening, he stayed close to her side, intent on showing his devotion and boasting of his new position.

Fabia wondered about the admiral who had chosen Guy as a flag lieutenant, and when she met that bluff overweight dignitary, her worst fears were confirmed. He did not appear to be a man who inspired respect or had the commanding presence she would have expected. Thank goodness for men like Nelson, Hood, and Rodney, who had proved doughty fighters. She disliked Guy's toadying manner to his chief, but allowed none of her distaste to show.

After making some suitable remarks and thanking the admiral for the evening, she suggested to Guy that they join the Meynells. Taking her arm in a proprietorial way she found annoying, they strolled toward the Saloon, where refreshments were being served.

Continuing her quest for information, Fabia asked Guy, "Have you seen much of Lieutenant Chalmers lately? He seems to have disappeared."

For a moment Fabia glimpsed an ugly expression in Guy's eyes, but he quickly masked whatever emotion her words had inspired and asked teasingly, "I do hope that gentleman is not the object of your interest, Fabia. I seem to have several rivals. And speaking of that, I have seen little of Captain Goring. I wonder what his real mission is in Weymouth, if not, of course, to court you."

Guy had hit too close to the mark to please Fabia, and she quickly countered, "That is not kind of you, Guy. I think, if it is not immodest of me, that Richard Goring is most *épris*. He has been quite devoted in his attendance on me." She hoped she did not sound like a conceited ninny, proud of her prowess in attracting men, but she must disarm Guy.

"Oh, dear. I can see I am in disgrace for not doing likewise. But I will remedy that. Perhaps you will ride out with me tomorrow."

Since this was the invitation she had been angling for, Fabia could not cavil at Guy's assumption that she yearned for more of his company, but she found his self-assurance irritating.

"I would be pleased to if Mrs. Meynell has no duties for me. She has first demands on my time."

Guy seemed satisfied with this tentative acceptance and promised to call at noon with his phaeton if that was agreeable. Fabia thanked him, and then they joined the Meynells, who were partaking of a light supper. Anne raised a rather wry eyebrow at Guy's evident appropriation of Fabia but greeted him pleasantly. Fabia wondered if she would ask him about Alan Chalmers, then realized that Guy had not answered her own questions about that elusive officer. Anne was not prepared to be so bold as to draw attention to her interest, but Fabia had no such qualms.

"Guy, you did not tell me if you had seen Lieutenant Chalmers. Is he still in Weymouth?" she asked, taking pity of Anne.

"As far as I know. I am a bit surprised he has not called on Miss Anne here lately. He seemed most *bouleversé* by her charms," he insisted in a tone Fabia found scornful and patronizing.

"I am sure Lieutenant Chalmers is an admirable officer, very devoted to his duties, whatever they may be," Fabia reproved sharply, and the subject was dropped.

Driving home that evening and barely hearing Mrs. Meynell's cheerful impression of the ship's tour, Fabia realized that she had a great deal to think about as the result of her conversation with Guy. Whether it revealed anything worth pursuing was another matter. She would be on her guard tomorrow when he drove her out and would attempt to extract more from him.

While Fabia had been delving into dangerous waters aboard the *Pegasus*, Richard had been enjoying a convivial evening with some fellow officers while trying to discover if any of them might lead him to the culprit he was seeking. Finally steering the conversation away from past battles and *on-dits* about various commanders, he turned to the present complement in Weymouth. Several bottles had been broached, and his companions, relaxed and off guard, had some scathing remarks about shore sailors, young men who wore the uniform but had never sighted an enemy sail.

"That Guy Fancher for one," Lieutenant Robert Ansell, a thin, weatherbeaten young man, veteran of several battles, scoffed, his disgust evident.

"I know Fancher. He has just been made a flag
lieutenant," Richard mentioned casually.

"Yes, and with very few credentials. But he is an
encroaching sort, and old Parkinson, his chief, is
not a good judge of men. Fancher would not be
my choice of a companion either at sea or ashore,"
Ansell insisted.

"What do you know about him?" Richard asked
bluntly.

"Not very much. Comes from a Shropshire family,
I think, but he must have influence to win such a
post. He has had no experience, I believe," offered
another officer. "What is your interest in him?" he
asked.

Richard, alarmed that he might have revealed
more than he wanted, admitted, seemingly reluctantly, that they were both interested in the same
young lady, no names mentioned.

"Ah, Richard, at last abandoning the benedict
state and eager to enter parson's noose," his companions teased.

Allowing them to think that Fancher was his rival
in a romantic affair, Richard laughingly agreed.

"Well, if he is serious about any respectable female, he had best be careful not to be seen in the
company of that light skirt I have seen him with
about town. A luscious piece she is and probably
costing him more than a year's pay," Ansell informed them.

"He has a woman in keeping then?" Richard
asked.

"Leona Langly, a former Covent Garden dancer,
I hear. What she is doing in a resort like Weymouth

is a puzzle. Her normal scene is among the London high flyers."

Satisfied that he had learned all he could from this convivial group, Richard made his adieux, pleading a report to write. On his way back to the Crown and Anchor, Richard digested the facts he had learned. It seemed obvious he must contact this Leona Langly. The prospect did not attract him, but she might be persuaded to reveal more of Guy Fancher than Richard could learn elsewhere. How Fabia would view this association with a known Cyprian did not cross Richard's mind. It should have.

Sixteen

True to his promise Guy arrived about noon the following day to take Fabia on the ride she had taken such pains to arrange. Not that she really thought she would discover any further clues to Potts's murder, but somehow she felt drawn to the site.

"Shall we drive along the Banks?" Fabia suggested as they rode out of town. "Some sea breezes would be delightful on such a fine day." To hide her eager expression, she unfurled her parasol, which matched her light blue redingote, reluctant to let Guy see how anxious she was to revisit the scene of the crime.

"As milady pleases," he agreed, twirling his whip flamboyantly. Fabia did not much care for his driving skills or for his horses, a high-mettled black pair looking a bit slender in the forelegs.

She chatted gaily, hoping Guy would not notice anything amiss. "I was most impressed with the *Pegasus*, Guy. It seems in trim shape," she offered as the last buildings of the town receded.

"*She*, not *it*, you landlubber," he teased. "You must always speak of a vessel in the feminine."

"I stand reproved. I really know very little about

naval life, this being my first visit to the seaside," she explained.

"And you are enjoying it, I believe. I find Weymouth a very boring place. If it were not for your presence, it would be quite unendurable," Guy said in what Fabia considered an unctuous tone. But she was prepared to humor him.

"Well, Wimborne was not exactly a nest of excitement."

"True, but there were certain distractions," he said, almost leering.

"Yes, my cousin Petra. She must be missing you."

"A rather trying girl after the first attraction paled. She is undoubtedly a beauty but rather shallow. I pity the man she finally snares. He will be nagged to death."

"How unkind. And I thought you were quite interested in her," she said with a smile.

"She introduced me to you, so I cannot fault her too much. And I am an ungrateful rogue to criticize her. She cannot help her nature, I suppose. Do you miss Wimborne?"

"Not as much as I should. My uncle and aunt were most kind to welcome me into their household, but I am enjoying my stay with the Meynells."

"He's in trade, I believe." Guy's sneering tone raised Fabia's hackles, and though she was prepared to allow him some license, she would brook no criticism of the Meynells.

"They are a delightful family, and Anne is an old schoolmate. She is most fortunate in her domestic circle. Her father is a very respected merchant, very successful, I understand, and no wonder. He appears quite astute as well as amiable."

"Rather a warm man, you think. That is interesting."

Fabia wondered if Guy realized how blatantly ambitious he sounded. He might take some pains to hide his snobbish and devious purposes, she thought, but as they were approaching the cove where she had discovered Potts's body, she only smiled as if in agreement. Really, she was becoming as calculating as Guy. "Do let us stop here. There is a nice stroll along the Banks below this outcrop," she suggested.

"I believe you have a macabre streak, Fabia. Isn't this where you found the body of that smuggler?" Guy said with surprising insight.

"Oh, you know about poor Mr. Potts. It really was rather dreadful. The authorities think he was in league with the smugglers."

"No doubt. There is quite a bit of it around here, and the Customs men are rather ineffective, I fear," Guy answered, drawing his horses to a halt, but not appearing eager to dismount.

Fabia could not help but wonder if his reluctance meant he had unpleasant memories of the place. Although she had no evidence, she felt Guy had a great deal to hide. He was just the type of man to accept money to betray his country, but she couldn't accuse him of that despicable behavior until she had more proof. Signifying that she intended to climb from the carriage and walk down to the cove, he perforce had to allow her, jumping down and tying his horses before assisting her. They scrambled down onto the bank and walked slowly toward the cove.

"And you found the body, Fabia?" Guy asked, lifting an eyebrow as if he thought such an action most ill-suited to a gently bred female.

"Richard Goring and I were taking a stroll and happened on him quite by chance," she admitted.

"I am surprised you can remember it with equanimity. It must have been an appalling shock," he said.

"He could do me no harm. The poor man had been dead some hours. I wonder if the authorities have made any progress in apprehending his killers," she asked guilelessly, but Guy's face was turned from her and she could not read his expression.

"I don't believe so. They seem singularly inept. Perhaps you hope to provide them with a clue and solve the mystery," he mocked.

"I would like to," she agreed simply, ignoring his condescending tone. "And just how did you hear about Richard and me discovering poor Mr. Potts?" she asked tartly.

"It's the current gossip. You could not expect it to be kept a secret in a town like Weymouth. Probably one of the investigating officers shot off his mouth," Guy said in some irritation.

Fabia wondered why he was so annoyed. But they were now nearing the cove where she had discovered the body, and she ignored him, looking intently about the ground. Of course the tide had ebbed and flowed in the period since the murder and washed away any signs of violence.

She strolled to the edge of the water and looked

out to sea. Several fishing smacks bobbed in the distance, but all appeared quiet and usual. Of course at night a small vessel might run into the shore undetected. Fabia had little faith in the expertise of the Customs men in watching out for strange craft. She had heard they were sometimes not above turning a blind eye to such illegal activities if properly compensated. No, the only reason for an alien ship broaching these waters was for smuggling or landing a foreign agent. She turned and looked behind her, where an outcrop loomed over the small cove. This appeared to be the only spot for some distance which might serve as a vantage point for a watcher.

Suddenly it occurred to her that Potts might have glimpsed a signal from that obvious perch. Either that or he had inadvertently come upon a man being landed. She tried to remember if she had seen any signs of a boat being beached when she had found the poor man. But, alas, she had been so concerned with the horrid sight she had made no effort to look. But this visit reinforced her belief that some skulduggery had transpired in this cove and that Potts had witnessed it, been discovered, then killed. Fabia turned away and indicated she had tarried long enough.

She looked at Guy with a searching eye. If he had been involved in Potts's murder or any other evil doing, he was remarkably sanguine, showing no evidence of uneasiness. She disliked the grin with which he watched her musings.

"Are you quite through investigating the scene of the crime, and have you come up with some star-

tling insight?" he asked, taking her arm and leading
her back toward the path to the carriage.

"I suppose you think it most unmaidenly of me
to be interested in such a dreadful spot?" Fabia
asked, ignoring his question.

"Never. I would not presume to question your
motives, and I would not expect you to behave as
most females in your position."

"Dear me, that sounds ominous."

"Not at all. You are not at all the usual thing,
and that, of course, is part of your charm," he insisted, squeezing her hand in a manner she found
most disagreeable.

On the surface Guy Fancher appeared an appealing young man, well-versed in attracting the ladies,
but somehow to her he seemed like an actor playing
a part. Was that why she distrusted him, or was she
just being foolish, suspecting him of dire deeds
when he was just a man looking out for the main
chance?

"Well, I am grateful you do not believe I have a
morbid interest in such affairs. And thank you for
being so patient. Now I think we had better return
to Weymouth. I must be back for luncheon." She
straightened her skirts after he had handed her up.

Guy clambered up beside her, then turned her
toward him. "Have you given any thought to what
I said to you the last time we were alone?" he asked,
looking so sincere Fabia had difficulty in resisting
him. Really, she might be behaving quite unfairly.
He might genuinely care for her, and she would
not want to hurt him.

"Guy, you must know that I have a prior commitment," she said kindly.

"Richard Goring, that estimable young man of impeccable background, destined for a brilliant future," he agreed bitterly.

"Perhaps if I had not met him first . . ." She trailed off, feeling miserable, for Fabia hated wounding anyone.

"I want you to know, Fabia, that if you should ever change your mind, if Goring should prove unreliable, should not come up to scratch, I am waiting," he said.

"Thank you, Guy. I am flattered that you regard me with such affection, but for now I am not hanging out for a husband. I want to enjoy this respite in Weymouth without any thoughts of my future."

"You may not be hanging out for a husband, my girl, but what other future do you have? I doubt that you will remain a spinster," he offered lightly.

He then appeared to abandon the topic, for which Fabia was grateful. His consideration tempered her doubts about him once again. She hated the thought that she had used him, had been unfair. She put on a cheerful face, determined to show him she still held him in regard, and they drove back to Weymouth in charity with one another.

Guy had induced just the feeling he had hoped he would, and he was smugly confident that he had made real progress with Fabia, although he was careful to hide his satisfaction. As they came into town, moving slowly down the crowded streets, Guy noticed, with a shock, Richard Goring on the doorstep of a boardinghouse with which he was very familiar.

"There is your friend Goring, and calling on a most fetching lady if I am not mistaken," he crowed.

Fabia, startled, looked toward the house Guy had indicated. Yes, that was undoubtedly Richard, and as she watched, he was admitted by a maidservant, and the door closed sharply behind him.

"What do you mean, Guy? Who lives there?" she asked, angry at her suspicion but unable to keep silent.

"Respectable females would not find Leona Langly acceptable. She has been in the keeping of some of London's most dissolute bucks, I understand," he informed her, repressing a laugh of satisfaction. What a coup. Now Fabia would have doubts about her lover, and that could only rebound to his credit.

"And how do *you* know Miss Langly, Guy? Are you one of those dissolute bucks?" Fabia asked, surprising him with her astuteness. He had hoped she would be so annoyed she would not notice he had some experience in such matters.

"The current *on-dit* in the officers' mess. Such a one as she would be the cynosure of many eyes, you can rely on that," he assured her. "I, myself, have not enjoyed her favors, if that is what you mean, and we should not be discussing her—not at all a suitable topic for your ears."

"Nonsense, I am not that much of a ninny. You would be surprised at what we respectable females discuss at times, I vow," Fabia said brightly in an attempt at sang-froid.

Guy wisely did not pursue his advantage, feeling

he had gained what he wanted from that fortuitous piece of luck. Goring would not find Fabia so welcoming on his next visit, he was sure.

Richard, from the purest of motives, would have been furious to learn of the hints Guy had dropped about his visit to Miss Langly. He had made up his mind that she would be able to tell him more of that gentleman, if what he had learned was true and Guy was one of her protectors. Why else would a woman of her stamp be in Weymouth? Well, he would wring some information from her, he determined.

Miss Langly, who had evidently not been long risen from her bed, received him in the parlor in a diaphanous silk gown which accented her very obvious charms. A blonde with a well-endowed figure, limpid blue eyes, and a complexion which owed quite a bit to the rouge pot, her profession was apparent. To her credit, she made no attempt to play the innocent.

"What can I do for you, Captain Goring?" she asked, not at all flirtatiously, but rather as if she were contemplating a business deal, as Richard supposed she often did.

"I want some information, Miss Langly, about a fellow officer with whom you are acquainted," he said equally straightforwardly.

"What a pity. I was hoping you had something else in mind. I rather like your looks. But enough of that. Why should I give you this information?" she asked, seating herself on a low chair and indicating that Richard should also take his ease. He remained standing, wanting to give this interview an official stamp. He had no intention of divulging his real motive in asking.

"As you may know, Lieutenant Guy Fancher has been assigned as flag lieutenant to an admiral of the Fleet, a very sensitive position," he said carefully.

"Guy Fancher, and what is he to me?" she asked guilelessly.

"Let us not fence, Miss Langly. I have it on good authority that he has you in keeping."

Richard's natural good manners made it difficult for him to pressure a woman, and to his surprise he found himself rather liking the fair Leona. She raised herself further in his esteem by her next words.

"Your information is quite correct. Lieutenant Fancher and I have that kind of relationship, otherwise I would not be in this tedious town. He has made it worth my while, and since that is the case, I would be most disloyal to gossip about him," she said, making no pretense of loving her protector. She had her standards, and if they seemed loose to Richard, he was forced to respect them.

"I wonder why a woman of your attractions and obvious good sense has adopted such a career," he said despite himself. "I intend no insult."

"None taken. It's a long story and a rather banal one. But suffice to say when I examined my options, I decided that becoming a dancer at Covent Garden would be the best way for me to accomplish my purpose. Lieutenant Fancher is not the first of my friends. He is fairly attractive, rather generous, and

I have had far worse lovers," she explained bluntly. "That is why I am reluctant to betray him."

"I am not asking you to betray him. Surely telling me something about his background can cause you little heart-searching," Richard argued.

"I suppose you have a good reason for asking, and I suspect it has a great deal to do with security. Believe it or not, I care deeply for my country and would do nothing to endanger it. But, really, Guy has not been very forthcoming. I know he must have a sufficient source of income, for I have benefited from it. I've always assumed he inherited it. He has not the style of a self-made man."

"I had heard he comes from Shropshire and still has family there," Richard confided.

"If so, he rarely visits them, but you could be right. All I know is that he came backstage at the theater and made me an offer that appealed at a time when I needed financial backing. What looks I have will not last forever, and a girl must provide for her future as best she can. He has made it quite worth my while to abandon my somewhat precarious career on stage to come down here and make myself available whenever he needs . . . relaxation," she said with a small chuckle.

"So you have no idea where his money comes from? He could hardly support you on a naval officer's pay," Richard insisted.

"I suppose not. As I said, I assume he must have an inheritance, money safely invested in the funds, on which he can draw when need be," she stated with a practical grasp of the problem. Then frowning a bit, "And you think the source of his income might not be too savory, based on smuggling, perhaps? There is quite a bit of that going on, and I must say I enjoy the fruits of it," she confessed, looking down at her gown which Richard thought might be fashioned of silk from Lille.

"That's a possibility, and as it is illegal, no matter how much winking at it goes on in these parts, his complicity in a smuggling ring would not be well-received in naval quarters."

"And what do you want me to do? Quiz him as we are nestled beneath the sheets?" she asked a bit coarsely.

Richard smiled, not at all offended. "How astute of you, Miss Langly. That might be very helpful."

"Well, I don't like it. But on the other hand I would not want to be mixed up in any shady activity. I will think about it. Give me a few days, and I will see what I can discover," she promised.

"I would be most grateful if you can discover anything which will clear Lieutenant Fancher's name, Miss Langly."

"It's a pity, really, that you are obviously occupied elsewhere, in a romantic sense. I believe we would deal very well together," she offered frankly.

"I am flattered, but you are correct. I am not available. But if I were, I would be tempted. You are quite an attractive female, and an honest one without the artifices I might have expected. I am grateful, Miss Langly, for your forbearance in listening to me. I think Lieutenant Fancher is a fortunate man," Richard concluded sincerely, rising to take his leave.

"It's been a pleasure, Captain Goring. We will meet again, I trust."

"Yes, indeed." Richard bowed over her hand as if she were the most respectable duchess before quitting her company.

Later, musing over that encounter, he decided it would serve his interests if Miss Langly believed Guy Fancher was involved in smuggling, a suitable distraction from his real suspicions about that gentleman. But he had to concede that Miss Langly had not really provided any evidence beyond the fact that Guy had an unexplained source of money. The man could be entirely innocent of any treasonable plots. Richard was honest enough to admit that he did not like the fellow, resented his pursuit of Fabia, and would not be unhappy to unmask him as the elusive spy. Well, he would just have to bring more pressure on Miss Langly to come up with some details. In the meantime he could not neglect other officers just because Guy so easily fitted his picture of a traitor in the pay of the enemy.

Seventeen

Fabia told herself she was foolish to be concerned over Richard's appearance on the doorstep of a well-known light skirt. She was not even certain she could believe Guy Fancher's story. She thought he was perfectly capable of seizing the opportunity to discredit his rival. Even if Richard had been calling on the woman, his motive might have been the purest. Still, the incident rankled despite her best attempts to dismiss it. To her relief the Meynells did not notice her distrait air, and Anne was once again in good spirits. Fabia believed her friend's happier mood had been induced by the arrival of Alan Chalmers, who blithely explained his absence as the press of duties. Fabia looked askance at this excuse, but Anne seemed to find it acceptable.

Fabia was happily planning an expedition to Corfe Castle, that imposing ruin which had been destroyed by Cromwellian forces during the Civil War after a valiant defense by Lady Bankes and her Royalist followers. Corfe Castle had finally been taken by the Puritans due to treachery by one of the garrison, Anne told Fabia, who concluded that traitors continued to threaten the safety of the realm.

Anne suggested that either Guy or Richard would make a pleasing companion on the trip to Corfe Castle, and Fabia finally agreed to invite Richard, penning him a note at the Crown and Anchor. She only hoped he was not too occupied to agree. Then, perhaps, she would find out what his business with the reputed light skirt had been. That Guy Fancher was the protector of the lady never crossed her mind.

On receiving Fabia's note, Richard felt guilty. He had neglected her recently, and was well-aware that Guy Fancher would take advantage of his absence to plead his case. He had visited Leona Langly again, trying to extract from her some more information, but either she was too loyal to Guy to betray him or she knew nothing. He wondered what Fabia's reaction would be if he told her that Guy, far from pining for Fabia, was consoling himself with Leona. Yet, much as he disliked and distrusted Guy, he knew he could not bring himself to discuss his rival's amatory pursuits with Fabia. However, he did promise to join the party to Corfe Castle.

Arriving at the Meynells on the appointed day, he was received quite coolly by Fabia, to his puzzlement. Henry Meynell was to join the group, escorting a fetching girl, Mary Anne Venner, and all three gentlemen would take their phaetons. Assisting Fabia into his vehicle, Richard was aware that Fabia was not responding to his lighthearted remarks and wondered if the spectre of his brother was again providing a barrier to their understanding.

As they trotted out of town eastward, he apologized for not seeing her. "I have been trying to check out the various officers posted in Weymouth to eliminate any possibilities. A tiresome job, but I have culled the list to about ten," he confided.

Fabia, feeling a bit ashamed of her bad humor, said with animation, "That's progress. I'm sorry, Richard, that I am so churlish, but I have several things on my mind."

"And are you going to tell me what they are?" he asked, looking at her appealingly. "I do hope you have not been brooding about our difficulties."

"Not exactly. Guy Fancher took me for a ride out to Chesil Banks, and I tried to discover what Mr. Potts was doing there when he met his death," she explained, unwilling to bring up the matter of Richard's unexplained appearance that day on the doorstep of the dubious woman. She hated the distance this knowledge gave her but could not bring herself to ask him what he was doing there.

"And did you discover anything of importance?" Richard asked, rather amused that Fabia should be trying to play detective.

"Not really," she admitted, but then continued, "Still, I think he must have either come upon your traitor welcoming a French agent who just landed, or saw a signal of some sort from the sea."

Richard, who had come to the same conclusion, was not surprised at Fabia's reasoning, but he frowned as he considered the danger to which she might be exposing herself if she delved any deeper into this conspiracy. "Yes, you are undoubtedly right, but I wish you would be careful."

He wanted to suggest that Guy Fancher, of whom he had deep suspicions, might not be the best companion for her on her jaunts, but knew she might think his warning was inspired by jealousy. So they were both quiet, both prey to emotions they did not want to admit.

After some minutes, as they trotted along the road leading to the rendezvous, well ahead of their companions, Fabia could no longer keep silent. "We saw you that day, entering a house on the quayside," she blurted out, determined to settle the matter one way or another.

Richard grimaced. He should have told her immediately. Obviously Guy had told her some scurrilous tale, making Richard out to be the worst deceiver. But how could he discuss Miss Langly with Fabia without exposing Guy? It was not the conduct of a gentleman, but then tracking spies did not demand gentlemanly conduct. Taking a deep breath, he explained, feeling the veriest cad.

"I was calling on Miss Langly, who had been reported to me by some fellow officers as a friend of Guy's. I have to admit that Fancher demands investigation. His source of income is mysterious, and Miss Langly confided that she had come to Weymouth at his invitation," Richard explained delicately.

Fabia, not at all shocked, barely repressed a sigh of relief. Perhaps she was being credulous, but she believed that of the two men it would be Guy who was capable of setting up a mistress, not Richard. Carefully she suggested, "And did you find out anything that strengthened your views?"

Richard laughed, relieved in his own way. "You never cease to surprise me, Fabia. Most young women would be appalled to discover that a man who was paying his addresses to her had a mistress in keeping."

"I think it is only to be expected of Guy. He has an inflated opinion of his prowess with my sex," Fabia said tartly. "And I would be a pea goose not to acknowledge that gentlemen often pursue other interests while paying assiduous attention to respectable women. Guy is somewhat of a rake, I think."

"And rakes are supposed to be very attractive to women," Richard conceded.

"It depends on the woman. I don't believe that old adage that they make the best husbands. Only too often they pretend to have abandoned such ways and then once married return to dalliance. But what I want to know is what light this Miss Langly threw on Guy's activities."

"Not much. She was a dancer in Covent Garden, and Guy is not her first protector. She has no idea where his money comes from and, I think, cares little as long as he provides her with a suitable life. She did not deny that Guy's unexplained funds might come from smuggling, and I let her think she was correct." Richard hesitated, wondering just what Fabia was thinking. Again she surprised him.

"And did you like her, Richard?" she asked whimsically.

"Yes, I did. She appeared quite honest about herself, making no apologies for her position. I think you would like her, too, Fabia, if you discount her profession."

"I probably would. Perhaps my island background is responsible, but I have no scorn of women less fortunate than myself who have had to make their way in the world as best they could without the support of a family or competence. And I think women like Miss Langly might have an easier time of it in some ways."

"I cannot see you as a light skirt, Fabia," Richard quipped, astonished at the line the conversation was taking.

"No, I can't either, but that does not mean I despise women of that sort. But it must be hard for them when they age. I take it Miss Langly is attractive?" she queried with a shade to her tone that Richard found endearing, for it assured him she was not disinterested in his reaction to Miss Langly.

"In a rather obvious way, but not to my taste. I like austere, determined women who give no quarter in the battle of the sexes," he teased.

"Am I austere? Dear me, I don't mean to be. Perhaps wary is a better description. But I will confess when Guy first told me of Miss Langly, I felt a very normal reaction, that you might find her appealing," she confided honestly.

"How satisfying, to think you cared enough. You quite encourage me, Fabia."

"Don't be ridiculous. You know I care for you, Richard. It's only this niggling horror about your brother, the feeling I might be disloyal to my sister, which prevents me from committing myself," Fabia insisted, determined to allay all doubts.

Richard reached across and laid a comforting hand on hers. "I know, my dear, and I honor you for it. I will just have to try harder to convince you. If only I could give my whole mind to it, instead of chasing after nebulous spies," he sighed in frustration.

But Fabia, her fears settled, only laughed. "I am quite flattered to think I can distract you from your duty. But seriously, Richard, do you think Guy Fancher is your traitor?"

"I don't know. There are certainly grounds for suspicion. But I could be wrong."

"He was wearing a splendid new uniform when we attended the *Pegasus* reception the other evening. Perhaps his old one has a missing gorget," Fabia suggested.

"You would make a fine intelligence agent yourself, Fabia. But do be careful with Guy. Whoever is conveying information to the French is ruthless. Look at poor Potts," Richard warned.

"Yes, I know. I often think of him, brave man," Fabia said. They were now approaching the crest of Corfe Castle, its impressive shattered walls reminding her of other battles and other treachery.

"We will say no more of this and try to enjoy our afternoon," Richard decided, and she agreed, as the other members of their party joined them.

The exploration of Corfe Castle proceeded successfully, the three couples scrambling over the ruins, exclaiming about the view, and generally enjoying themselves. Finally, having exhausted the rugged scene, they repaired for a picnic on one of the castle slopes. After a hearty meal of cold pigeon, beef, and strawberries, they lay back and talked idly. Finally Alan Chalmers rose to his feet and announced he must walk off this indulgence, inviting Anne to accompany him and giving her a

meaningful look. Much too eagerly, in Fabia's opinion, her friend agreed, and they strode off, Alan
holding Anne's arm in a firm grip. Fabia, finding
this masterfulness not to her taste, turned to Richard, stretched out by her side.

"I hope Anne is not going to be too acquiescent
with that young man. He has neglected her shame-
fully after having given her expectations, I fear,"
she said, not wanting Anne's brother to hear, although there was little fear of that as he was engaged in a spirited discussion with Miss Venner on
the chances of an invasion and Napoleon murdering
them all in their beds.

"Don't you like him?" Richard asked idly, not really concerned.

"No, I don't, and I think Anne is too tender-
hearted not to be hurt. After all, she knows little
about him. Charles Cartwright is a much steadier
fellow and adores her," Fabia insisted fiercely, then
smiled and admitted, "It is really not my business
except that I am fond of Anne." Then she remembered and taking a cautionary glance at Henry, confided, "I meant to tell you before this but forgot."

"Well, what is it? You have thoroughly aroused
my curiosity," Richard asked, lulled by the lovely
weather and Fabia's intent face. He watched her
speaking eyes with much enjoyment, thinking what
an arresting girl she was, even if a bit too stubborn.

"I have discovered a French émigré, M. Puissant,
a musician who we heard at a concert a few days
ago. He seems a disingenuous type. Later I noticed
him having a rather lengthy and serious conversa-

tion with Charles Cartwright in the High Street," she offered triumphantly.

"Really, Fabia, you must curb this unmaidenly interest in conspiracy. It does not bode well for married bliss," Richard teased.

"I will not dignify that remark with comment. But do you think Charles could be involved in some skulduggery? It seems most unlikely, and I like him so much."

"Dear me, another rival. The ground is thick with them," Richard mocked, then seeing Fabia was becoming annoyed, "I am a beast to tease you. But I really think M. Puissant is what he seems, a pathetic émigré trying to make his way in an alien world. French émigrés are rather thin on the ground in Weymouth, and I checked him out some time ago. He appears to lead a blameless, even dull life."

"But what about Charles Cartwright?" Fabia protested.

"I doubt very much if he is in a position to learn any naval secrets. No, it must be a serving officer. That is why Fancher is such a possibility. He is in a strong position, as flag lieutenant, to discover maneuvers and strategy. He's still my favorite candidate."

Before Fabia could argue the merits of either M. Puissant or Charles Cartwright, Anne and Alan Chalmers returned. Fabia noticed her friend looking quite overwhelmed. Had Alan made her an offer? Fabia looked at Henry to see if he noticed his sister's mood, but with brotherly indifference he continued his discussion with Miss Venner, not at all concerned.

As a brisk wind had begun to blow in from the sea, the party decided it was time to take their leave. Soon they were riding back to town, Richard's phaeton trailing the others, a deliberate ploy on his part. He had only the most cursory interest in Anne Meynell's romantic affairs, but he could see that Fabia was concerned about her friend.

"Do you think Miss Meynell wants to marry Chalmers?" he asked, deciding that topic was safer than any more discussion of spies. He worried that Fabia might decide, on whatever information he provided, to do some dangerous investigating, and he wanted to distract her.

"I'm afraid so, and I think it would be a grave mistake," Fabia said with a frown. "She knows so little about him. Most men are charming when they are courting, but that does not always mean they would make devoted husbands once the union is a fact."

"Such a cynic. I hope you do not believe I have dark passages beneath my kind exterior and will beat you or be niggardly with the household money when we have sealed the vows," he mocked.

"Oh, Richard, don't joke. I am quite worried about Anne. She seems mesmerized by Alan Chalmers. And as far as that goes, marriage can be a fearful lottery for a woman."

Suddenly serious, Richard nodded. "Yes, you are right. The most intimate of ties can sometimes produce ogres or bullies, not ever visible to the world outside the home. I agree that Chalmers's quite evident charm could be a masquerade similar to that of Guy Fancher's." He could not rid himself of the feeling that Fabia entertained warm emotions about that officer.

"Guy's facade is easily pierced. I am sure he is a gambler and a rake, if not worse," she said in a decided manner that settled Richard's doubts temporarily. They proceeded on their way without coming to any more conclusions about either Anne Meynell's future, their own, or the possible apprehension of the spy.

On reaching the Meynells', Richard bid her a lingering farewell, promising to see her soon, but Chalmers accompanied Anne into the house on learning that Mr. Meynell had returned from his office.

As Anne and Fabia walked upstairs to their rooms, Fabia could no longer restrain herself. "Has Alan Chalmers offered for you?" she asked bluntly.

"Yes, and oh, Fabia, he is now seeing Father. I don't know what Father will say. You know the parents favor Charles Cartwright, but friendship is not a basis for marriage, only love is," Anne insisted, blushing at her ardor.

"Come in and tell me all about it," Fabia invited, determined not to put her own objections before her bemused friend until she had heard the full story.

Anne settled herself on the bed, Fabia taking a nearby chair. "When we went for that walk above the castle, he asked me to marry him, and he was so strong, even demanding. What could I do but confess my love and agree?" Anne said simply.

"Are you sure, Anne?" Fabia asked, remembering her own doubts and her rejection of Richard. If she had loved him as Anne confessed to loving Alan Chalmers, would not she have dismissed his brother and all that meant and accepted him with similar eagerness? She envied Anne her certainty, the product of a warm and caring home. Her friend could not conceive of treachery or cruelty.

"Yes, I am. And if Father does not consent, I have agreed to elope with him. You will not break my confidence, Fabia?" Anne asked, worried that she had said too much.

Fabia, appalled, wanted to object but knew that if she did, Anne would turn from her, disappointed and reluctant to say more.

Carefully Fabia chose her words. "If you are convinced that Alan Chalmers alone can make you happy, then I will say no more. I am no doubt a crabby pea goose to cast a pall on your romance, but I fear life has taught me some hard lessons."

"I know, Fabia, and I understand, but Alan has no wicked brother or other horrid secrets in his past. I know I can trust him," she said with engaging if foolish candor.

"Then I will wish you happy and hope your father agrees," Fabia conceded, not at all sure that the canny Mr. Meynell would be so obliging.

Eighteen

Dinner that evening was a rather tense meal, Anne brooding, Mr. Meynell abstracted, and Mrs. Meynell unhappy. Only Henry remained impervious to the undercurrents, or at least prepared to ignore them, whether he sensed them or not. Fabia felt most uncomfortable being in Anne's confidence, believing that Mr. Meynell had not given his consent to Anne's marriage. Although she agreed that Mr. Meynell was wise to delay, she wondered what her friend might do. After the poached peaches Mr. Meynell, pleading business, left abruptly, summoning Henry to accompany him. This was so unlike his usual relaxed host that Fabia became seriously concerned. She dreaded a rift between Anne and her parents, and it very much looked as though it could not be avoided.

The ladies adjourned to the drawing room, where Mrs. Meynell took up her tapestry and then, after a few stitches, threw it down in disgust. She turned to her daughter in gentle reproach. "I know you think your father is being difficult about young Chalmers, Anne, but really he is just trying to protect you," she pleaded.

Anne, usually so agreeable and pleasant, looked

fiercely angry and was about to rush into uncon-
sidered words when Fabia intervened. "I am sure
you and Anne have much to discuss of a private
nature, Mrs. Meynell. I have some letters to write."
After offering the time-honored excuse, she stood,
preparing to leave mother and daughter to sort out
the problem. But Anne would have none of it.

"Nonsense, Fabia, you know all about it, so don't
pretend differently."

Mrs. Meynell, a bit taken aback by her daughter's
opposition, sighed and nodded at Fabia. "I would
prefer that you stay, Fabia, as you seem to know all
about our trouble and could, perhaps, have a calming effect."

Fabia sat down again and folded her hands in her
lap. This was most disconcerting. The Meynells, always so affectionate and warm in their regard for
one another, were miserable, and she tended to side
with the parents, which made her position vis-à-vis
Anne uncomfortable.

"Anne, my dear," Mrs. Meynell said, "your father
is only acting for your benefit. He has suggested
that you and Alan wait for six months to see if this
relationship is really a constant one. That is not
asking too much of you, certainly," she explained.

"In six months Alan could be at sea, in danger
of his very life. All the officers feel that a major
battle with the French cannot be long delayed,"
Anne said mutinously.

"Does Captain Goring believe there may be a battle soon?" Mrs. Meynell asked Fabia, hoping for
some support.

"I believe so, Mrs. Meynell. Of course, he does

not tell me any news of importance as such secrets are best not shared," she replied carefully, hoping to avoid trouble.

"I want to marry Alan before he sails away. Who knows what might happen to him? I could easily become a widow without having any happiness. I will never love anyone else," Anne moaned.

If Mrs. Meynell thought this was nonsense, she was wise enough not to say so, and Fabia applauded her good sense while seeing the justice of Anne's demands.

"I think, Anne, you must be guided by your father in this matter. He has your welfare at heart, and it is his duty to see that you make a sensible choice of a life's partner," Anne's mother said.

"You hate Alan just because you have not known him for ages and because you want me to marry Charles Cartwright," Anne said in a fury. She jumped to her feet, her face flushed and tears gathering in her eyes. Without another word she fled from the room, slamming the door behind her.

"Oh, dear, I handled that badly. Whatever are we to do, Fabia? Surely you see that we cannot let Anne marry a man we barely know. She only met him several months ago, and he has told us nothing about his background. I hope you do not think we are behaving in a gothic fashion. I want Anne to be happy. It is true we prefer Charles, but we would never force her to marry any man repugnant to her," Mrs. Meynell confided, her usual cheerful face marked by worry.

"Anne does seem truly in love with Lieutenant Chalmers, Mrs. Meynell, but I think you are quite right to insist on a six-month waiting period. You have a responsibility to guard her against future sorrow."

"We really have nothing against the young man and have not denied him the house or anything drastic like that," Mrs. Meynell explained. "Young people naturally are so impetuous and want to grasp their happiness eagerly, especially when they are in love. I cannot fault them for that, even if Anne believes we have forgotten all about such feelings." She looked to Fabia for support. "You do agree, don't you, Fabia?"

"Yes, I do, Mrs. Meynell, and I don't think for a moment you are being cruel or despotic. I am a bit surprised that Anne's natural common sense has been swamped by her more passionate emotions, but I suppose it is understandable."

"Thank you, my dear. I know it is unfair of me, but you appear to have considerable influence with our daughter, and I hope I can rely on you to persuade her that what we are asking is not so dreadful," she pleaded. A startled look crossed her face. "You don't think she might elope, do you?"

Since Fabia was quite sure that Anne would, she found herself with a dilemma. She wanted to tell Mrs. Meynell there was no possibility of such a scandalous action on her daughter's part, but she could not be convincing. All she could offer was the bare comfort that she would do her best to prevent it.

"I really don't know, Mrs. Meynell, but you can be assured I would do my best to counsel against it. I think Anne will be in a better frame of mind after she has slept on this situation. She has a good fund of common sense."

"Which can easily fly out the window when love is involved," Mrs. Meynell said with a sigh. "I know I can trust you to advise her that marriage requires more than passion. Your own experience will be invaluable."

"I think we must be patient and not give the appearance of disliking Alan, which will only solidify Anne's determination to stay loyal to him," Fabia cautioned.

"You are quite right, and I must admit the man has a great deal of charm, if only he were not so secretive about his past. Surely he has nothing to be ashamed of, and it is not as if Anne needs to marry a wealthy man. If Alan is all he appears, we would have no objection just because he does not have a large competence," Mrs. Meynell said kindly.

"You are a very wise and good woman, Mrs Meynell, and I entirely agree with your sentiments I will suggest gently to Anne that a waiting period is not too much to ask."

"Thank you, my dear, you relieve my mind. And now all this turmoil has quite exhausted me, and I think I will retire early. I will tell my husband of our little talk, if you don't mind. It might calm his fears," she said in her usual sensible fashion.

"Of course. Good night, Mrs. Meynell." Fabia stood and watched her well-intentioned hostess retire, leaving her prey to some very mixed emotions. She wandered over to the window, restless and uneasy, drawing aside the draperies and unlatching the doors so that she could walk out onto the terrace as she needed a breath of air. The night was starry and brilliant with a crescent of moon peeking over the horizon. On such a lovely evening, it was hard to realize that turbulent emotions stirred in this benevolent household and that out there some villain plotted to betray his country.

Sighing with uncertainty about her own role in all this trouble and remembering that she had yet to come to a decision about her own future, about Richard, she paced up and down the terrace, her mind in turmoil. For the past weeks she had drifted, allowing Richard to soothe her worries and woo her with soft words and patience. She knew she loved him, but did she love him enough to chance marriage when the spectre of her sister's tragedy still haunted her?

Then she chided herself. For the past few weeks she had hardly given Stella a thought, completely immersed in the business of unmasking the traitor. Certainly the years had mellowed her memories of that tragic event, and Richard's manner had shown none of his brother's regrettable behavior. He must truly care for her, or he would not have pursued her with such diligence. She was ashamed that she had dithered and dallied when he had acted with such restraint. She had told Anne that waiting to see how her relationship with Alan developed was wise because that was the advice she had given herself, but Anne had reminded her that time was not on their side. Both these young officers might soon encounter danger and even death. Had she been selfish to deny Richard? Now he was occupied with his duty, discovering the spy in their midst, but she had every confidence he would succeed, and she would do her best to help.

Perhaps when their onerous task was completed, she would give him the answer he desired. Her every inclination was to do so. She only hoped she would be spared seeing him sail away without making that commitment. Feeling that somehow she had come to a decision and feeling cheered by the resolution, she made her way to bed.

Evidently Anne had decided to temper her enthusiasm for elopement and abide by her parents' wish, for she appeared in the next few days more her equitable self. Fabia doubted Anne was capable of deception, so if she was still thinking of an elopement, she hid her plans well. Alan Chalmers called frequently at the house where he was welcomed, if not with enthusiasm, at least not with coolness.

Richard continued to pursue his investigations into Guy Fancher's activities but was most disheartened by a lack of evidence pointing to shady business, as he confided to Fabia. Despite his concerns he remained calm and determined, his demeanor toward Fabia as cheerful and possessive as ever, and she could not help responding to his devotion. She almost told him that she had decided to marry him, but she restrained herself, believing that the spy affair must be solved before they could claim their happiness. In the back of her mind lurked the dreadful possibility that chance might rob her of Richard. He could be recalled to his ship at any moment.

The weather continued exceptionally balmy as May drew to a close, and one day Fabia joined Anne in the Meynells' sunny garden. Her friend had a bundle of sewing on her lap and greeted Fabia cheerfully.

"Isn't it a beautiful morning? I could not bear to sit inside, so have taken my sewing into the garden," she informed Fabia, indicating that her friend should sit down on a stone seat nearby.

"Quite right. May I help you with any of that?"

"No, these are just some shirts I am mending for Alan. Poor boy, his clothes are in a dreadful state. His landlady is not very obliging," Anne explained.

Fabia hesitated but, convinced there should be no reticence between them, asked, "And have you come to some resolution about your engagement, Anne?"

"Well, yes. Alan thinks we must abide by Father's decree, although I tried to persuade him I was not reluctant to elope."

"I am glad to see one of you is sensible," Fabia said, tempering her remark with a smile. Silently she thought Alan was unwilling to chance the Meynells cutting off their daughter without a florin, although he did not know those parents as well as Fabia did. For whatever reason, Fabia was pleased that Anne had decided not to do anything outrageous. An elopement to Gretna Green would create a dreadful scandal, and the Meynells did not deserve that.

"Well, I am perhaps more amenable since he has told me there is small chance of his ship being ordered to sea soon. His admiral has been ordered to protect the port," Anne said with honesty. As she talked, she continued to ply her needle industriously. She finished sewing the sleeves of a shirt and, folding it carefully, put it to one side.

Then to Fabia's dismay, she noticed Anne take a navy blue uniform jacket from her pile of mending. Rooting in her sewing basket, Anne found a gorget which she proceeded to attach to the neck of the jacket.

Fabia barely suppressed a gasp. But marshaling her senses, she asked in a careful voice, "What is that you are attaching there?"

"A gorget. Alan is so careless. He said it fell off the other day and he could not find it, so he had to buy a new one for me to sew on. He has a new uniform but insists he needs this spare, too, so I agreed to make repairs," she offered cheerfully, not having any idea how shocking this proof of Alan Chalmers's perfidy was to Fabia.

Her first instinct was to snatch up the offending garment and run to the Crown and Anchor with it, but prudence prevailed. She watched in mounting horror as Anne, with neat stitches, replaced the gorget, and so skillfully did she do it that no one would ever realize that it was a replacement.

Fabia, her pulse racing, tried to collect her senses. She must not reveal what she had learned to her friend. Almost incoherent with impatience, she stood up. "Well, I must write some letters. I have been most dilatory in writing to my uncle and aunt. Lovely as it is out here, duty calls." And she hastened to her room to ponder this development.

On reaching her room she shut the door softly and sat down on the window seat, completely oversee by what she had learned in the garden. She mus get this news to Richard. But she could hardly call on him, even in a respectable hostelry like the Crown and Anchor. She had no recourse but to write him a note begging him to call upon her at the earliest opportunity. And then they could put their heads together about this latest evidence. Richard had been mistaken, tracking Guy Fancher. The lieutenant might be guilty of wrongdoing, but at least he had not betrayed his country, unless he was allied with Alan Chalmers in his schemes, a possibility Fabia could not ignore.

Quickly she wrote a message to Richard imploring him to come to the Meynells immediately. She must send a maid to the inn with the note, and she hurried downstairs to find a messenger. Unfortunately she ran into her hostess just crossing the hall toward the garden.

"Oh, Mrs. Meynell, do you think that one of the servants could deliver this note to the Crown and Anchor?" she asked, careful not to sound too urgent.

"Of course, my dear. I suppose you wish to get in touch with that Captain Goring. Well, perhaps this will help you. It was just delivered by a footman from the Crown and Anchor," Mrs. Meynell said, handing over an envelope. "I was just on my way to the garden as I thought you were out there with Anne."

"Thank you, Mrs. Meynell," Fabia said pocketing the letter and hoping she did not show her impatience to read it.

"If you have a moment, Fabia, I would like to talk to you," Mrs. Meynell asked.

Despite her eagerness to learn what Richard said, courtesy demanded she acquiesce to Mrs. Meynell's request.

"Of course," she agreed, and trailed her hostess into the morning room.

Seating herself on a sofa, Mrs. Meynell patted the cushion beside her. Fabia sat down, restraining her irritation at the delay.

"Anne seems a little more reconciled to our advice, don't you think?" Mrs. Meynell asked.

Anxious as she was to rush away, Fabia was too kind-hearted not to listen to Anne's mother and to reassure her. What would the poor woman do if she knew that her dear daughter had become embroiled with a traitor? It did not bear thinking about.

"Yes, I think so. She has learned that there is little possibility of Alan Chalmers putting to sea in the near future, so although she wants to wed him, she is prepared to give in to your demands at least for the present."

"Thank goodness. I am sure you were a factor in restraining her, and I cannot tell you how grateful we are for your attempts to make Anne agree to our wishes."

"You have been so kind to me, Mrs. Meynell, all of you, offering me shelter when my own life seemed in a turmoil, it was the least I could do."

Mrs. Meynell smiled. "I hope you have resolved your own problem with Captain Goring. We all admire him so much and your good sense in allowing time to settle your differences with him over his brother. It must have been a difficult decision for you."

"Yes, but I think I would be foolish to persevere in my intention to refuse him because of that tragedy. Richard is in no way like his brother. And I am grateful to you for allowing me this period to look at matters realistically," Fabia insisted sincerely. And now she was to be the instrument of bringing unhappiness to Anne and her family, for how could she ignore the evidence of the gorget? She could not confess to this kindly woman that her daughter was probably facing an even graver tragedy.

"Well, I will not keep you any longer. I am sure you are dying to get away and read your letter in privacy," Mrs. Meynell said with a twinkle.

"Thank you, Mrs. Meynell. You have always been the best of friends to me, and I want you to know how much I appreciate your tact and kindness." Nodding to her hostess, she left the room, barely able to keep from running so anxious was she to make her escape.

Again gaining the privacy of her room, she tore open Richard's letter.

My dear Fabia,

Just a quick note to tell you I have been recalled to London on Admiralty business. I should only be gone a day or two. See that you stay out of trouble while I am not on hand to rescue you!

Seriously, I have every confidence that you will not expose yourself to any danger, and I pray you will not meet anyone to challenge my claim to your affections.

Your obedient and impatient servant,
Richard.

Oh dear, thought Fabia. What should she do now?
Could she afford to wait with her news until Richard
returned? What option did she have? She could
hardly approach Alan Chalmers on her own, nor
could she enlist the Meynells in her affairs, for Richard had warned her to keep her own counsel. Not
that she suspected the Meynells of untoward behavior, but could they keep this matter from Anne? And
what would that young lady's reaction be to any slur
on the reputation of her beloved? This situation was
rife with problems. And she could be wrong about
Alan Chalmers. To expose him on the scanty evidence of a torn gorget was unthinkable. There could
be another, completely unexceptional, excuse for the
missing gorget. But she doubted that, remembering
her initial distrust of Alan and the secrecy surround-
ing his background.

What could she do but bide her time and wait
for Richard's return? She fervently hoped that Anne
would not take some dramatic step, having lured
her family and Fabia into believing she was content
to wait for her marriage. And with every hour that
passed, if Alan was the culprit, he would be further
endangering the safety of hundreds of sailors.
Then, too, there was the death of Potts. If Alan
had killed once to protect his secret, he would probably not flinch at another murder. Fabia groaned,
thinking of this terrible stalemate. Still, she could
not sit idly by and allow Alan Chalmers to continue
his nefarious work.

Nineteen

Richard had been called to London by Admiral Hood, impatient at the progress of the investigation. Ruefully Richard had to admit to his godfather that he had a suspect but was not entirely certain of his guilt.

"All I am really sure is that the culprit has to be a Navy officer. And unfortunately he appears to be a ruthless scoundrel, willing to kill to protect his secret. An able seaman, who served under me, was murdered while he was investigating for me. The authorities insist it was a case of smugglers dispatching one of their own, and I have not disabused them," Richard reported.

"How can you be sure it is a naval officer?" Hood asked.

Richard told him of Fabia's find, the gorget. His godfather was annoyed that Richard had enlisted the help of an innocent bystander in the affair, but acknowledged that Richard had been in a difficult position, finding Potts's body while on a ride with the lady.

"Can this female be trusted to keep her mouth closed about this affair? My experience is that ladies rattle on interminably about matters better kept quiet," the admiral complained.

"The lady is my intended wife," Richard informed him shortly, not wanting to hear any criticism of Fabia. "And a very sensible girl. She is quite aware of the danger inherent in loose talk. I trust her implicitly."

If the admiral was tempted to say that a man in love was not the best judge of his betrothed's discretion, he bit his tongue. No point in getting Richard's back up at this juncture.

"And whom do you suspect?" he asked calmly.

"There is an officer, a flag lieutenant on an admiral's ship, one Guy Fancher, who I suspect of shady behavior. He seems to have plenty of money with no known means of income except his pay, hardly enough to support the light skirt he is funding in Weymouth. And he is in a position to give the French the information they need."

"An officer in His Majesty's service. How shocking. Well, he sounds promising, but how are you going to proceed?"

"We have some evidence. The seaman I enlisted, with the torn gorget. The Customs men have not taken his death seriously."

"I have never entirely trusted the Customs men. Many of them are as corrupt as their quarries."

"The problem is that smuggling is rife on the Dorset coast and only confuses the issue, for the natives see nothing wrong in the trade and will protect the villains. Many of these men are in direct contact with the French and are not hindered by feelings of patriotism, so it is all quite difficult."

"You seem to have made a great deal of progress. Quite frankly I did not expect much from your investigations, and I am pleased that you have accomplished so much. Somehow you will have to lay a trap for this Fancher, I suppose," Admiral Hood suggested, frowning deeply. "The matter is becoming urgent because we believe Nelson will face the French in a major battle before too long."

"He is in the Caribbean now, sir, I understand."

"Yes, and too many people seem to know what he is about. A lot of loose tongues, if not real traitors, out there," the admiral grumbled.

"Well, all I can do is track Fancher and hope to catch him in the act. That's probably what Potts did, and it led to his death. Either he saw suspicious activity, such as the landing of an agent, or he discovered a set of signals. It is all too easy for a foreign fishing ketch to invade the waters around Portland," Richard suggested.

"Take care, Richard. These men will not cavil at another murder, and I hope the young lady in question is equally cautious. I don't want innocent deaths on my conscience."

"Fabia is a sensible girl, sir, and I trust her to behave with circumspection," Richard assured his godfather.

Admiral Hood disliked having civilians involved in these affairs, but he must trust Richard to handle the business. Still, another warning would not come amiss. "Do take care, Richard, and especially warn your young lady not to expose herself to peril. These men are ruthless because if caught they know they will die. How an Englishman can behave so is beyond me."

"Greed is the primary motivation, sir, and Napoleon is quite generous in his payments. I suppose we have French agents engaged in the same trade, but we call them patriots."

"Quite right; I stand reproved. But it is a very worrying situation. We cannot allow Napoleon to dominate the sea lanes, or we will be enslaved under his jackboots just as so many people on the Continent are. We must unmask this spy."

"I am doing my best, sir. Could you run some sort of check on Fancher through the Admiralty?" Richard asked.

"I will attend to it immediately. I wish you success, Richard. So much rides on your discovering this man. Keep me informed," the admiral ordered and bid his godchild an affectionate farewell.

As Richard left the room, Admiral Hood wondered if he was not exposing Richard to the same fate as poor Potts. Well, he would just have to take his chances. This was a different, secret type of war, but vitally important to the security of the nation. Spying was a dirty business. Sailors could expect to die in battle, but to be murdered in some dark alley by unseen foes was a nasty risk, and only a brave man would expose himself to such a possibility. Still, Richard was a clever as well as brave man and might yet prevail.

Having convinced Admiral Hood that Guy Fancher was the culprit, Richard, upon leaving the admiral, began to wonder if his own dislike of the man might have colored his thinking. He knew he was jealous of Fancher's interest in Fabia, although she had tried to reassure him on this point. Then, too, he had exposed her to danger. If Guy was the spy and thought Fabia was a threat to him, he would have little compunction in killing her. The thought terrified Richard. At last he had convinced Fabia that she might trust him, that he was not the cad his loose-living brother had been, and now he had enlisted her in this search for the spy. Knowing how resolute she was did not help. She had no idea of what she was facing.

A deep worry overtook him. Who knew what she could be up to when he was not there to protect her? He had thought of staying in London a few more days but suddenly he had the urgent desire to return to Weymouth and assure himself that she was all right. He had a premonition that events might have developed in his absence that could threaten her. Within an hour Richard was riding posthaste to Weymouth.

Meanwhile Fabia was in a fever of impatience but tried to control her apprehension. That evening Alan Chalmers was coming to dinner. She must hide her unease and see if she could discover more about this officer. The thought that her friend could be contemplating marrying a traitor appalled her. How could she spare Anne if this were true? And how could she find proof that Alan Chalmers was involved? As she dressed for dinner that evening, a plan evolved in her mind.

Whatever the Meynells' feeling about Alan Chalmers, they received him kindly. It was a family party, just the six of them, and at first the atmosphere was a bit subdued. Anne appeared not to notice, basking in the presence of Alan and looking quite charming in a white muslin gown ruched at hem and sleeves.

Fabia, determined to wrest from Alan some significant proof of his treachery, masked her fear with a bright smile and welcoming chat. "And is there any possibility of you going to sea soon, Lieutenant Chalmers?" she asked as they waited for dinner.

"I'm not sure. My admiral is confined to port here, so it seems unlikely. Some force has to stay in the Channel, and we all cannot be dashing about the Atlantic chasing the French, who I must say are most elusive. But such a depressing topic for ladies' ears. Tell me, I want your advice. Do you think the Meynells are any more resigned to my marriage with Anne?" he enquired boldly.

"They are naturally not eager to allow a much-loved daughter to marry a man who until several months ago was unknown to them and who will probably take her miles away. I understand your people come from Shropshire, Lieutenant Chalmers. That is half the country away from here."

"I thought a mother's chief desire was to see her daughter make a good marriage," he replied coolly. But Fabia was not to be drawn. "The Meynells are not ambitious in that way." She noticed he refused to offer any information about his Shropshire roots, if indeed that was his background. Obviously the man had a great deal to hide and proved a clever dissembler. Knowing what she did about him, she was not surprised.

Lieutenant Chalmers did not find Fabia's arguments acceptable and frowned. "Do you think there is any chance they will relax their six-month waiting period? I believe Anne is quite determined to persuade them."

"She will abide by her parents' decrees, I am sure," she said firmly.

"A pity. Who knows where I will be in six months."

The implication that some other girl's family might be more amenable to welcoming him as a son-in-law was an attitude Fabia found insufferable. The man had an amazing conceit. Was his proposal just a ploy to keep him on the scene where he could continue to betray his country? How she wished Richard was here so that she could discuss this latest development with him.

Before she could continue her quizzing, dinner was announced, and as Henry escorted her from the drawing room, she realized that Alan Chalmers had not really answered any of her questions satisfactorily. Well, he should not escape so easily. She meant to wrest some information from him, however hard he tried to elude her.

Conversation at dinner, with an officer as guest, naturally concerned the war. Mr. Meynell asked Alan what he thought the chances of a naval battle were in the near future, and how it would affect Weymouth.

"Unfortunately you are quite vulnerable here, sir, as are all seacoast towns. The French could invade, you know," Alan said importantly as if confiding information that he was in a special position to provide. Seeing her father's frown and sensing he disliked this suggestion, Anne leaped to defend her lover. "Alan is privy to all kinds of secrets, Father, being in such a confidential post," she said proudly.

Alas, yes, thought Fabia, and in a position to bring about just the dreadful prospect he had mentioned. What did he hope to gain from a French victory or invasion? Really, the man was quite unpleasant, and Fabia wondered, not for the first time, what her friend found so attractive about him. But to be fair, he was a handsome man with more than his fair share of charm, and Anne, dear as she was, had little discernment. Naturally he seemed more romantic and exciting than Charles Cartwright, upright and respectable as that young man was, who she had known all her life.

"I see you are not in uniform tonight, Lieutenant Chalmers. I understand officers are not required to wear them when not actually on duty," Fabia offered, hoping for she knew not what from this provocative statement, but aware of that mended uniform in Anne's sewing basket.

"I needn't wear it when dining *en famille*," Alan agreed, but Fabia was certain she saw a flicker of uneasiness cross his face.

"I have your mended jacket for you, Alan. Remind me to give it to you," Anne injected artlessly. And then Fabia could not doubt his annoyance, much as he tried to hide it. He did not want a discussion of that uniform, she was sure.

"That's kind of you, Anne," he said briefly, turning the conversation. "Has the war affected your business, sir?" he asked Mr. Meynell.

"Of course, since the French ships threaten all

trade, but we manage." If Mr. Meynell found the young man's question impertinent, he did not indicate it.

"Smuggling probably helps. I understand that the Dorset coast is a hotbed of such activity," Alan suggested.

"I do not deal with smugglers," Mr. Meynell replied, admirably hiding his annoyance. "It would not serve us in the long run."

"I understand that a man was killed the other evening on the Banks. The Customs people believe he was a smuggler," Henry said.

Fabia, watching Alan closely, could only applaud his insouciance. If he had been the murderer of poor Potts, he showed little remorse, or even interest.

"Well, they are a quarrelsome lot, smugglers. Probably there was an argument about the division of spoils and this man was the loser," Alan offered as if bored with the whole business.

"I think we should speak of more pleasant topics," Mrs. Meynell reproved, and for the rest of the meal they did just that.

The evening broke up early as there was a certain distance in the Meynells' reception of Alan, although they did their best to seem welcoming. But Fabia, knowing them so well, realized they had not abandoned their reservations about him, and well they might be cautious.

Just before he left, Alan approached Fabia and asked about the absence of Richard Goring.

"I understand he is a devoted suitor, and I expected him to be here tonight. I wanted to pick his

brains about some naval matters," he said candidly,
to Fabia's surprise. Was he so sure of his own in-
fallibility that he could make such a statement?

"I believe he was called away on family business,"
Fabia replied curtly, unwilling to let Chalmers know
that the Admiralty had summoned Richard. Even
that tidbit of news would be reported to unfriendly
ears, she thought a bit wildly.

"Gives Guy Fancher an innings, I think, or has
Captain Goring cooled off?" Alan asked insolently.

"I don't believe my affairs are any concern of
yours, Lieutenant Chalmers," Fabia replied, as-
tounded at his animosity.

"Oh, dear, I have offended. You are a very forthright lady, Miss Thurston. I find my Anne's sweet
and kindly nature not as challenging, but then we
men are apt to prefer gentleness in the object of
our devotion," he insisted, implying Fabia was a
vinegary harridan. Yes, he sensed her opposition to
his suit and would give no quarter in the battle
between them to influence Anne.

"Ah, but then, only the most unusual man is able
to meet a woman on equal terms. Anything else is
too wounding to their conceit," Fabia riposted.

"I stand corrected and admit you have won this
passage at arms, Miss Thurston," Lieutenant Chalmers said, bowing and turning away, but not before
Fabia had seen the angry look in his eye and a
sudden flush to his cheek.

Alan, balked in his efforts to get Anne alone,
asked if she might ride out with him on the following day. Fabia's first instinct was to try to wring
an invitation to accompany them, but at the last

moment bit her tongue. If Alan was absent from his lodgings, it might be the perfect occasion for her to investigate and discover some incriminating evidence of his complicity in this spy business. That such a daring plot could be perilous never crossed her mind.

Anne retired early, and Fabia was about to follow her when Henry stopped her, requesting a few moments of her time.

"Tell me, Fabia, what do you think of this Chalmers chap? She is so set on marrying him," Henry said worriedly.

"I don't completely trust him to make Anne happy. She is such a gentle girl and could easily be dominated by a demanding husband," Fabia said, careful not to say too much.

"And we know so little about him. Father was quite right to insist on a waiting period. I can't say I take to him myself. Not like your beau, Captain Goring, a thoroughly nice fellow and a man who would be a stalwart ally in a fight, I suspect," Henry replied, giving Fabia a teasing smile.

"No, Alan Chalmers does not have Richard's sterling qualities, I think, but then I am prejudiced, and we must remember Anne thinks differently. She is deeply in love."

"I know, and I wish for her sake he was more open about his affairs. If he hurts Anne, is playing with her affections, he will answer to me," Henry said with brotherly bravado, which Fabia could only honor.

Much as she would like to confide in Henry about what she suspected of Alan Chalmers's machinations, she held her tongue. She owed it to Richard to keep silent, a decision which might have surprised Admiral Hood, but one that Richard would have expected.

"Don't worry, Henry. Six months is a long time. A great deal can change in that period," Fabia said comfortingly, with the only assurance she felt free to give.

Twenty

The next day Anne dutifully asked Fabia if she would like to accompany them on the ride Alan Chalmers had suggested. Fabia pleaded the necessity of domestic chores, knowing Anne would prefer her absence to her presence.

"Will you be gone long?" she asked casually, although eager to know how many hours she would have to search Alan's lodging, which she had decided to do, desperate as the venture appeared.

"Well, Alan mentioned driving to Dorchester on some business, so I cannot say. I am not a very thoughtful hostess, abandoning you so cavalierly," Anne said a bit ruefully.

"Nonsense, you need some time alone with Alan. It is so difficult with all these rules about proper behavior for a girl to have the opportunity for private conversation with any man. Riding is about the only privacy we have," Fabia grumbled. Remembering the free and easy manners of the island, she sometimes found the rules of English society very constricting but was too polite to rebel openly.

"Well, I suppose parents have to protect their daughters from unwelcome advances. Mine seem to have accepted Alan, and since we are almost engaged, they have relaxed a bit," Anne agreed happily.

Fabia, concerned for her friend, hoped that Anne's trust in her lover would not be betrayed, but somehow she could not believe that. She saw nothing but sorrow ahead for Anne, who deserved better of life.

"Well, since you will not join us, I will be off soon. I do feel guilty, but you are so obliging, Fabia."

If Fabia felt any guilt at her deception, she stifled it. Much as she hated deceiving Anne, the question of Alan Chalmers's treasonous acts was much more important. With final assurances that she would be happily employed during Anne's absence, Fabia bid her goodbye. She felt she could not face Alan Chalmers this morning in case her intentions were writ large on her face for him to see. Alas, she thought as Anne left on her expedition, she did not make a good dissembler, having a dislike for subterfuge. Then an idea occurred to her that would make her plan easier.

She caught Anne just as she was emerging from her room with her bonnet and shawl. "Oh, Anne, I just thought of something. I will be taking a walk later, and if you have not given Alan his mending, I might drop it at his lodgings. You will not want to be bothered with it, I am sure," she suggested, wondering if Anne would suspect any impropriety in this weak excuse.

"Oh, Fabia, I am glad you reminded me. That would be so thoughtful. Just a moment and I will get it. It does make quite a bundle, and I am so scatterbrained I forgot to give it to him last night. And I must give you his direction. He lives quite near the Crown and Anchor, on Market Street at the house of Mrs. Perkins. I really would appreciate it. It is so kind of you."

Fabia barely repressed a blush of shame at her ploy but managed to say, "I really will need an excuse for an outing after writing my letters. Think nothing of it. There is so little I can do for you."

Anne bustled away, returning with a neat but bulky package. "It's quite awkward but not too heavy. I am sure Mother will spare Gladys to carry it, if it is too much trouble for you."

"Not at all. Now be off with a clear conscience and have a happy tête-à-tête with Alan," Fabia urged, quelling her guilt.

She stood irresolute in the hall as Anne sped down the stairs, eager for her rendezvous. Well, she had committed herself now, and she must go through with her idea of searching Alan's room, if only she could visit it without rousing his landlady's suspicions. There was also a certain dread that Alan might ask Anne for his mending when he arrived to take her on the outing or that Anne might mention she had given it to Fabia to deliver, which should arouse his suspicion. Well, if she were to behave in this faint-hearted fashion, she would never discover anything.

She lurked in her room, hoping to avoid any awkward questions until she was certain that Anne and Alan had left. Finally she heard Alan's arrival and then the clop of the horses' hooves on the cobblestones as Alan's hired carriage drove off down the

road. Giving them about a half an hour to be sure
they would not return for some reason, she donned
her bonnet and gloves, took up the bundle, and
prepared to depart. As she came downstairs, she
noticed the parlor maid responding to a knock on
the front door. Ducking into the morning room,
her heart pounding in fear that Anne and Alan had
returned, she peeked out and, to her surprise, saw
a tall familiar figure. It was Richard, whom she had
not expected for several days. Interrupting the
maid's explanations, she ran into the hall and with
difficulty prevented herself from throwing her arms
around him.

"Oh, Richard, I am so glad to see you. I did not
expect you for ages. That's all right, Annie, I will
see Captain Goring in the morning room," she
blurted out, anxious to explain matters to him without delay.

Ignoring the maid's raised eyebrows and Richard's
attempts at a greeting, she tugged at his arm and
dragged him off to the morning room, shutting the
door behind them with a resounding slam.

"Well, Fabia, you seem most anxious to greet me.
Can it be that you missed me?" Richard asked
whimsically, a bit amused at her enthusiasm.

"Of course I missed you, and especially since I
have some important news."

Richard, seeing that she was in earnest, said
calmly, "Well, can we sit comfortably to hear this
vital information?" He waited, but she made no attempt to compose herself, pacing up and down in
a fever of impatience. Since he could not in politeness sit down himself, he crossed to her side and,

putting his hands on her shoulder, tried to soothe her. "What can be so disturbing?"

"Richard, I think I have discovered your spy. And it is not Guy Fancher. Oh, I am all at sixes and sevens. Please forgive my lack of ceremony, but I have been yearning for your return and am not quite sure what to do."

"Well, this is a surprise. I hoped you would behave yourself while I was gone and not get up to any dangerous japes. What have you ferreted out?" he asked, convinced she was embroidering facts in order to help him.

"Yes, let us sit down and I will try to compose myself." And suiting action to words, she settled herself on a nearby chair and indicated he should do the same. Then she launched into her tale about the missing gorget on Alan Chalmers's uniform and Anne's mending of a new one.

Listening to her tale, Richard could not but be impressed by her reasoning, but a nasty idea crossed his mind as she insisted on Alan Chalmers's guilt.

"And what were you intending to do about it before my timely arrival?" he enquired sternly.

A bit tentatively Fabia informed him of the bundle, which she had placed on a table near the window, and confessed her plan to search Alan's room.

Richard, with difficulty, restrained his anger. "I applaud your courage, but I will not have it. Don't you realize the danger you would have been exposing yourself to?"

"But how else are we to find proof of his treachery?" Fabia asked, a bit chagrined at Richard's attitude.

"Not by having you poking about his effects and risking discovery. If Alan Chalmers is the man, and certainly this gorget is damning, there must be an easier and safer way to force him into the open. I will not have you meddling in this affair. Surely you understand how ruthless this man is?" Richard insisted, thoroughly angry at Fabia's indifference to the danger she was facing.

Fabia flushed, angry, too. "Really, is that all the thanks I get for trying to help you?"

Richard rose and crossed to stand in front of her, looking at her almost with dislike. "You will drive me mad, Fabia."

And before she could protest, he had dragged her up from her chair and smothered her in a hard embrace, kissing her with a passion he had not displayed since their tempestuous argument when she broke their engagement. Despite her fury she found herself responding with a warmth she had not realized she was capable of feeling. Emerging from the hard clasp of his arms, gasping and flustered, all thoughts of Alan Chalmers forgotten, she pleaded with him to listen to her.

"If I hurt you, I am sorry, but really, Fabia, you would try the patience of a saint," Richard said a bit ruefully.

"Perhaps I was behaving foolishly, but I was so excited to have some concrete evidence to help you," she pleaded.

Mollified, Richard smiled. "I know, and I do appreciate it, but I am glad I returned in time to

prevent you from committing some indiscretion or
worse. Now listen to me. I have the means to bring
Alan Chalmers to brook if he is indeed our man.
But we must be careful. We cannot entirely rely on
this business of the gorget. There might be an innocent explanation. It is not impossible that the gorget could have fallen off Chalmers's uniform and
that the incident had nothing to do with Potts's
death."

"That seems highly unlikely, too much of a coincidence," Fabia insisted, clinging to her belief that
Chalmers was their man.

Richard pondered her words as he began to pace
back and forward in a quandary. "I never suspected
Chalmers. He seemed such a lightweight. My money
was on Fancher," he confided.

"Yes, I thought Guy might be the one, but now
that I have thought it over, I think Alan Chalmers
is just as likely. Of course, they could be in it together," Fabia suggested, unwilling to abandon
Chalmers.

"I will go with you to deliver this bundle, and
we will see if we can learn anything from Mrs.
Perkins. But we must be very circumspect. And I
will institute enquiries into Chalmers's record
through the Admiralty."

Glad that she would not have to investigate Chalmers's room alone, Fabia sighed in relief. She was
not as brave as she pretended, she thought. "You
know, Richard, I am so accustomed to making my
own decisions, to fending for myself, it is a distinct
relief that I now have someone to shoulder some

of these problems," she admitted a bit cravenly, ashamed of her need.

"Does that mean you will agree to marry me and allow me to continue shouldering your problems?" Richard asked, for the moment all thoughts of spies and treachery forgotten in this more exciting prospect.

"Yes, I think so. I have been behaving badly, not considering your wishes at all. And as for the matter of your brother, I was a gudgeon. Please be patient with me, and I will try to be the kind of wife you want," she said humbly, at last aware that she had almost sacrificed her happiness for a loyalty to her sister which made little sense.

"Thank goodness. I could not stand much more of this," Richard sighed and kissed her again, this time slowly, savoring the triumph.

Fabia, after a long pause, released herself with lingering regret. "But that does not mean I will sit back and do nothing about Alan Chalmers. He must be apprehended. The safety of you and thousands of others depends on it," she insisted severely.

"We will see. Now let us deliver this bundle and try to learn more about the rogue."

"I am so relieved," Fabia admitted.

"That you have settled our future or that you will not have to delve into these intricate matters alone?" Richard asked, not entirely in jest.

"Both, and I must say you have been most forbearing."

"I wonder what made you decide in my favor," Richard mused, taking up the bundle as Fabia straightened her bonnet, which had slipped off her head in the fervor of their lovemaking. Eager to lighten the emotion that had threatened to get out of hand, she gave him a wicked look and said, "I began to think if I procrastinated much longer you might take up with Miss Langly or some other likely lady."

"Nonsense. You knew you had me completely enslaved. But enough of this riposting. We must be about our errand," Richard said and shepherded her toward the door. "You know, I intended to stay in London a few more days when I had this compelling feeling that you needed me immediately and rushed pell-mell to your side. A good thing, too," he insisted, trying to be stern.

Although Fabia agreed, she would not tamely accept it. "Nonsense. I would have contrived some scheme and discovered evidence to prove Alan Chalmers is our spy, and then I could have presented it to you," she said with a pride that Richard found both foolish and endearing.

"I wish my godfather could hear you. He warned me about taking you into my confidence, but it appears he was wrong. You should be enlisted in Naval Intelligence," he mocked, as they left the house, Anne's bundle of sewing stowed carefully under Richard's arm. As the distance was but a few blocks, he suggested they walk, and they set out briskly, still arguing about the matter of Fabia's involvement. So intent were they on their discussion, they did not notice Guy Fancher strolling on the other side of the street and watching them with interest. He was about to approach them when Fabia looked up and saw him, giving a wave. Richard bowed austerely but did not look as if he welcomed an interruption. Guy bowed in return and walked on, wondering if Fabia and her escort were indulging in a row that might somehow rebound in his favor.

"You know, Fabia, I have the greatest reluctance in abandoning Fancher as our chief suspect. That fellow is up to something, I am convinced," Richard confided.

"Possibly. But I am inclined to think his illicit money comes from some other source, smuggling or even blackmail," she insisted.

"Your opinion of him has suffered a sea change, then."

"Not really. I have always known he was capable of any double-dealing that might reward him, but I think he is too selfish, too self-indulgent, to put his neck in real jeopardy," she conceded.

Richard chuckled. "Then I need not have feared him as a rival."

"Although it does no good to pander to your conceit, I have to admit Guy Fancher never seriously attracted me." She smiled and might have said more, but they had now reached Mrs. Perkins's house. "Just how are we to approach the landlady? What excuse can we give for examining Alan Chalmers's room?"

"A good tactician relies on chance as well as planning. We will just see what can be contrived," Richard said as he rapped sharply on the door of the lodging. Looking at the facade of the house, he murmured, "At least Chalmers is not spending his money on luxurious living. This is a rather shabby house."

Before Fabia could answer, the door flew open and a scared little tweeny, her lank hair falling over a pale face with dull eyes, looked out vacantly at the visitors.

"Is this Mrs. Perkins's house?" Richard asked kindly.

"Yes, sir, but the mistress is not at home."

"You have a Lieutenant Chalmers lodging here, do you not?" Richard asked.

"The naval gentleman, yes, sir." She bobbed a curtsy.

"Well, we have a package to deliver for him. Perhaps you could indicate his rooms and we could leave this for him. I must write him a note," Richard insisted firmly, stepping forward and forcing the servant girl to retreat into the hall.

"Oh, I don't know, sir, what Mrs. Perkins would say. She is most particular," the tweeny whined.

If Richard thought otherwise, after a cursory glance around the dim, dusty hallway, he did not demur. "I can't believe she would object. Lieutenant Chalmers is a fellow officer, and you can be sure I would not ask you to do anything that would cause trouble with Mrs. Perkins," Richard coaxed, giving her a winning smile. Fabia, almost amused at this deliberate exercise of charm, realized that Richard had talents she had not really appreciated.

"Well, I guess it would cause no harm. He has the best bedroom and sitting room, just here," she said, and threw open a door on the left.

"And what is your name?" Richard asked, as she stood hesitating in the doorway.

"Maisie, sir. Oh, thank you so much." The girl

bobbed as Richard slipped her a coin. Still, she obviously intended to guard the door and watch as Richard wrote his note. Fabia wondered just how he would rid himself of her presence when there came a bellow from the back of the house.

"Maisie! Where is that dratted girl? Get down here right away, you lazy little madam," came a stentorian voice.

"That's Cook. She'll give me a clout if I don't run," Maisie said and scuttled off.

"Good. Now I am just going to peek through this desk and you keep a sharp eye and ear out for the landlady," Richard ordered.

In a neat-fingered and rapid fashion, he leafed through the papers in the secretary after placing the bundle of sewing on a nearby table. Fabia marveled at his coolness and conceded that she would not have handled the matter so adroitly.

The sitting room was plainly furnished with a few chairs, a faded divan, and a table obviously used for dining. Alan Chalmers had done little to stamp his personality on his environment, for there were few personal objects, just some books and a portable writing case left casually on one of the chairs.

Richard sighed. "There is little that's damning here, except possibly this bill from his tailor for a new uniform. Certainly no evidence to convict him. I was hoping for a code book or even a hint as to how he received payment or what he did with the money he received, if indeed he is our man." Richard finished his task and turned away in disgust.

"Perhaps this writing case?" Fabia indicated, feeling uncomfortable at pawing through Alan's effects

Richard, sensing her distaste, looked up and frowned. "It's a dirty business, no doubt about it, but so is spying, and we cannot be guided by our ideas of personal probity, you know." He opened the unlocked case and gave a snort of disgust. "There is nothing here but some writing paper. Well, our last recourse is the bedroom."

Without more ado he walked briskly into the inner room. Fabia followed reluctantly, despising this whole matter but unable to repress the feeling that there must be some clue to Alan Chalmers's treachery in these dreary rooms.

The bedroom, quite Spartan, with a narrow bed covered by a well-worn quilt and a table holding toilet articles and a candle, appeared as innocuous as the sitting room. But on the chest stood a small portrait of a lovely dark-haired woman with a small child standing by her side.

While Richard investigated the wardrobe, to no avail, Fabia picked up the portrait. "I wonder who this can be? His sister, perhaps. She is quite lovely," Fabia offered.

Richard crossed to her side and looked at the portrait. "Let us hope so. If she is a wife, then your friend Anne is going to encounter real unhappiness." Then his ears, sharper than Fabia's, heard something to alert him, and he urged her back into the sitting room, where he hurriedly scrawled a note and dropped it casually atop the bundle of sewing. Just in time, for as they turned toward the door, they met a stout lady in forbidding black bombazine who had the most ferocious expression.

"And what, pray, are you doing, sir, in the officer's room?"

"We have just dropped off a parcel for Lieutenant Chalmers, Mrs. Perkins. I am Captain Goring and this is Miss Thurston, friends of his, and we were entrusted with this errand. I do hope we have not alarmed you," he said with that winning smile that Fabia was beginning to suspect he could turn off and on at will.

Evidently Mrs. Perkins was as easily charmed as her tweeny, for she apologized for her remarks. "Sorry, sir, I am sure, but you cannot be too careful with all these clever rogues about. But I can see you are a high stickler," she gushed, obviously impressed by Richard's manner.

"Not at all, Mrs. Perkins. I am delighted to see that you keep such a stern eye on the premises. Well, we will not delay you any further from your duties. Come, Fabia," he insisted, taking her by the arm and high-handedly sweeping from the room.

Mrs. Perkins followed them into the hall, all obsequiousness, to which Richard paid only the most perfunctory notice, and within moments they were in the street.

Fabia, who had been holding her breath, let it out in a great sigh of relief. "You surprise me, Richard, with your devious methods, but thank goodness you had your wits about you. I was terrified that she would accuse us of stealing or worse, even call the constable."

"Nonsense. That type of woman is always overawed by an air of command and would never suffer the disgrace of letting the neighbors see a constable at her door. But come, let us return to the Meynells and discuss what we have learned." And so saying, he quickly escorted her down the street.

Twenty-one

Any consultation about Alan Chalmers's complicity in a treasonable plot was foiled when Fabia and Richard returned to the Meynells to be welcomed by Mrs. Meynell, who was in a most perturbed state. She barely acknowledged Richard's presence, so unlike her hospitable manner, and quizzed Fabia almost before she could remove her bonnet.

"I understand that Anne has gone out with Lieutenant Chalmers, Fabia, and will be gone until the afternoon. I assumed you were with her. She really cannot go careening around the countryside unchaperoned with that young man. Do you know anything about it?" she asked in an accusatory tone.

"Not really, Mrs. Meynell. She mentioned they would be driving to Dorchester, where Alan had some business to contract, but surely there is little to worry you. Anne is so sensible," Fabia soothed, determined not to rouse Mrs. Meynell's fears.

"Not where that man is concerned. We have given her too much latitude. But how were we to know she would defy convention in this shocking manner?" Mrs. Meynell, flustered and annoyed, would not be placated.

"Anne has sensibly complied with your wishes to

wait six months before marrying Lieutenant Chalmers. I doubt she would do anything foolish," Fabia said, wondering if Mrs. Meynell believed her daughter might elope.

Realizing that Richard must find this conversation both puzzling and too personal, Mrs. Meynell tried to regain her usual equanimity. "I am sorry, Captain Goring. Since you have been away, you will not know of Anne's determination to wed Lieutenant Chalmers and our request that they postpone the wedding for six months since we know so little of the young man and had hoped Anne might become engaged to Charles Cartwright," she explained.

Richard, anxious to calm Mrs. Meynell, whom he thought had every reason to be concerned about her daughter's future with Lieutenant Chalmers, hurried to allay her fears. "Fabia had mentioned to me that Anne favored Chalmers. I think you were wise to postpone a marriage," he said abruptly, hoping he would not have to explain further.

"Do you know anything to his detriment?" Mrs. Meynell asked sharply, her natural common sense seizing on the implication of Richard's words.

"Not really, just that his background is a bit mysterious, but I have told Fabia I will make some enquiries at the Admiralty. Certainly he would not have received a commission if the authorities doubted his probity. It just might be that his background is rather humble and he is a bit ashamed of it."

"I think there's more to it than that," Mrs. Meynell said shrewdly.

"We have some news for you, Mrs. Meynell," Fabia offered, eager to distract her from the dangerous topic of Lieutenant Chalmers. "Richard and I have decided to marry, and soon, I think, since he will be putting to sea before long." Her revelation surprised Richard if not her hostess.

"That's wonderful, my dear. I am sure you are well-suited, and you are a fortunate man, Captain Goring," Mrs. Meynell congratulated. "Of course, you will inform your relatives of this exciting development. I suppose you will be wanting to return to Wimborne? We will miss you."

"I think I will remain here for the moment, if you will have me, dear Mrs. Meynell. You have been such a kind and thoughtful hostess, and I feel so comfortable here."

Any appeal to Mrs. Meynell's good nature was received well, and she began to plan the wedding enthusiastically, putting aside her concerns for her own daughter in the light of this satisfying development. Henry and Mr. Meynell joined them for luncheon, during which the discussion centered around the upcoming nuptials. If the Meynells could not help but contrast the satisfying conclusion of Richard's courtship of Fabia to their own daughter's choice, they were too kind and unselfish to express it.

After luncheon Henry and Mr. Meynell returned to the office, and Mrs. Meynell excused herself on some household duties, leaving Richard and Fabia alone in the drawing room.

"I felt I had to tell the Meynells our news, but I had some compunction in parading our happiness when they are so worried about Anne," Fabia confessed.

"Yes, and they have cause to be. Can you not dissuade her from committing herself so thoroughly to Chalmers?" Richard asked.

"I have tried, but she is adamant. Anne is singularly loyal and would not entertain any aspersion on Alan," Fabia admitted unhappily. "What can we do?"

"Wait until I hear from the Admiralty and keep a close eye on the fellow and on Anne. I fear that is all we can do for the moment unless he makes some move which will betray his intentions," Richard said. "And I must be off immediately to put that investigation in train. I will contact you later today, and I suppose I must write to your uncle and let him know of our plans. You are still in his charge, and he might refuse his consent."

"Very unlikely. I will write, too, of course, but Uncle Aubrey will pose no difficulties unless his wife influences him. She might not welcome this news," Fabia said, remembering her aunt's jealousy.

"It might be better for you to return to Wimborne. Of course, you will want your uncle to perform the ceremony. And you will be safe there," Richard insisted, not wanting Fabia to be involved anymore in the investigation.

"There will be no wedding until your spy is unmasked," Fabia insisted, and even when Richard took her in his arms and tried to coax her with passionate kisses into changing her mind, she persevered.

"You are a stubborn, unyielding menace to my peace of mind. Whatever will I do when we are wed and you oppose me?" he groaned, only half in jest.

"I will be the most docile of wives once this horrid situation is behind us," Fabia promised.

"Hah, I don't believe that, but for the moment will accept that promise. And seriously, Fabia, I would not want you any different. Well, I must be off, but I will call on you tomorrow. Perhaps you will have learned a bit more from Anne when she returns."

Fabia, submitting to one more embrace, sighed and bid him farewell, knowing the hours would pass slowly until they met again.

Alone later she thought over what they had learned that day. Not much really. But there was that portrait of the mysterious attractive dark-haired woman in Chalmers's lodgings. She was convinced Alan's past had a great deal to do with his present activity. She was not entirely convinced that Richard had abandoned his interest in Guy Fancher as their villain and only hoped his suspicion of that officer was not founded on any doubts he had of her own interest in Guy. Certainly Guy had much to explain about himself to settle their doubts, but in her own mind she had tried and convicted Alan Chalmers. Restless and unhappy at her lack of action, she spent the afternoon waiting anxiously for Anne, who finally arrived just before tea. Fabia was in her room when she heard the curricle approaching and hurried into the hall, only to find Anne alone, having already said her farewell to Alan.

Barely repressing her desire to quiz her friend about her expedition, she managed to ask blandly, "Did you have a nice day, Anne?"

"Oh, yes. Alan is such an entertaining companion. We had a perfect day for our drive to Dorchester. And we visited Maiden Castle," she reported rather hesitantly. If she had intended to say more, she thought better of it and hurriedly asked Fabia about her own day.

Suspecting that Anne could tell her a great deal more, Fabia, frustrated at her friend's reticence, had no recourse but to tell her about Richard's return and her agreement to marry him. Anne was full of good wishes and genuinely delighted for Fabia's happiness with a bit of wistful jealousy that her own lover was not as acceptable as her friend's. But she did not allow her feelings to intrude on her enthusiastic reception of Fabia's news, and plied Fabia with questions about the arrangements.

"Come, Anne, we just decided today. But I will tell you we will not delay with conditions as they are," Fabia assured her.

"Alan says there will be a big battle by fall. I do wish I could be married if there is any possibility of his ship leaving port soon," Anne moaned.

How was Alan so sure of a battle and the time, Fabia wondered? What had he inadvertently let out to Anne? How miserable she was to indulge in her own plans when Anne's own future appeared so problematical. And there was an air about her friend that concerned her, as if Anne were keeping a secret. An open, trusting girl, who had no experience of tragedy or the deception of men, she would be easily gulled, Fabia was sure. What did Anne know and what was she hiding? Somehow she must discover what lay behind that ingenuous facade. But Anne's loyalty now lay with Alan Chalmers, and

Fabia doubted it would be an easy matter to gain her confidence. It was a worrying affair, and as the girls parted to dress for dinner, Fabia's foreboding increased.

After dinner Anne sat demurely in the drawing room with her family, stitching on some tapestry and smiling pleasantly, if abstractedly, at her mother's trials with a planned Bring and Buy sale to benefit the church organ fund. As this was an ongoing effort which Mrs. Meynell had championed for years, her audience paid only the most cursory attention, each of them occupied with their own thoughts. Mr. Meynell appeared deeply troubled, but whether it was business or his personal affairs Fabia could not tell. Even Henry was unusually quiet. As for Fabia, she had decided that she would visit Anne in her room before retiring and try to win her confidence. Fabia disliked intruding when it was obvious Anne preferred to keep her own counsel, but she felt she must take some action. She greatly feared Anne was becoming involved in an action that might shadow her whole life, and Fabia could not let that happen, mindful as she was of all Anne's kindness to her and her own debt to the Meynells for their hospitality and friendship.

Mr. Meynell, who had been in a brown study for some time, suddenly jumped to his feet and with a murmured excuse left the room, much to Mrs. Meynell's irritation. But that good lady was not one to harbor a grudge and only murmured to the girls and Henry, "I suppose your father is worried about business again, but it is too mean of him to dash off right in the middle of my story about the Reverend Mr. Osgood and Mrs. Phipps."

"I think he has heard it all before, Mother. And I can't think what business Father could be concerned about. Everything is quite in order, although this war has cast a pall over all commerce." Henry tried to mollify his mother, but his usual cheerful humor appeared to have deserted him as well. "I think I will just drop around to the club, if you will excuse me." And bowing to the ladies, Henry took his leave, bound for that solace Englishmen always seek when events on the domestic front become too much for them.

Fabia wished she had such a refuge, for she felt oppressed by the mood. She was almost ashamed that her own happiness appeared secure, but then was overcome by the thought of Richard's sailing away before their wedding and not returning. Well, enough of this brooding. She yawned and excused herself. "For some reason I am quite sleepy. If you don't mind, I think I will retire. I can't imagine why I feel so listless," she said.

"It's this weather. Much too warm and no breeze off the sea to relieve us. Very unusual. The air has a positive malignant closeness," Mrs. Meynell said, surprising Fabia with her perception. She, too, must sense the uneasiness of the household even if she was uncertain as to the reason for it.

Fabia made her escape, only to sit pensively on the window seat in her bedroom, trying to sort out the various strands of this affair that was threatening to consume her. The idea of an Englishman, a possible acquaintance or even friend, being engaged in such treason appalled her. How could anyone in their small circle here behave so wickedly? Until now she had been eager to accuse Alan Chalmers, but doubts had arisen since her visit to his rooms. Perhaps they were traducing a perfectly innocent man, despite the evidence of the gorget. Richard had mentioned that there might be a perfectly valid reason for that suspicious circumstance. And then there was Anne. What was she hiding? She could not possibly know of any action on Alan's part, for if she did, she would undoubtedly reveal it. Oh, dear, what a coil it was. An hour or so passed in this fruitless musing before Fabia decided Anne must have left the drawing room and retired. Bracing herself for an uncomfortable interview, she hurried from the room, determined to quiz Anne.

Anne answered Fabia's tentative knock with permission to enter, and Fabia found her friend already in her nightgown, brushing her hair and gazing thoughtfully into her mirror.

"I hope I am not disturbing you, Anne, but I could not settle and thought we might have a little coze," Fabia offered, realizing how feeble her excuse for the visit sounded.

"Of course, Fabia. It has been a strange day, as Mother said. Too oppressive tonight."

"Yet you enjoyed your expedition to Dorchester," Fabia replied, waiting for Anne to elaborate on her outing. But Anne only smiled, unwilling to share her thoughts.

"I know you find this restriction about waiting six months to marry very tiresome, Anne, and I will say no more on the subject," Fabia began, only to be interrupted, somewhat waspishly by the usually gentle Anne.

"Especially since you can wed Richard when you wish. Everyone is thrilled at your choice."

"Well, I am not sure that my Wetherell relatives would share that view, but I don't think Uncle Aubrey will try to forbid the marriage. He's probably only too eager to see the back of me," Fabia said with an effort to lighten Anne's bitterness.

"Mother, Father, even Henry are all against Alan, and for no reason except that he has few expectations. I suspect Mother views him as a Detrimental," Anne complained.

"Oh, I don't think worldly considerations influence your parents. They are conscious of their duty to provide for your happiness," Fabia said gently.

"Well, Alan will provide for my happiness if they would allow it. They had best realize that if I can't marry Alan, I will wed no one. And they had best not force me into making a choice," she said stubbornly.

Like many gentle and usually amiable souls, Anne had an intractable streak and would not be easily swayed from a position she had taken no matter what arguments were marshaled against it. Suddenly Fabia had a dreadful thought. Was that the secret Anne was hiding? Was she planning to elope with Alan Chalmers? Surely she would not be so foolish to chance a scandal, all because her parents were insisting on this waiting period. And an elopement would do little to enhance Alan's chances of promotion in the Navy. Superior officers did not look kindly on such affairs. But she must be careful not to alert Anne that she might suspect her intentions.

"Dear Anne," Fabia said, crossing to her side and putting a comforting hand on her shoulder. "I do understand your frustration and anger at the delay, especially since we are at war and our men in danger, but do take care. Do not threaten your future happiness with any reckless action. I know you are too sensible and too caring of your family to risk bringing disgrace upon them." She wondered if she had gone too far, for Anne turned her head away and Fabia could not see her expression.

"My parents would never abandon me, I know. And you are absolutely right. It would be cruel to treat them shabbily when they have always been the dearest and most understanding of people."

Fabia, knowing Anne hoped to reassure her, wondered if her friend would withstand Alan's pleas to disobey her parents. She was not certain that the claims of a lover might exert more power than the care and concern of even the most devoted family. Well, she had done her best. Now all she could do was keep a sharp eye upon Anne so that the opportunity to elope would not be open to her. And just how was she to do that?

Bidding her friend an affectionate good-night, Fabia retired to spend a restless night dogged by wretched dreams of spies, duels, careening coaches, and frantic pursuits.

Twenty-two

Exhausted by her troubled night and her inconclusive chat with Anne, the next morning Fabia eagerly accepted a commission from Mrs. Meynell to deliver a note to Mrs. Meynell's co-chairwoman of the Bring and Buy sale. Urging Anne to accompany her, Fabia insisted the outing would be a good tonic, especially as the day was less sultry than the day before. Although obviously reluctant, Anne agreed. The girls accomplished their task, congratulating themselves that Mrs. Hobson, a stout matron of a talkative nature, was not at home, so they could leave the message with a clear conscience and be away.

"Mrs. Hobson is really a very nice woman, industrious about good works and a great help to mother, but she can prose on forever. Now we can pride ourselves on having done our duty and return to more cheerful chores," Anne said as they left.

"Let us stroll down toward the front," Fabia suggested. "There will be a breeze along the water, and I am not inclined to spend the next few hours doing my needlework."

Anne assented, and the girls walked toward the sea, feeling much more in charity with one another.

The streets were crowded, for it was market day, and a host of farmers' carts and wagons jostled each other as the vehicles slowly wended their way toward the stalls. Some of the men had already made long visits to neighboring taverns and were boisterous in their good spirits, not taking prudent care of their carts as they swore and yelled at one another to give way. The progress of pedestrians was much impeded by the traffic, and Fabia was beginning to doubt the wisdom of trying to reach the waterfront.

As they neared the crossroad that would lead them away from the market scene, people pressed closer around them, driven from the roadway by a herd of sheep massing down the main avenue. Just ahead of them a blond-haired woman carrying a shopping basket screamed as a harried drayman lost control of his maddened horse and ran up onto the pavement, knocking the woman against the side of an ironmonger's establishment. At first it looked as if no one would come to the poor woman's aid, as all the bystanders were too busy securing their own safety.

Fabia shouldered her way to the woman's side, trailed by Anne. She knelt down by the woman, clearing a space around her and speaking sharply to those about her. "This woman is injured. We must get her to safety. Don't stand there like dolts, but help me raise her," she said to two burly clerks who had run from the ironmonger's store at the sight of the accident. The drayman responsible had gone on his way, either not aware of the accident or uncaring.

As Fabia lifted the woman's head, she was heart-

ened to see her eyelids flutter and a little color rival
the paint on her cheeks.

"Would someone fetch some water?" Fabia ordered in a tone that brooked no nonsense, and
within moments a man returned with a brimming
cup. Fabia managed to get a little down the
woman's throat and chafed her hands, hoping to
restore her. She could not tell if her injuries were
serious but could see no sign of blood.

"Oh, dear, what happened? Where am I?" the
woman asked in a frightened voice.

"You have had a slight accident. A careless drayman lost control of his horse, but I believe you will
be better shortly. Can you move your arms and
legs?" Fabia asked.

"Yes, yes, I think so," the woman said, running
a shaking hand down her side and testing her legs
gingerly before attempting to sit up.

"If you live nearby, it might be best to allow us
to help you home," Fabia suggested. She assisted
the woman to her feet. Beyond a certain paleness
and evidently a bruise on her hip, which she mas-
saged gently, the woman appeared to be none the
worse for her accident.

"Yes, yes, I must get home, but where is my shopping basket?" She looked around distractedly, seem-
ing to be more worried about her possessions than
her state of health.

"Here it is." Anne proffered it to her, having
rescued it from the cobblestones, where the woman
had dropped it when she fell.

"Oh, thank goodness. It would never done for me
to have lost it," she said. "And thank you both for

coming to my aid. Perhaps if you could just see me to my lodgings, not two blocks from here, that would not be too much of a trespass on your kindness," she asked, then as if remembering her manners, "My name is Leona Langly."

Somehow this information did not surprise Fabia. What did surprise her was Miss Langly's genteel air, her lack of coarseness, which Fabia might have expected in a woman of her type. Reproving herself for being so prejudiced, Fabia hurriedly offered to guide Miss Langly home and took the shopping basket from her. The trio walked slowly away, no longer hindered by the crowd, who had lost interest once Miss Langly had regained her senses.

Anne, much more at ease in the role of a savior than Fabia, whose interest in the woman did not lay in her injury, encouraged Miss Langly and kept a firm hand on her arm. Fabia, glancing idly into the shopping basket to make sure the contents had not been ruined in any way, was surprised to see only a stoutly wrapped brown paper packet.

Her curiosity aroused, she poked idly at it with a finger. It seemed to be a collection of papers, and she turned over the package, trying to decipher the address. Seeing that Leona Langly was occupied in assuring Anne of her recovery, Fabia surreptitiously peeked again into the basket and was taken aback by her discovery. In spidery black ink was the single line: *Lt. Guy Fancher, Weymouth.* Her head reeling with the possible meaning of this odd happenstance, Fabia was barely aware that they had reached Miss Langly's lodgings, the very house Guy had pointed out to her when they had returned from Chesil Banks and seen Richard on the doorstep.

When Miss Langly's landlady had heard of the accident, she clucked over the incident, full of sympathy. She would have swept Leona into her rooms and banished Fabia and Anne if she could, but Miss Langly, conscious of her debt to the two girls, insisted they come in and have some refreshment.

"What you needs is a nice lie-down, not chattering away," Mrs. Morton insisted, but Leona was not to be forestalled.

"What I need is a nice cup of tea, Mrs. Morton, and I am sure these kind ladies would like one, too. Could you please oblige us?" she said with a gracious smile but a determined stare. Mrs. Morton was not proof against her star boarder's demands and, muttering, went off to brew the tea.

"A nice woman, but apt to be overly interested in my activities," Leona exclaimed, settling down in a comfortable chair with a sigh and indicating that her visitors also be seated.

"Are you sure we should not call a physician?" Anne asked, always practical. If she found the company of Miss Langly embarrassing, she showed no signs of it for which Fabia applauded her good sense. Many girls would be quick to shun such a woman, but Fabia had no intention of leaving until she had asked Miss Langly some questions, no matter the state of her health.

"Not at all," Miss Langly replied. "I am feeling very much better. I believe it was just the sudden shock of the horse and cart mounting the pavement, almost out of nowhere. I must admit my mind was occupied and I was not paying attention to my direction," Miss Langly explained cheerfully as if the mishap was all her fault.

Before Fabia could delicately probe as to the thoughts that had so thoroughly absorbed Miss Langly, the landlady had returned with the tea tray. Putting it before Fabia, the older woman watched as the cups were poured and handed about, standing akimbo and evidently prepared to remain until she learned every detail of the accident.

But Leona Langly was not intimidated by her curious landlady, and after a few moments during which she assured the woman she was recovering from her ordeal, she skillfully dismissed her. Short of disobeying Leona's tactful order, Mrs. Morton had no choice but to leave. Fabia was impressed with Miss Langly's manner and had begun to think that she was probably much too nice for Guy Fancher, whatever their relationship. Although she was in little doubt as to that situation. But what was in the packet? And how was she to find out? As if Leona Langly could follow Fabia's thoughts, she suddenly turned to her, almost interrupting a comment by Anne, and asked, "My shopping basket? Where is it?"

Fabia reached down by her side and picked up the basket, handing it over reluctantly.

"Thank you for rescuing it. I was on my way to the market, but the purchases will have to wait, I fear, until I feel more the thing," she explained.

Deciding that she must risk a rebuff, if not worse, Fabia boldly remarked, "There is nothing in there but that packet. I do hope nothing rolled out and was lost during all the confusion of the accident."

"No, I had not as yet done any shopping, only collected this packet for a friend," Leona Langly confided serenely. If she suspected any chicanery concerning the parcel, Fabia thought she hid it well. And, of course, she was probably entirely innocent of anything but a desire to do her protector a favor.

"I could not help but notice the packet was addressed to Lieutenant Fancher, who happens, by coincidence, to be a friend of mine also," Fabia said blithely as if there were nothing exceptional in Guy pursuing an acquaintance with the respectable Fabia while keeping Miss Langly in some style.

"Oh, you know Guy. I suppose I shouldn't mention such business before you two obviously proper ladies. I do not want to shock you, but you seem sensible and not prone to the silly vapors well-bred ladies have when faced with women of my type," Leona said a bit defiantly.

"I see nothing embarrassing about rescuing a victim of a nasty accident and then escorting her home and accepting her hospitality," Fabia said firmly, wondering what Anne was making of all this, for she must be puzzled by Leona's allusions.

"That is very kind of you," Leona said. "And may I learn the names of my Good Samaritans?" she asked as if prepared for a rebuff.

"I am Fabia Thurston and my friend is Anne Meynell," Fabia obliged.

"Ah, yes, I have heard of you both," Leona said, but did not say how. Had Guy mentioned them? Fabia wondered. But, still, she was no closer to learning about this mysterious errand which had sent Miss Langly out with her shopping basket. Obviously Guy had asked his mistress to accommodate him by collecting this packet and she had consented, seeing nothing strange in such a request. Did that mean he could not collect it himself for some reason or that he hoped to evade scrutiny by any bystander or watcher? And where had she picked up the packet? Certainly Guy would not dispatch Leona Langly on an innocent errand. Did the packet contain letters used to blackmail some victim of Guy's, or did the information in that bundle have a more sinister purpose? It was all Fabia could do not to snatch up the packet and examine its contents, but she managed to restrain herself, only suggesting that she and Anne had best take their leave and allow Miss Langly to rest.

"I thank you again for your charity. I don't suppose we will meet again, but I wish you both all the best," Miss Langly said, holding out a hand in farewell but behaving as if she doubted they would take it. Both Anne and Fabia shook it heartily and wished her well. Fabia could not resist saying as they parted, "I will stop in and see how you are coming on in a few days, Miss Langly."

"Do you think that wise, Miss Thurston? It would be poor recompense for your kindness to have your presence on my doorstep misinterpreted and your reputation impugned," she said with a grin.

"I care nothing for that," Fabia insisted robustly and, taking Anne by the arm, withdrew gracefully.

Once outside the house and walking back toward the Meynells, having decided to abandon any further expeditions, Fabia was quite taken aback when Anne congratulated her on her intention to make a future sympathy call on Miss Langly.

"I know Mother would say it was shocking of us to make the acquaintance of such a woman, but under the circumstances what else could we do? I found her very honest and quite interesting. If she is a light skirt, and she seemed quite frank about it, I see nothing to cause alarm," Anne said, amazing Fabia with her tolerance.

"I agree, and somehow I don't think your mother, generous woman that she is, would object to us helping a victim of that accident. It is what any Christian would do, I hope," Fabia answered, wondering if she sounded smug, although she did not intend that impression. Like Anne she had been impressed with Miss Langly and wished circumstances would allow a closer acquaintance, for she wondered what had brought this woman to her present pass.

"Men really are so stupid, thinking we have no idea of their other . . . well, I guess you might call them relationships. And, really, well-bred women have a boring time of it, surrounded by all these strict rules of behavior. Miss Langly certainly looked cheerful, as if she enjoys life," Anne continued with surprising force.

"Yes, now she does, but there is the problem of the years ahead when her charms pale. I suppose we have to sacrifice freedom now for affection and security later. And not all men pursue such women, although I am not entirely convinced that even the best of them do not stray," Fabia admitted, hoping she was not destroying Anne's innocence with her cynicism.

"Even Richard?" Anne asked roguishly.

"Even Richard," Fabia agreed, and then laughed. "We are noodles to carry on this way. Think how appalled the staid matrons of Weymouth would be if they overheard us."

"Too true, but I am glad we met Miss Langly. It has opened my eyes to a certain reality," Anne confessed, again surprising Fabia. But they had reached the Meynell house now. By tacit agreement the subject was dropped as Fabia left Anne to make an abbreviated explanation to her mother of their adventure.

Reaching her room, Fabia threw off her bonnet and gloves, and sat down to puzzle out what her next move should be. She must contact Richard immediately, but what was the best way to do that? She could hardly visit the Crown and Anchor alone. And even then he might not be there at this time of day, for she suspected he was busy investigating Alan Chalmers. Could she entrust a note to one of the Meynells' servants, stressing the urgency of the matter? For she was convinced it was urgent. Guy Fancher would be impatient to retrieve his packet from Leona Langly. Even now it might be too late.

In a welter of indecision, Fabia paced back and forth, frantic to take some action. Should she confide in Anne? Ask her to accompany her to the Crown and Anchor? Richard had mentioned coming around today, but could she wait until he called? And if she asked Anne to come with her to the Crown and Anchor, she would have to tell her about her suspicions. And those suspicions were still very nebulous. For if Guy Fancher was involved, where did that leave their theories about Alan Chalmers? No, she could not involve Anne. She must just chance her reputation and go alone.

If Richard was not at the Crown and Anchor, she could hope that a note would bring him posthaste to her side. Angry and frustrated, Fabia once more donned her bonnet. Picking up her gloves, she prepared to slip out of the house. As she hesitated in the hall, wondering what excuse she could give for being absent at the luncheon table, she heard the front door open. Peeking around the banister, she saw Henry Meynell enter, home for luncheon from his office, no doubt. Could she ask Henry to escort her? And how would she explain the urgency of her mission?

Deciding that this was no time to behave in a missish fashion, she slipped down the stairs and hailed Henry.

"Could I ask you a favor, Henry?" she said as he placed his hat and stick on the hall table.

"Of course, Fabia, as long as it is not accompanying you to shops. I have a horror of milliners and drapers," he joked, then noting her grave face, apologized. "I can see it is a serious matter."

"Yes, Henry, I must locate Richard immediately. An emergency has arisen, and he is the only one who can cope with it."

"Well, I think I can help you. I just left the club and saw him there with some other officers."

"I can hardly go to him in that sanctum," Fabia declared.

"No, but I can. You can wait in the carriage or here if you prefer, and I will try to bring him as soon as possible," Henry offered, always obliging. If he wondered at Fabia's insistence, he did not question it, for which she was grateful.

"I will wait in the carriage. Time is very important. I regret you might miss your meal," she admitted ruefully.

"Not to worry. A missed meal will not harm me. I am developing an *embonpoint* anyway. Some fasting will benefit me," he said affably.

"Thank you, Henry. I cannot tell you how much I appreciate your help. Later I might be able to tell you all about the problem," she promised, feeling she owed him some recompense.

Seeing her perturbation, Henry said no more, but shepherded her out the door after sending a maid to alert his groom to rig up the horses.

Impatient as she was, Fabia recognized the necessity for the horse and carriage. She could hardly lurk in the street while Henry wrested Richard from the club. Within a few moments they were on their way, the club a bare quarter-mile from the Meynell house. Henry tactfully talked of the weather and other commonplaces as he drove through the streets, taking a circuitous route to avoid the market traffic. Reaching the dignified red-brick building which housed Randall's, he jumped down and secured the reins to a hitching post. Reassuring her he would be quick, he entered the club.

Fabia, left alone, could hardly contain her impatience. Every moment that passed endangered their effort to apprehend Guy and the packet. Then, as

she fumed, she saw Guy himself emerge from the
club and walk leisurely away. Was he bound for
Leona Langly's lodging? She watched him turn the
corner, walking toward the center of town, her worst
fears realized.

Twenty-three

Unable to wait any longer, Fabia leaped from the carriage, determined to follow Guy and discover his destination. She had almost reached the corner of the street when Richard and Henry emerged from the club. Richard, looking in the empty carriage, raised his eyebrows at Henry, who pointed out Fabia's disappearing back as she turned the corner. Running after her, after a hurried word to Henry, Richard caught up with her as she ducked into a doorway, panting.

"For heaven's sake, Fabia, what are you doing dashing pell-mell down the street like a hoyden?" Richard asked, taking her by the arm.

"Quick, we must follow him. It's Guy Fancher. We have been wrong about him. You must hear what I have learned. That is why I sent Henry in to fetch you," she gasped, almost incoherent in her urgency.

Richard, realizing that some event of momentous nature had engaged her, tried to calm her. "Whatever the business, it can wait. Just tell me why you are in such a state."

Calming under Richard's presence and his command, Fabia took a deep breath and tried to explain what she had learned as a result of Leona Langly' mishap. "It's the packet, Richard. I really feel it is the answer to our search for evidence, and we must retrieve it before he does. He might be on his way to Miss Langly's at this moment," she urged, tugging at his arm.

"If so, we will be in time to apprehend him, but are you sure we have any grounds for taking charge of his private papers?" he reasoned. "And what about Lieutenant Chalmers? We appear to have a plethora of suspects."

Fabia, under Richard's calm effort to settle her, began to see that they must behave with some circumspection. As they walked around the corner, she tried to explain her feelings while keeping an eye out for Guy, but he appeared to have eluded them.

"I don't think for one moment Miss Langly is involved in any conspiracy. She is just an unknowing, obliging victim, sent by Guy to collect important papers and protect him from any discovery," she argued.

"Perhaps, but have you thought it might be an entirely innocent packet?" Richard insisted, not convinced.

"If it is not evidence of his complicity in the treason, it could be blackmail letters that he has come by in some way," she protested.

"But we cannot commandeer Guy's mail on the assumption it is illegal, you know."

"I think you are being overly cautious. We have a great opportunity to catch your spy, and all you do is put up objections," Fabia complained.

"Not objections. Just an attempt to restrain your rash actions. Do you realize what could have hap-

pened if Guy is our spy and he caught you pur-
loining the package from the hapless Miss Langly?"

"Well, no, in my enthusiasm I did not think of
that," Fabia conceded a bit wryly, seeing Richard's
point. "But do you believe that you can persuade
Miss Langly to hand over the documents?" she persisted.

"I am not going to try, and neither are you.
There is another way of handling this matter that
does not involve you putting your head in the lion's
mouth," he explained patiently.

They had, during their argument, finally arrived
at Miss Langly's lodgings, and Richard paused,
bringing Fabia to a standstill. "If Guy is inside, we
are already too late. If he is not, I believe I have a
way to keep him from contacting Miss Langly, to
keep him out of circulation for the moment. You
must let me judge whether this is feasible," he
warned sternly.

Accepting that Richard intended to manage this
affair his own way, Fabia conceded that her impetuous actions might just have precipitated the very
situation they wanted to prevent. If Guy were indeed guilty and learned of Fabia's interest in his
packet, he would take care to cover his tracks. And
of course, maddeningly, Richard was right: they
could not simply wrest the packet from either Guy
or Leona. But what did Richard have in mind?

"We will just call and inquire about Miss Langly's
health after her mishap. If Guy is with her, we will
know it is too late. If not, we can make other arrangements," Richard insisted, his brow furrowing

as he worked out possible methods to circumvent Guy obtaining the packet.

Suiting his action to his words, Richard mounted the steps, a reluctant Fabia in his wake, and raised the knocker, giving it a resounding bang. After a few moments the door opened and Mrs. Morton stood before them. Recognizing Fabia, she said without more ado, "You cannot see Miss Langly now, Miss. I have just given her some laudanum and she's off to sleep. She would not let me call the doctor, and I think rest is what she needs. I will tell her you and the gentleman called?" she said, her voicing rising as she looked at Richard, no doubt recognizing him.

"Yes, do, Mrs. Morton. This is Captain Goring, who is also concerned for Miss Langly's condition. Perhaps we may call back later when she is more herself," Fabia said.

Whatever Richard's plan to prevent Guy from reaching Miss Langly, he did not confide them to Fabia, which irked her.

"Really, Richard, I think I should know what is going on as I am the one who discovered this evidence against Guy," she insisted as he escorted her home.

"We don't know if it is evidence. I have distrusted Guy from the beginning and believe he is a much more likely candidate for my spy than Alan Chalmers, who appears to be nothing but a rather shallow charmer, but I could be wrong. Have you forgotten the gorget?" he reminded her as they walked along.

"No, of course not. But I agree Guy seems much

more capable of organizing a large-scale conspirac
than Alan Chalmers. Still, they could be in it to
gether.

"I doubt it. Guy would never trust Chalmers tha
far or give him that kind of advantage. Think wha
Chalmers could do if he knew that Guy was en
gaged in treasonable activity?"

They had, by now, arrived back at the Meynells
and Richard refused her invitation to come in wit
her. Taking her by the shoulders, he looked at he
sternly. "Promise me, Fabia, you will not run o
on any more hazardous missions, seeking evidence
I am quite serious about this. It is not a game bu
a dangerous enterprise with many lives at stake, an
I do not want yours to be one of them. Remembe
you are now my promised wife and owe me som
consideration. I sometimes doubt if I will ever g
you to the altar," he concluded, trying to take th
edge from words Fabia considered little less tha
an order.

She sighed and wrinkled her nose in disgust. '
suppose you are right, and I promise not to st
unless I hear from you."

"Well, I don't propose that you sulk in yot
room. But do take care. I am off to see Fancher
commanding officer, a rather bullheaded man, b
perhaps he will cooperate. If we can keep Guy clo:
to his duties, to his ship, for the next few days, th
will give me time to investigate this business of Mi
Langly's involvement."

"Ah, I see. That will be a most pleasant task
she mocked, then feeling ashamed, said, "That w
unfair. I trust you not to become enslaved by Mi

Langly. And I must say she is a provocative, yet sensible woman. I quite liked her and think that in other circumstances we could become friends. I do hope no harm comes to her through this association with Guy."

Richard looked at Fabia with amazement. "You are a singularly honest and tolerant girl. And I assure you that although I share your sentiments about Miss Langly, I have all I can handle with one Miss Thurston."

He looked at her searchingly, and Fabia thought if they were not standing on a public street, he might have given her a bruising kiss. Alas, that was not possible, and she gave him a reassuring handclasp and disappeared into the Meynell house, leaving Richard yearning for a more intimate farewell.

The rest of that day seemed interminable to Fabia, but she obeyed Richard's strictures and remained at home. She felt guilty about Henry Meynell and tried to think of how she could explain her frantic chase of Richard to him. But Henry, never one to pry, appeared to have forgotten the incident or tactfully had decided not to refer to it. In her preoccupation with this new problem, Fabia did not notice Anne's barely concealed excitement. If her thoughts had not been centered on Miss Langly and Guy Fancher, Fabia would have been concerned by Anne's manner, but for once her perception failed her. After a pleasant evening playing cards, the household adjourned. Exhausted by the dramatic events of the day, Fabia fell asleep immediately, and no dreams haunted her rest.

Mrs. Meynell had asked Anne and Fabia to help her with her arrangements at the parish hall for the upcoming Bring and Buy sale. There was a great deal of sorting and pricing to be done, and unsuitable items diplomatically pushed behind the stalls. Although Mrs. Meynell, herself a capable and ruthless organizer, tried to marshal her workers efficiently, a great deal of time was wasted in gossiping. Fabia was asked by several matrons about Richard, and Anne about Lieutenant Chalmers. Fabia laughingly admitted that a wedding was planned, but Anne just smiled mysteriously and refused to satisfy their curiosity.

All in all the day was pleasant and served as a distraction to Fabia's confused ideas about the identity of Richard's spy, as she had begun to call the traitor. She was rather disappointed not to hear from Richard that day or on the day following but conceded he had heavy responsibilities and no time for her. She thought tartly that now that he had secured her consent to marry him, he could concentrate on weightier matters, then reproved herself for such meanness of spirit. The problem was that this mystery made her edgy. The thought of either Guy or Alan as a spy was repugnant, and she feared for Anne if the latter should be unmasked. The next few days, burdened by no message from Richard but a hurried note with some flowers, did little to relieve her anxieties.

After three days her frustration was mounting but she managed to conceal her concern from the

Meynells. Arriving at the breakfast table, she greeted the Meynells and Henry, and was surprised to find Anne absent. While Henry politely served her some ham and toast from the sideboard, Mrs. Meynell, in reply to Fabia's query about Anne, said her daughter had a bad headache and was trying to go back to sleep after a disturbed night.

"I will look in on her later. Is there anything I can do for you today, Mrs. Meynell?" Fabia asked.

"No, my dear, but thank you. I think I have my committee under my thumb now. They will follow orders," she twinkled, and returned to a pile of letters by her plate. "Here are some letters for you, Fabia, and a message that Gladys picked up that did not come with the post."

She handed Fabia her letters, barely able to keep from asking who would send such a missive. Fabia smiled but kept her own counsel. Mrs. Meynell was all that was kind and helpful, but she had an insatiable curiosity about her household's doings, and often Henry, in particular, had to tell her politely to mind her own business, which Mrs. Meynell always took in good part.

Seeing that the one letter was from Wimborne, and no doubt a reply to her letter to her uncle and aunt about her coming marriage, and the other, franked, from Richard's parents, Fabia laid them aside to read at her leisure. The one that had been delivered by hand showed no hint of its sender, merely Fabia's name scrawled on the folded paper of good quality, and sealed with wax. She opened it not knowing what to expect.

Dear Miss Thurston,

*I do wish you would call upon me as soon as
possible. I feel quite indebted to you for your help
when I suffered that mishap on market day. I am
in need of a confidante, and since I am a stranger
here and not accepted by many, I hope I can prevail
upon your charity to visit me and listen to my tale.
The nature of the affair is quite worrying. Of course
I know I am asking a great deal of your tolerance
and will understand if you feel that any exchange
between us would be unsuitable. But somehow I
know you will take pity on me. I will be home this
morning and expect you at any time that is convenient.*

> *Your grateful acquaintance,*
> *Leona Langly*

Whatever could this mean? What did Miss Langly
have to confide in her? Did she have some damning
evidence of Guy's machinations, and if she did, why
would she trust Fabia with such information? She
had not struck Fabia as a disloyal type, out for her
own ends, but if she had discovered Guy in treasonable activity perhaps that overcame her affection
and loyalty to him.

Then Fabia remembered her promise to Richard.
But surely calling on Miss Langly represented no
danger. And this might be the final proof of Guy's
treachery or evidence of his innocence. She would
go, she decided. But first she must look in on Anne.

However, when she knocked softly on Anne's
door, requesting permission to enter, Anne's muffled voice begged her to go away. She heard a mut

tered complaint that all she wanted was to sleep. Not deterred, Fabia tried the door only to discover it was locked. More than a little surprised, she was tempted to insist on entrance, for Anne had never, to her knowledge, done such a thing before. But concluding that Mrs. Meynell was the one to deal with this disturbing occurrence, Fabia went off to find that lady. She was anxious to be off to her meeting with Leona Langly but felt she could not desert Anne if her friend was suffering. Finding Mrs. Meynell in the morning room completing her shopping list, Fabia mentioned that she had tried to see Anne, but the door was locked.

"Oh, dear. That must mean she not only has the headache but is brooding. She rarely denies me admittance or you, I trust, but sometimes she retires to her room and refuses to allow anyone to disturb her. I suppose we all desire privacy occasionally, and I have always honored her wishes in this matter," Mrs. Meynell explained, as if she found the necessity for withdrawal from the communal family life a mystery.

"Yes, but if she is really ill, I think someone should see to her," Fabia said.

"Well, I did see her this morning, and she claimed it was only a bad headache. But I will try to persuade her to open the door after a bit. But I think you have no need to worry, Fabia," Mrs. Meynell assured her kindly.

Fabia did not share Mrs. Meynell's conviction, but she could hardly argue with Anne's mother over her daughter's behavior. Also, Fabia, impatient to meet Miss Langly, decided she must leave the problem of Anne in her mother's capable hands.

"Is there anyway I can assist you, Mrs. Meynell?" she asked.

"Well, my dear, I must be off to the church, and this list needs to be delivered to the butcher. I would send Gladys, but I have set her to turn out the linen closet and cannot interrupt her at this stage, or it will never be done till after Whitsun. If you could deliver this, it would be such a help. I would take it myself, but the church is quite in the opposite direction from Mr. Porter's shop. Can you oblige me?"

"Of course, Mrs. Meynell." Fabia thought this offered a good excuse for her to slip along to Miss Langly's after her errand. She hoped none of Mrs. Meynell's cronies would notice her direction, but she was determined to answer Miss Langly's pressing invitation.

The butcher promised to deliver the Meynell order promptly, and Fabia walked off quickly, feeling a bit foolish as she kept darting looks behind her until she reached Miss Langly's door. It was most unlikely that anyone she knew would see her now. The door was opened by a shawled Mrs. Morton who looked at her impatiently.

"Oh, it's you, miss. I suppose you have come to see Miss Langly. I am just off to my niece's, an emergency, but you can go right in, as you know the way," she informed Fabia somewhat harriedly.

"Thank you, Mrs. Morton," Fabia said and watched as the landlady scurried out on her mission. Crossing the hall, she knocked on Leona Langly's door and was invited to enter.

On the street outside Charles Cartwright paused, puzzled. He had been just about to hail Fabia when he realized her destination. Normally he would not be in this neighborhood at this time of day, but he had been sent to confer with a shipping owner about legal matters. He could not imagine what Fabia's business could be at this time of day and in this street. It was a respectable-enough address, but Charles, not unworldly, knew that some ladies of dubious virtue lived in the area. Surely Fabia could have no commerce with such women, and she was alone, most unusual. He hesitated. He could hardly pound on the door and insist on admittance, but he was troubled. There was some mystery here.

Despite her efforts to call on Leona Langly without discovery, she might have been reassured to know that Charles Cartwright had seen her. For when she entered Miss Langly's sitting room, her hostess had barely greeted her when the door of the adjoining room opened and Guy Fancher appeared.

"I must say you are prompt, my dear Fabia. We thought you might not appear until the afternoon, meaning a tedious wait on my part. And due to our industrious betrothed's work, I had a devil of time escaping my duties in order to be here to greet you," he said affably, settling himself in a chair.

Despite his casual tone Fabia knew immediately that she had unwisely stepped into an ambush. No one knew where she was, and despite Richard's warning she had rushed headlong to meet the very

danger about which he had been concerned. One
look at Leona Langly's face told her that this sum
mons had not been her idea but had been forced
upon her by Guy Fancher, who sat smugly regarding
Fabia much as a spider did a fly.

Twenty-four

Guy continued to regard her smugly, as if his cleverness had solved a troublesome problem. Whatever her fears she would not allow him to frighten her, and decided to brave it out.

"What a surprise to find you here, Guy. I understood from Miss Langly's importuning letter she wanted to consult me on a very private matter," Fabia said calmly, lifting her eyebrows as if to convey that Guy had committed a solecism of some sort by intruding on this meeting.

"You really delight me, Fabia," he drawled. "But alas, I can only play your game for a few moments. You must have figured out, with your perceptive, enquiring mind, that Miss Langly's letter was written on my insistence."

"Really, and why was that?" Fabia asked, hoping to delay any action. She had a sinking feeling that Guy Fancher would not allow her to leave this room until he had wrested from her whatever damaging information he believed she had. She looked away from him with an effort to meet the shamefaced grimace of Leona Langly, who dropped her eyes and muttered, "I didn't want to do it, Miss Thurson, but Guy was quite demanding."

"Yes, I can imagine," Fabia said dryly.

"He said no harm would come to you," Leona continued. "He just wanted to question you abou some matters where he would not be interrupted.'

"And you believed him?" Fabia said skeptically.

"Not really. I was frightened," Leona admitted bowing her head.

"What nonsense, Leona. You must not give th redoubtable Fabia the impression that I terrorizec you," Guy insisted, amused.

Sitting up straight in her chair and fixing Gu with a quelling look, Fabia said calmly, "I can quit believe you did terrorize her, but now that I an here, you may practice your skills of persuasion o me, although I cannot imagine what you want t discuss."

"Enough of the subterfuge, Fabia. Unfortunatel you caught a glimpse of that packet I sent Leon to collect, and I do not doubt that you have re ported your finding to that prig of a captain yo fancy. I suspect his mission in Weymouth is not t wait about for his ship but to poke his long nos into matters that do not concern him."

"And you are a judge of what should concer him?" Fabia could not resist twitting him haughti! although she conceded she might be wiser to try t placate him, but his sneering reference to Richar angered her.

"Yes, I think so. My work here is almost finishec I would have preferred to put off my departure fc a few more weeks, but that would not be wise no" But before I depart, I will settle with you. For son time I sensed that you might be trouble with you insatiable prying and your indifference to my best efforts to charm you," he explained.

Now that he had decided to reveal his real identity, Fabia knew that he had no intention of letting her escape, so whatever she said would not alter her fate. He meant to kill her; she had no doubt of that.

"Yes, I imagine that your charm has taken you a long way, but I wonder why you were willing to sacrifice a secure commission in His Majesty's Navy for the dubious profit of spying for the Corsican." Fabia knew that to any passionate defender of Napoleon such a sobriquet would raise one's hackles, and she was correct.

Guy flushed and abandoned his pose of patronizing superiority. "You sanctimonious English egotists cannot recognize a real genius when you see one. But you will all pay the price for your stupidity. Napoleon will be sitting in the House of Lords before the year is out," he fumed, rising to his feet threateningly.

Fabia, not to be intimidated, rose, too, and walked across to the window before turning to face her adversary. "And I suppose you think you will be by his side. What a fool you are, Guy, trusting that mountebank. He has used you and will discard you when he has wrung all advantage from your treachery," she said with scorn.

Guy's hands clenched, and he looked as if he would throttle her, but he quickly regained his composure, realizing he was reacting as she wanted. "Sit down, Fabia, and stop trying to make me lose my temper. You will be a casualty of war, and your captain, too."

"And I suppose you intend to dispose of me as you did poor Mr. Potts," she goaded. Thinking to discover more, she added, "Or was that the doing of Lieutenant Chalmers?"

"No, the fool tried to prevent me from dispatching the simpleton. Not that Chalmers is above a little conspiracy, but he and his smuggling friends have been of use to me, so I treated him quite gently. But I am afraid your friend Miss Meynell has cast her lot with a rogue."

So that was how Alan Chalmers had lost his gorget, in a struggle to prevent Potts's death at the hands of this villain. Fabia prevented herself with difficulty from lashing out, believing that was just the reaction Guy wanted.

Instead she turned to Leona Langly and said scathingly, "Were you aware that your protector was a spy, Miss Langly?"

"No, no, of course not. Oh, Guy, say that isn't so," pleaded Leona, twisting her hands and looking beseechingly at him.

"Very clever, Fabia, trying to turn Leona against me, but it will avail you little. You should have accepted my proposal, you know, then you would have been safe."

"I had enough sense to realize you were a deceiver and a cad, Guy. I was only amused by your efforts to bring me under your spell," Fabia ridiculed, knowing that was the reaction he would find most unacceptable. She moved to stand behind the desk as if hoping that would protect her from his advances. How was she to escape? What a fool she had been not to tell someone where she had gone.

Now she had to rely on her own resources to get out of this nasty situation, and she did not think Leona would be of much help. She had a passing sympathy for her, sitting there with tears falling down her cheeks, incapable of action.

"Enough of this nonsense. You will pay the price for your meddling," Guy promised chillingly, and crossed toward Fabia, a thin scarf in his hands. She realized he intended to strangle her, and she doubted she had the strength to fight him off. Anger rather than fear inspired her as Guy faced her across the desk.

Almost without thought Fabia leaned down and picked up the glass inkpot sitting on the desk and threw it full in his face. He shouted as the glass hit his eyes and the black ink dripped down his cheeks. Fabia, quick to react, ran around the table as he sputtered and tried to dash the blinding liquid away. She reached the door, but before she could move, she felt his hand on her shoulder, and twisted vainly to get away.

Just as she felt him forcing her back, the door flew open and several men crowded in, thrusting her aside. She backed toward the wall to give them space. It was Richard, Henry Meynell, and Charles Cartwright. Within moments they had subdued the struggling, cursing Guy and bound his hands with the very scarf with which he intended to strangle her. Gasping with relief, she watched his fruitless efforts to escape, but Henry, with great adroitness, tore a tasseled tieback from the window and bound Fancher's feet, then threw him to the floor.

Richard, ignoring Fabia, who stood shaking to

one side, turned to Miss Langly, who had watched the proceedings without moving. "Where is the packet, Miss Langly?"

Fabia, although a bit piqued by his lack of concern for her welfare, realized his first responsibility was the evidence of Guy's perfidy.

"Come, Miss Langly, we know you collected a packet for him, and he came here today not only to get rid of Fabia but to get the package. Surely you do not want to be accused of abetting a spy and traitor?" Richard insisted, staring at the distraught woman sternly.

"No, no, he has the packet. In his pocket," she stammered, turning aside, unable to meet Richard's accusing eyes. Richard knelt, and ignoring Guy's rage and efforts to elude his search, he drew out the packet and ripped it open, scanning it hurriedly.

"Yes, it's all here, the code, directions for future messages, and the date of the landing of several agents. Just what we need to convict this miserable scum," he informed his fascinated audience.

"I think, Cartwright, you or Meynell had best go for the constable to take this man into custody. For the moment we will lay accusations of assault and robbery against him, for we are not anxious to have his real activities bruited about. Neither do I want Fabia involved in this business."

He turned then and looked at her strangely, then crossed to put comforting arms around her. "I should have known you would get embroiled in some dreadful attempt to expose Guy. You would not listen to my warnings, and if Cartwright here had not seen you entering this house and had the good sense to inform me, who knows what would have happened?"

"He meant to strangle me," Fabia gasped into Richard's shoulder.

"And I suppose to thwart him you threw that ink bottle and while he was blinded tried to run away. You probably would have succeeded and did not need our intervention at all," Richard mocked, trying to reduce the tensions aroused by this lamentable affair.

Fabia managed a weak smile. "Something like that. Do you suppose I could sit down? Then you can continue to berate me in comfort."

"I'm sorry, my dear. You have suffered an ordeal." He guided her to a divan and placed her in it tenderly, although Fabia believed his real inclination was to turn her over his knee and give her a good paddling.

The next half-hour was one of frustrating inaction. Guy ceased his struggle, giving only baleful looks at his captors. Finally Fabia tried to comfort Leona, but that poor woman was so dazed and unhappy there was little help she could offer. Eventually, Fabia persuaded her to go into the bedroom and lie down as she seemed unable to grasp what had happened. Fabia hoped that Leona would be protected from punishment.

At last the constable arrived with some reinforcements, and Guy was dragged off to prison. Fabia had a host of questions she wanted to ask her fiancé, but she could see that Richard was interested only in sorting out Guy's arrest.

Deciding that she could be of most assistance by

allowing him to get on with his job of clearing up matters, she agreed to allow Charles and Henry to escort her home. Richard, giving her a perfunctory kiss, promised faithfully to report as soon as possible on the outcome of Guy's arrest. Just before leaving she told him of Lieutenant Chalmers's smuggling, and Henry, overhearing this damning news looked stricken. Fabia was surprised to see the normally genial Henry so aroused.

On their way home she asked him how he was going to tell Anne. "She must be shielded from as much pain as possible. It will be a dreadful shock," Fabia insisted.

"It would have been worse if she had wed him and then learned of it," Henry growled, obviously upset. "I know it's cowardly of me, Fabia, but could you tell her? It will come better from you."

"I will try, but it will be difficult news. I wonder what prompted Alan to engage in such activity? If only there was some reason."

"Greed, probably," Charles offered, looking sad. His devotion to Anne inspired him with pity for her, but he could not help but think that the revelation of Alan Chalmers's illegal doings would eventually help his cause.

At the Meynells', while Henry explained matters to his parents, Fabia finally gained admission to Anne's room by pounding insistently and threatening to have the door broken down. What she found reinforced her fears. Anne was sitting on the bed surrounded by portmanteaux, obviously having used the ruse of a headache to pack her belongings in preparation for departure.

Fabia sat down beside her and took her hand. "You are planning to elope with Alan after all you had promised," she said sadly, disappointed at Anne's deceit.

"Yes, I am. I cannot wait, and neither can he," Anne answered with defiance.

Gently Fabia related the events of the morning, Miss Langly's part in the affair, and Guy's revelations about Alan. To her surprise Anne did not seem horrified.

"Alan told me about the smuggling, but it was not because he wanted money. He was trying to get the smugglers to bring his sister and her little boy from Calais. She was the mistress of a French count who had been guillotined, and she just managed to escape to the port. Her family had disowned her, but Alan wanted to save her and his nephew. That was his secret, and I suppose Guy Fancher discovered it and tried to blackmail him into cooperating with his own evil plans."

Fabia was amazed at the calm acceptance in Anne's voice. Surely she could not excuse him, no matter what the reason for his wrongdoing. "But you cannot marry him now, Anne. He will be arrested and, at the very least, cashiered from the Navy."

"I suppose so, and his poor sister never rescued, but I cannot condemn him," Anne said gently. "I love him."

Sighing for her friend's unhappiness, but not quite able to see how she could remain so devoted to a man who had behaved with so little compunction, Fabia wondered what Alan Chalmers's really felt for Anne. Did he truly care for her or see her only as an advantageous match. And would they ever know?

Later that day Richard arrived, looking tired but triumphant. He knew the Meynells would be all agog, awaiting explanations, and he patiently answered their questions. Guy had been taken from the constables and dispatched under guard to London, to the Tower, where he would be executed in due course. There was no reprieve for traitors.

Alan Chalmers would be given a dishonorable discharge from the Navy, but his testimony, buttressed by Guy's admission about his effort to save Potts, might help him escape the ultimate penalty. Richard was well-aware of what this news meant to the Meynells and pitied them, but he could only offer the suggestion that at least Anne had not married the man. Whatever her suffering she would eventually recover and perhaps even come to see the worth of Charles Cartwright.

At last alone with Fabia, he looked at her searchingly and then sighed with relief. "I should be so angry with you that I would cast you off without another word, but unfortunately I love you too much to manage my life without you."

"You have every right to be angry, Richard, but you must believe me when I say I never thought for one moment that Leona Langly's request for me to visit her held any danger. If I had thought Guy was behind it, I would have let you know immediately. And I thought you had successfully thwarted his freedom, that he was safely aboard his ship."

"Yes, you are right; my best efforts failed there.

He was able to get around that stupid chief of his
and claim pressing family business."

"I do hope Leona will be all right," Fabia said,
pity for the woman overcoming her distaste for her
actions and her inability to stand up to Guy.

"Leona Langly is a survivor," Richard said
brusquely. "I do not doubt she already has plans to
provide herself with another protector. Deep emotion is not a luxury she allows herself."

"Such a cynic, Richard," Fabia reproved.

"Not about you, milady. And in order to see that
you become embroiled in no more disasters, I insist
we be married within the month, either here or in
Wimborne. That will give us over a month before
I sail. I heard today that the *Andromeda* will be ready
by August first," he said, taking her in his arms to
soften the blow. Fabia, determined not to show her
dismay at this news, raised her arms and placed
them around his neck, for once taking the initiative
in their lovemaking.

Richard, confident and relieved that all problems
had been settled, kissed her with a passion that could
barely be restrained and to which she made no protest. At last they were free to follow their own happiness, and should it only last for a month, Fabia was
prepared to bear it. If Mrs. Meynell had interrupted
the scene, she might have been shocked by their conduct. But that good woman had enough sense to leave
the lovers alone so that they could settle their affairs
in the most satisfactory way possible.

Epilogue

The sun, with its usual tropical speed, was setting quickly over Nevis as Fabia and Richard watched from the veranda of Eden Hall.

"There you can see the green flash, a phenomenon of the island sunsets," Fabia pointed out to Richard as in a last brilliant flare the fiery ball descended into the ocean. "You can only see it when there are no clouds. I feel it is a good omen for our holiday here."

"Is that what you consider it, a holiday?" Richard asked, smiling at his wife.

"Of course. I know we must return to Dorset so you can help your father with the estate. And I think this place will have to be sold. It can have no part in our future life," Fabia said. Then looking at him with concern: "Will you miss the Navy dreadfully? Beechwood is charming, but farming does not hold the drama of life at sea." Fabia refused to think of the worry and fears she had had when Richard sailed off in the *Andromeda* after their wedding and brief married life to join Nelson in the Battle of Trafalgar.

"I have had enough of war. Trafalgar was a mighty victory, and I am glad I could be a part of it, but we paid a dreadful price, the death of Nelson and so many good men," he sighed, remembering that tremendous struggle and the death of what many were calling "that immortal hero."

"Yes, and you paid your own price with that wound in your arm. It seems still a little stiff after all these months," Fabia remarked gently, remembering her own horror when Richard returned from the battle, pale and in pain, his arm shattered by a French bullet. She could only give heartfelt thanks that those ghastly hours of waiting for news and the days following his return were behind them.

"This tropical heat is a tonic. I feel nothing but a slight twinge now and then," Richard reassured her. "Yours was the most difficult part, I know, waiting for news and dreading to hear the worst."

Fabia refused to dwell on those anxious days and hurried to change the subject. "I think we must accept the offer for Eden Hall that Mr. Bristow has made. It is a generous one. Fortunately Anderson has done a good job as overseer, and the sugar yields have continued high," she said, looking out over the field, now ripening in the spring sunshine. Fabia and Richard had arrived in Nevis just three days ago, a final visit to bury her ghosts before she took up her life with Richard at Beechwood, where Sir Thomas was eagerly awaiting their joining him and Serena.

"Does it make you unhappy to look down the hill at the house Stella was to have occupied?" Richard asked.

"In some ways, but it was so long ago, and so much has happened since I left here that sometimes it appears but a dream, a nightmare, but one which no longer causes me deep unhappiness."

Richard hesitated, not wanting to remind her of his brother. Fabia sensed his concern and hastened to put his fears at rest. "For some reason that business with Guy Fancher in Weymouth put it all in perspective. I realized that more important issues were at stake. I behaved like a pea goose, holding you responsible for all that happened to my family. I fear that Paul Beaumont would have caused Stella grief one way or another, even if he had lived. He was hotheaded and, alas, had a fondness for the bottle, but, of course, we cannot know how the marriage would have turned out." She sighed, thinking of her sister and her parents.

"Now that you have returned to Nevis, will you be content in Dorset, in our winter storms and wet?" Richard asked, thinking it best not to dwell on the long-ago tragedy.

"Oh yes. Somehow this does not seem like home anymore. While you were at sea, I became quite attached to Beechwood. Your parents were so kind and thoughtful, so eager to help me when they must have been just as concerned as I was. I dearly love your parents, Richard," she said, remembering their support during those worrying days.

"Well, we must just try to enjoy this holiday. We have both earned it," Richard said with satisfaction, feeling that at last his life lay in pleasant lines. His only worry had been that Fabia might find this return to the island where she had spent her childhood a grim reminder of all she lost. But she appeared not to find it a trial, nor had she shown any signs of brooding over that tragedy. He looked at the house once destined for Stella and her husband.

As if reading his thoughts, she said, "Since Mr. Anderson and his family have been living in Stella's house, much of the haunted quality of the place has disappeared. Once I only wanted to tear it down, but now I am happy that a family has lived in it and removed much of the curse. You know, the natives think it is haunted and refuse to go near it, very trying for Mrs. Anderson."

"They are a superstitious lot, but eventually they will forget, I suppose," Richard offered, not very hopefully.

"Perhaps, but it is not my concern any longer," Fabia said. Laying a hand on Richard's, she insisted, "Do not worry that memories of the past will dog our married life. I have so much for which to be thankful."

"I like to think all has turned out amazingly well," Richard replied. "Now that Anne Meynell will marry Charles Cartwright, even those days in Weymouth have lost their anguish, but I did feel sorry for her. She did her best to appear cheerful during our wedding, but I know it was an ordeal for her. And I greatly fear that Alan Chalmers's defection was a blow. She would have remained loyal to the end."

"I think she realized finally that his affection for her was very limited and that her income was more important to him than her love, very disillusioning," Fabia admitted. "But she is a girl with a great deal of character. When she and Charles are married, we must have them at Beechwood."

"Yes, of course. I owe Charles a lot. If he had not had the sense to appraise me of your call on Miss Langly that day, I greatly fear you would not have survived Guy Fancher's attempts to kill you, despite your valiant defense with the inkpot." Richard smiled faintly.

"Charles will make Anne happy, I know," Fabia said with finality.

"I wonder if your cousin Petra will settle as well. I was quite surprised when she married that rather pompous colonel."

"He has a lot of money and a certain position, so that should help. And she likes being a reigning hostess in London. But I found Colonel Acton a dreadful bore," Fabia admitted ruefully.

"He will have his hands full with that little minx. She was quite odious at our wedding, with her airs and jealous tantrums."

"I hardly noticed. It was all such a rush, and I was so concerned with your safety since I knew you would be leaving shortly for the battle," Fabia confessed.

"We might have waited. I had great qualms about you becoming a wife when there was every chance you would soon become a widow," Richard responded. "Very selfish of me, but I do not regret it."

"Nor do I since all has turned out so well." She hesitated, then, feeling that the time was most opportune, added, "And in six months I will become a mother and you a father."

Richard jumped from his chair, his face radiating joy. "Oh, Fabia, is it true? That is all I need to feel that life has rewarded me beyond my deserts. Are you sure?"

"Yes." She smiled. "I was almost sure before we sailed but hesitated to tell you in case you thought the journey might be taxing. Actually, it did me a great deal of good, and you, too. We had a very pleasant voyage."

"I rather want a girl," Richard mused, dreaming of the future.

"I want a boy, with his father's courage and handsome looks," Fabia twinkled.

"Yes, that might be nice, too. But we will have many years ahead to raise a family. Now I want to enjoy this time, a respite from all cares, with you. I sometimes thought we would never win through," Richard said with satisfaction.

"You were too much for me, so determined, so patient. I don't expect our married life will be without problems, but it is a comfort to know I will not have to solve them alone," Fabia said, looking at her husband with deep affection. "But here comes Mattie to announce our dinner." And rising, she took one more look into the distance, seeing not a haunted house but a fruitful plantation and a memory of a hoyden girl who had never once expected her life to offer such bountiful pleasures.

ZEBRA'S REGENCY ROMANCES
DAZZLE AND DELIGHT

A BEGUILING INTRIGUE   (4441, $3.99)
by Olivia Sumner

Pretty as a picture Justine Riggs cared nothing for propriety. She dressed as a boy, sat on her horse like a jockey, and pondered the stars like a scientist. But when she tried to best the handsome Quenton Fletcher, Marquess of Devon, by proving that she was the better equestrian, he would try to prove Justine's antics were pure folly. The game he had in mind was seduction—never imagining that he might lose his heart in the process!

AN INCONVENIENT ENGAGEMENT   (4442, $3.99)
by Joy Reed

Rebecca Wentworth was furious when she saw her betrothed waltzing with another. So she decides to make him jealous by flirting with the handsomest man at the ball, John Collinwood, Earl of Stanford. The "wicked" nobleman knew exactly what the enticing miss was up to—and he was only too happy to play along. But as Rebecca gazed into his magnificent eyes, her errant fiancé was soon utterly forgotten!

SCANDAL'S LADY   (4472, $3.99)
by Mary Kingsley

Cassandra was shocked to learn that the new Earl of Lynton was her childhood friend, Nicholas St. John. After years at sea and mixed feelings Nicholas had come home to take the family title. And although Cassandra knew her place as a governess, she could not help the thrill that went through her each time he was near. Nicholas was pleased to find that his old friend Cassandra was his new next door neighbor, but after being near her, he wondered if mere friendship would be enough . . .

HIS LORDSHIP'S REWARD   (4473, $3.99)
by Carola Dunn

As the daughter of a seasoned soldier, Fanny Ingram was accustomed to the vagaries of military life and cared not a whit about matters of rank and social standing. So she certainly never foresaw her *tendre* for handsome Viscount Roworth of Kent with whom she was forced to share lodgings, while he carried out his clandestine activities on behalf of the British Army. And though good sense told Roworth to keep his distance, he couldn't stop from taking Fanny in his arms for a kiss that made all hearts equal!

Available wherever paperbacks are sold, or order direct from the Publisher. Send cover price plus 50¢ per copy for mailing and handling to Penguin USA, P.O. Box 999, c/o Dept. 17109, Bergenfield, NJ 07621. Residents of New York and Tennessee must include sales tax. DO NOT SEND CASH.

Taylor—made Romance From Zebra Books

WHISPERED KISSES   **(3830, $4.99/5.99)**
Beautiful Texas heiress Laura Leigh Webster never imagined that her biggest worry on her African safari would be the handsome Jace Elliot, her tour guide. Laura's guardian, Lord Chadwick Hamilton, warns her of Jace's dangerous past; she simply cannot resist the lure of his strong arms and the passion of his *Whispered Kisses*.

KISS OF THE NIGHT WIND   **(3831, $4.99/$5.99)**
Carrie Sue Strover thought she was leaving trouble behind her when she deserted her brother's outlaw gang to live her life as schoolmarm Carolyn Starns. On her journey, her stagecoach was attacked and she was rescued by handsome T.J. Rogue. T.J. plots to have Carrie lead him to her brother's cohorts who murdered his family. T.J., however, soon succumbs to the beautiful runaway's charms and loving caresses.

FORTUNE'S FLAMES   **(3825, $4.99/$5.99)**
Impatient to begin her journey back home to New Orleans, beautiful Maren James was furious when Captain Hawk delayed the voyage by searching for stowaways. Impatience gave way to uncontrollable desire once the handsome captain searched *her* cabin. He was looking for illegal passengers; what he found was wild passion with a woman he knew was unlike all those he had known before!

PASSIONS WILD AND FREE   **(3828, $4.99/$5.99)**
After seeing her family and home destroyed by the cruel and hateful Epson gang, Randee Hollis swore revenge. She knew she found the perfect man to help her—gunslinger Marsh Logan. Not only strong and brave, Marsh had the ebony hair and light blue eyes to make Randee forget her hate and seek the love and passion that only he could give her.

Available wherever paperbacks are sold, or order direct from the Publisher. Send cover price plus 50¢ per copy for mailing and handling to Penguin USA, P.O. Box 999, c/o Dept. 17109, Bergenfield, NJ 07621. Residents of New York and Tennessee must include sales tax. DO NOT SEND CASH.

TODAY'S HOTTEST READS
ARE TOMORROW'S SUPERSTARS

VICTORY'S WOMAN   (4484, $4.50)
by Gretchen Genet
Andrew—the carefree soldier who sought glory on the battlefield, and returned a shattered man . . . Niall—the legandary frontiersman and a former Shawnee captive, tormented by his past . . . Roger—the troubled youth, who would rise up to claim a shocking legacy . . . and Clarice—the passionate beauty bound by one man, and hopelessly in love with another. Set against the backdrop of the American revolution, three men fight for their heritage—and one woman is destined to change all their lives forever!

FORBIDDEN   (4488, $4.99)
by Jo Beverley
While fleeing from her brothers, who are attempting to sell her into a loveless marriage, Serena Riverton accepts a carriage ride from a stranger—who is the handsomest man she has ever seen. Lord Middlethorpe, himself, is actually contemplating marriage to a dull daughter of the aristocracy, when he encounters the breathtaking Serena. She arouses him as no woman ever has. And after a night of thrilling intimacy—a forbidden liaison—Serena must choose between a lady's place and a woman's passion!

WINDS OF DESTINY   (4489, $4.99)
by Victoria Thompson
Becky Tate is a half-breed outcast—branded by her Comanche heritage. Then she meets a rugged stranger who awakens her heart to the magic and mystery of passion. Hiding a desperate past, Texas Ranger Clint Masterson has ridden into cattle country to bring peace to a divided land. But a greater battle rages inside him when he dares to desire the beautiful Becky!

WILDEST HEART   (4456, $4.99)
by Virginia Brown
Maggie Malone had come to cattle country to forge her future as a healer. Now she was faced by Devon Conrad, an outlaw wounded body and soul by his shadowy past . . . whose eyes blazed with fury even as his burning caress sent her spiraling with desire. They came together in a Texas town about to explode in sin and scandal. Danger was their destiny—and there was nothing they wouldn't dare for love!

Available wherever paperbacks are sold, or order direct from the Publisher. Send cover price plus 50¢ per copy for mailing and handling to Penguin USA, P.O. Box 999, c/o Dept. 17109, Bergenfield, NJ 07621. Residents of New York and Tennessee must include sales tax. DO NOT SEND CASH.